Watchers on the Hill

Books by Stephanie Grace Whitson

Prairie Winds

Walks the Fire

Soaring Eagle

Red Bird

Keepsake Legacies

Sarah's Patchwork

Karyn's Memory Box

Nora's Ribbon of Memories

Dakota Moons

Valley of the Shadow

Edge of the Wilderness

Heart of the Sandhills

Pine Ridge Portraits

Secrets on the Wind

Watchers on the Hill

04B

STEPHANIE GRACE
WHITSON
Watchers
on
the Hill

BETHANYHOUSE
PUBLISHERS
MINNEAPOLIS, MINNESOTA

Watchers on the Hill
Copyright © 2004
Stephanie Grace Whitson

Cover design by Dan Thornberg

Background images of the Pine Ridge from NEBRASKAland Magazine/Nebraska Game and Parks Commission photo.

Unless otherwise identified, Scripture quotations are from the King James Version of the Bible.

Published by Bethany House Publishers
11400 Hampshire Avenue South
Bloomington, Minnesota 55438
www.bethanyhouse.com

Bethany House Publishers is a Division of
Baker Book House Company, Grand Rapids, Michigan.

Printed in the United States of America

Library of Congress Cataloging-in-Publication Data

Whitson, Stephanie Grace.
Watchers on the hill / by Stephanie Grace Whitson.
p. cm. —(Pine Ridge portraits ; 2)
ISBN 0-7642-2786-6 (pbk.)
1. Triangles (Interpersonal relations)—Fiction. 2. Fort Robinson (Neb.)—Fiction. 3. Women pioneers—Fiction. 4. Single women—Fiction. 5. Nebraska—Fiction. I. Title II. Series: Whitson, Stephanie Grace. Pine Ridge portraits ; 2.
PS3573.H555W38 2004
813'.54—dc22 2004006539

Dedication

To *myDaniel*
who gave me tomorrow
when I thought my life was all yesterdays

With thanks
to everyone at Bethany House Publishers
who made the impossible possible,
who modeled a servant's heart
when this writer needed help most,
and who exemplified Philippians 2:3–4

About Stephanie

A native of southern Illinois, Stephanie Grace Whitson has resided in Nebraska since 1975. It was when she was teaching her homeschooled children their state history unit that Stephanie became interested in the lives of the women who settled her adopted state. What she likes to call "playing with imaginary friends" eventually became her first book, *Walks the Fire,* published in 1995 by Thomas Nelson Publishers. Stephanie's books have appeared on the ECPA bestseller list and been finalists for the Christy Award (*www.christyawards.com*). She founded a home-based inspirational gift company and has also been involved in quilt pattern and sewing-related jewelry design (pewter at *www.lorarocke.com*). Widowed in 2001, Stephanie remarried in 2003 and now pursues a full-time writing and speaking ministry from her home studio in Lincoln, Nebraska. Visit her at *www.stephaniegracewhitson.com*. You may also contact her at: WhitsonInk, 3800 Old Cheney Road, #101–178, Lincoln, Nebraska 68516.

Chapter One

My soul is weary of my life;
I will leave my complaint upon myself;
I will speak in the bitterness of my soul.

Job 10:1

They were lowering her husband's casket into the grave, and the only emotion Charlotte Bishop could manage was relief; relief diluted with just the slightest tincture of guilt perhaps, but relief nonetheless. She had protested at first when her mother-in-law insisted on the old-fashioned mourning garb, but now Charlotte was grateful for the long black veil covering her face. If she kept her eyes lowered and refused to meet anyone's gaze, perhaps she would be able to maintain the facade and earn her Widow Who is Still in Shock moniker. Thankfully, everyone seemed to think her lack of emotion since Emory's sudden death was evidence of a vast sea of grief.

The fall breeze wafted the scent of roses her way. Charlotte closed her eyes and inhaled deeply. The boy at her side reached up and took her hand. He squeezed. She squeezed back, turning her head just enough to be able to see the dark curls cascading from beneath his wool cap and over the collar of his dark suit. Her mother-in-law cleared her throat, and Charlotte looked down again, this time noticing the shoes.

Will's were impossibly old-fashioned, as were the knickers he despised.

She continued looking around the circle of shoes ringing the grave and thought about how much could be revealed about a person just by their shoes. The Colonel's two ancient uncles had donned full dress for the occasion. Their military boots shone with new polish, but still looked dated beside Major Peyton Riley's. The proximity of Riley's dress boots to Mother Bishop rankled. Charlotte suspected he would come calling under the guise of comforting the grieving widow. Probably in less than a week. She had caught him leering at her from behind the hymnal in church. *At the Colonel's funeral. How dare he.*

Aunt Daisy's shoes weren't visible, but picturing them necessitated suppressing a smile. Charlotte had heard the shouts of agony earlier that morning as one of the servants helped Daisy cram her size-ten feet into the size-eight shoes she'd always worn to funerals "because I'm too old to be paying for special-occasion shoes." Aunt Daisy walked with a cane, so hobbling around in too-tight shoes fit the image.

Mother Bishop cleared her throat again. Charlotte started at the sound and realized the casket had landed and everyone was waiting. Taking a deep breath, she squeezed Will's hand. He squeezed back again and held out his rose, reminding her of what came next. Together, Charlotte and her son stepped forward. Together, they dropped their roses into the grave. Together, they stepped back. Charlotte bowed her head.

Good-bye, Colonel. I am supposed to be praying for your soul. Perhaps someday I shall. But not today. Today I can't seem to stop thinking you deserve a little time in hell for the things you've done.

•••◆•••

"All I'm saying is"—Aunt Daisy gestured with her butter knife—"in my day children showed more respect for their elders." Charlotte's eyes followed the clump of butter on Daisy's knife as it plopped into a bowl of fresh blackberries, splattering dark juice onto the white linen breakfast cloth. In an effort to recover the butter, the elderly woman tipped her overfull teacup. Amber stains joined the deep blue ones around Daisy's place at the table.

"Please, Daisy," Ella Bishop snapped. "Between Will's pranks and your clumsiness, Edgar has just about had his fill. With all that has happened, we don't need him giving notice, too."

"Let him give notice," Daisy blustered. "In my day, people didn't allow themselves to be ruled by the help."

Mother Bishop sighed. "I'm doing my best to reestablish a peaceful home." Her voice trembled. She dabbed at the corner of each eye with her napkin. "Although heaven knows without Emory it's going to be a difficult task."

Charlotte shoved her napkin off her lap. She bent down to retrieve it instead of meeting Mother Bishop's gaze.

"I apologize if I sound harsh, Daisy. It's just that Edgar's been with us for years, and we don't want to lose him." She looked pointedly at the empty seat beside Charlotte. "I see we are once again off to a disorganized beginning to our day." She looked down her nose at Charlotte. "May I remind you, dear, that we agreed that Master Will would cease dawdling in the morning and join us for breakfast precisely at seven?"

Charlotte twisted the napkin in her lap while she formulated a reply.

"You do recall that conversation?" Mother Bishop intoned.

"Of course I do," Charlotte snapped. Mother Bishop's left eyebrow arched. Charlotte felt goose bumps rising on her arms. She touched the scar on her left wrist where the surgeon had operated to repair a broken bone. Just before Charlotte had "fallen," her husband had arched his left eyebrow exactly that way. Forcing herself to look into her mother-in-law's eyes, she replied, "I do remember, Mother Bishop. But Will had a headache when he woke this morning, and I told him to stay in bed."

A shriek from the kitchen caught everyone's attention. Will bolted like lightning from the butler's pantry, followed by the cook in hot pursuit, her cap askew, a rolling pin wielded like a sword.

Charlotte jumped up, but not before Garnet Irvin came to the top of the stairs, glided down to the landing, and intercepted Will. Small in stature but strong as a horse, Garnet wrapped one hand around the boy's shoulders. Charlotte saw her whisper something in his ear just before she let go. The cook paused to catch her breath. Will skittered up the stairs and escaped to his room at the far end of the expansive upper hall, slamming the door shut behind him.

Charlotte instinctively started to follow after him, but she sensed Mother Bishop's approach and turned around, grateful she was almost halfway up the stairs so the woman couldn't loom over her, as was her habit. Even so, her heart thumped when she saw the tightly pressed lips, the tilt of the head, the way the older woman's left hand clenched her walking stick. No one had ever been able to tell Charlotte why Mother Bishop required a walking stick, but she had an impressive collection of them. This morning, she was using the ebony one with the brass dragon head at the top. If it was going to be what Will called a "dragon-lady day," Charlotte was in for it. She backed up one step and put her hand on the railing, grateful when Garnet descended from the upstairs landing and stood behind her, close enough for Charlotte to feel her comforting presence.

"In my day, Charlotte," Mother Bishop said, her voice terrible in its studied self-control, "children were taught to be seen and not heard. My son would be appalled by the demonstration we've just witnessed. But even more disturbing would be the realization that the behavior was enabled by a lie told by the child's *own mother*." The gray hair piled atop Mother Bishop's head trembled as she punctuated the chastisement with a tap of the walking stick on the inlaid wood floor.

Charlotte looked down at the hem of Mother Bishop's black silk dress. Across the hall in the dining room, china clinked as Aunt Daisy continued her breakfast. Good old Aunt Daisy. Nothing ever came between her and a good meal. The doorbell rang. Cook retreated to her kitchen, muttering unhappily. Mother Bishop glared at the door and waited for Edgar.

Edgar opened the door, bowed, and announced the caller. With a warning glance up the stairs to where Charlotte stood gripping the handrail and trying to suppress a sense of overwhelming dread, Mother Bishop advanced toward the entryway, her hand extended, her genteel-lady-of-the-manor expression easing into her version of a welcoming smile.

"Major Riley," she purred, "what a delightful surprise."

November 3, 1889
Detroit City, Michigan
Dearest Papa,

I received a letter from Dinah only yesterday, and she seems to be thriving in Philadelphia. It doesn't seem so long ago that I heard you lament the fact that the family tradition in medicine was destined to end with your generation and the birth of two girls. And now we have Dinah planning to seek admission to medical school as soon as she is old enough. Who would have thought that my little sister the tomboy would brave a world only recently opened to women. I, for one, am proud of her, and I hope you share that sentiment. Miss James says Dinah is applying herself well in all her studies. Aunt Hazel seems pleased with Dinah as a houseguest. Our little girl certainly has a bright future ahead.

Will and I have not been quite so fortunate in our adjustment to life without the Colonel. Of course his death was a shock. The jump was low, and how he came unseated I will never understand. It is even harder to comprehend that such a minor spill could kill a man. There are days when I wake and almost convince myself it was all a dream, and a silly one at that. But then I look around at my little room and I am forced to accept reality. Moving into the manse permanently has proven to be very different from when we used to stay here for holidays or when the Colonel was on leave. There is little more to say appropriate for my pen.

Papa dearest, I well remember what a challenge I was to you in the past. In the summer of 1879 when you said good-bye to Mama and Dinah and me, I know you were relieved to have me away from Fort Robinson. Since then I have done my best to learn from my mistakes and to become someone of whom you might be proud.

Charlotte's hand trembled. She raised the pen from the paper, but not before leaving a smudge. "Blast," she muttered. Looking up from her writing desk, she was struck once again by the recent change in the view from her bedroom window. The Colonel and she had once occupied nearly an entire wing of the house whenever they came to stay. From their sitting room, they had enjoyed a view of the distant hills forested with oak and pine trees through which ran a stream that shone like a silver ribbon at daybreak. The day after the Colonel's funeral, Mother Bishop had instructed the servants to close off that wing of the house and move Charlotte's things into the small room next to Will's.

"It will be better for the boy's adjustment to have you nearby, don't you think," Mother had asked, in the tone of voice that was not a question.

Seated at the tiny desk she had positioned in front of the only window in her new room, Charlotte looked out on the stone courtyard between the back of the house and the stables. On a clear day, she could still see the hills in the distance if she leaned far enough out the window. Today, a gray mist obscured the view of anything beyond the stables and the groundkeeper's residence. For the first time, Charlotte realized the groundkeeper probably had more space of his own than both she and Will combined. She leaned her head on her hand, thinking back to the days when she used to complain about having to share a room with Dinah.

"Why do we always have to share?"

"Will we ever get to live in a real house?"

"Nothing ever happens here."

"When I grow up, I'm leaving Fort Robinson and I'm never coming back!"

Watching the rain wash over the stone courtyard at the back of Bishop House, Charlotte sighed. Fort Robinson was certainly a far cry from this. Built on a broad valley between the White River and a ridge of high bluffs way out in western Nebraska, the fort had been little more than a collection of canvas tents that first winter when Charlotte's father reported for duty. Even when the family finally joined him the next year, Fort Robinson hadn't been much. But it grew. It had been named regimental headquarters for the Ninth Cavalry with hundreds of soldiers stationed there now—most of them the black troops called "buffalo soldiers." Father had explained the moniker, which had evidently come via the Cheyenne and had something to do with the men's thick, curly hair and what the Indians thought was its resemblance to the fur between a buffalo's horns.

Father practiced medicine in a brick hospital now. He even had his own house. And they were building a new set of officers' quarters and more barracks around a larger parade ground to the west of the one Charlotte remembered. The railroad had arrived, and a town had sprouted up nearby.

Papa was alone now. Charlotte's mother had died only last year. Colonel Bishop hadn't allowed her and Will to travel west to the funeral. Charlotte pictured the Fort Robinson cemetery. Papa said it was fenced now and had neat rows of gravestones. He assured her that he had ordered a fine one for Mama.

Winter lay ahead, bleak and frigid in Nebraska until spring when the vast prairie would be alive with wild flowers, bursting with color. Charlotte remembered how she and Dinah had delighted in gathering them by the armfuls, adorning the dining table at home and even the men's mess hall tables, making bracelets and garlands, once even scattering petals across the front steps when Sergeant Nathan Boone came to dinner. *Nathan Boone*. Charlotte's cheeks still colored with embarrassment when she thought about her adolescent flirtations with the handsome widower. He'd been gone from Fort Robinson for years now. Papa had written news of him once, saying Sergeant Boone had been promoted to lieutenant.

Looking out through the raindrops clattering against her window, Charlotte also remembered the seas of mud that were part of every spring at Fort Robinson. Battles with mud usually subsided just in time for the hot summer wind to layer every flat surface with dust. When the wind died down, the air grew heavy with the oppressive odor of stable manure and outhouses. In spring everyone rushed to get gardens planted and then spent the summer hauling water to coax life into seedlings and transplanted trees, longing for shade in a land where a person could see the heat rising from the earth come July. *"Fort Robinson,"* Charlotte's mother used to say, *"is not the end of the earth, but you can see it from there."*

Charlotte picked up her pen, wiped off the nib, and dipping it back in the inkpot, she brought her letter to a close.

Please, Papa, I am begging you. Please may I come home?

Always your devoted and loving daughter,
Charlotte Mae Valentine Bishop

CHAPTER TWO

Woe unto them that decree unrighteous decrees . . . that widows may be their prey, and that they may rob the fatherless!

ISAIAH 10:1–2

SIX FEET TALL WITH STRIKING BLUE EYES AND THICK blond hair, Major Preston Riley was what women called a fine figure of a man. He danced with grace and dined with the impeccable manners of a gentleman. When in the company of men, he displayed a good grasp of the chief political issues of the day, and when in the company of women, he could discuss the newest variety of roses being imported from England. He was sought after as a dinner guest, admired as a military leader, and generally expected to become great.

Charlotte Valentine Bishop was neither blind nor ignorant, and therefore she was aware of the major's assets. If it were not for two things, she would have perhaps been able to convince herself to smile more when he visited. The first thing was that Mother Bishop smiled quite enough for the both of them when Major Riley stopped in. The second was that his presence made Charlotte's skin crawl.

Mother Bishop found a need for financial advice regarding her son's estate just a week after his funeral. Major Riley knew the bank president. Of course, Emory's widow must be included in the meetings. Charlotte hated the way Riley stood behind her chair at the bank, as if he had applied for and had been hired to fill the position of The Widow's Protector. With the only man who had ever harmed her in the grave, Charlotte felt no need for protection. She resented Riley for applying for a position she had not advertised. It soon became clear to Charlotte that someone was, indeed, "advertising" on her behalf.

When Mother Bishop decided to purchase a different team of horses to draw her carriage, Major Riley assisted in the decision. This especially rankled Charlotte, who had become an expert horsewoman in her own right and knew almost as much about horseflesh as Emory had. She didn't see the need to change teams and she told Mother Bishop as much.

"A four-in-hand is just too much, now," the older woman said. "We must economize."

Major Riley arranged the sale and arrived late one December evening with flowers for both Charlotte and Mother Bishop, under the guise of celebrating the good price he had gotten for their four matched bays. "Everyone knows those horses," he said. "There was practically a bidding war." He was invited to dinner and was seated next to Charlotte.

Will took one look at the seating arrangement and declared he was not hungry. He marched out of the dining room and up the stairs to his room and did not come down again even though he knew dessert was to be his favorite, coconut cake.

As winter unfolded, Major Riley's attentions became more persistent and Mother Bishop's intention to make the match became more evident. Scarcely a day went by that mention was not made of the need to economize. Mother Bishop made the shocking suggestion that Charlotte ignore local mourning custom and attend a holiday ball with the Major.

"I'm not saying she should *dance,*" she explained when Aunt Daisy expressed her dismay at the possibility of such unheard-of behavior. "But Charlotte is young. I don't think it's right for the old guard to make such old-fashioned demands on the younger generation."

Charlotte began a desperate kind of avoidance while watching the mail for the letter that would say *come home*. If only Papa would say it, she could wire him for a loan, buy a train ticket, and be free once and for all of everything about the Bishops, save the name.

⁂

Shortly after the New Year, Mother Bishop hinted at letting Garnet go. Charlotte's unhappiness almost reached panic mode.

"But you can't replace Garnet," she protested at tea one afternoon. "I don't know what I'd do without her. She's practically family."

"That's precisely the problem," Mother Bishop sniffed. "She's begun to think she *is* a member of the family. I don't care for her uppity ways one bit. It just doesn't do for one to become too close to one's *servants,*" she said.

So that was it, Charlotte realized. It had nothing to do with finances or Garnet's performance of her duties, and everything to do with the relationship Garnet and Charlotte had forged over the years since that first time Emory had stormed out of the house, angry again over one of his young wife's errors. Charlotte had slunk down the back stairs to the kitchen to make herself a cup of tea. Halfway down the stairs, she had heard singing. When the last step creaked, Garnet whirled around. Even when her lips were closed, the tip of one of Garnet's terribly crooked teeth tended to show. She had a habit of covering her mouth when she talked or smiled. Her hands and forearms were dusted with flour, and when Garnet reached up to cover her mouth, she left a floury imprint on her chin.

"Please," Charlotte said, "please don't stop singing. I only wanted to make a cup of tea. I . . . Emory . . . the Colonel . . ." Her voice began to tremble. Clasping her hands together, Charlotte blinked away tears.

"Yes, ma'am," Garnet said. "I know. He came through here on his way out."

"I made him so angry," Charlotte said, biting her lip.

Garnet shook her head. She turned back around and punched the dough. "Colonel Bishop has always been an angry man, missus." She ducked her head and brushed her chin against the shoulder of her apron. "I used to make the first Mrs. Bishop my special tea when the 'angries' were visiting. Would you like to try it?"

Charlotte nodded. "I would. But, please . . ." She unclasped her hands and gripped the back of a chair. "If you'll just show me where . . . Keep at your work . . . and keep singing." She forced a smile. "My mother liked to sing. It's very soothing."

Garnet nodded toward the door leading into the butler's pantry. "There's a jar on the bottom shelf. Part of the blue and white set. Says R-I-Z on it. That's my special tea."

Charlotte headed to the cupboard. While she made tea, Garnet shaped the dough into loaves, singing while she worked. Sitting at the kitchen table that day, sipping Garnet's special tea, Charlotte closed her eyes and gave herself to Garnet's music and the warmth of the sunshine pouring in the window.

After that day, whenever she and her husband were staying at the Bishop manse, Charlotte often asked Garnet to sing. She soon discovered that, contrary to her assumption, Garnet was neither illiterate nor unschooled. In fact, one of the primary reasons she stayed with the Bishop family, in addition to having been needed by the Colonel's first wife when the "angries" visited, was that Emory Bishop's now deceased father had amassed an impressive personal library, and Garnet was allowed access to the books.

Most people thought Garnet, who was small in stature and quiet by nature, was painfully shy. But Charlotte soon learned that Garnet had an independent streak and a will of iron. She moved about Bishop House with an ease that belied the complexities of pleasing a domineering older woman and her equally demanding, quick-tempered adult son. Charlotte was drawn to Garnet's inner strength. Although about the same age as Charlotte, Garnet soon took the young woman under her more experienced wing, becoming her confidante and, when necessary, her encourager. It wasn't long before Garnet was reading aloud to Charlotte while Charlotte struggled with the fancywork Mother Bishop seemed to think so necessary to a lady's résumé.

"I hate sewing," Charlotte had tried to explain to her mother-in-law. "I made one ugly quilt before I was married because my mother insisted. I'm just no good at it." She had appealed to Emory, "I much prefer riding with you, dear, to being housebound with the sewing circle."

It didn't work. Colonel Emory Bishop might command regiments but he had no talent for resisting his mother. Charlotte learned needlepoint and filet crochet. She started a quilt with velvets and satins. And had it not been for Garnet's reading aloud to her while she poked and stabbed fabric with needles, Charlotte was quite certain she would have gone *crazy* while working on her "crazy quilt."

Garnet read when Emory broke his wife's wrist. *"Lead me, O Lord, in thy righteousness because of mine enemies; make thy way straight before my face. For there is no faithfulness in their mouth; their inward part is very wickedness; their throat is an open sepulchre; they flatter with their tongue."*

Garnet read when each of the three babies died and the Colonel sent his wife across town to recover at the Bishop manse. *"I am weary with my groaning; all the night I make my bed to swim; I water my couch with my tears. Mine eye is consumed because of grief."*

Garnet read after the Colonel died and Charlotte's state of mind affected her ability to sleep. *"I will both lay me down in peace, and sleep: for thou, Lord, only makest me dwell in safety."*

Since the Colonel's death, Garnet had taken to reading aloud to Will on nights when the boy was especially upset. She could calm him like no other person in the world, simply by crooning in her low, mellow voice while Will tossed from side to side in his narrow bed.

It often struck Charlotte just how applicable the Scripture passages Garnet read were to a given event. "I've got nothing to do with that, missus," Garnet would protest. "I just open up the book and read. I'm partial to the Psalms, but I'm no preacher. If the verses mean something to you, I'm glad. Lord knows you need comfort and strength."

Garnet had, in many ways, become Charlotte's only friend. And now Mother Bishop was hinting that Garnet might be let go.

There had to be a better way.

* * *

No letter.

Charlotte stood in the foyer of the grand old house blinking back tears of frustration. It had been this way every day for weeks. She had given the letter plenty of time to reach Fort Robinson and plenty of time for Papa to send his reply. Why, she wondered, didn't Papa answer?

Perhaps the letter was lost. What if it had never arrived at Fort Robinson? Charlotte wondered if she should telegraph the fort. But she couldn't think of how she would explain that to Mother Bishop, especially if Papa *answered* in a telegram.

Maybe Papa was away on some kind of drill. Charlotte couldn't think of a reason for her father to be called away in the dead of winter.

There could be any number of reasons. Charlotte turned to go back up the stairs, trying not to think the worst. *Maybe he doesn't want us.*

Certainly her father had never anticipated helping his daughter raise a ten-year-old boy. He was probably looking forward to an undisturbed retirement, and here she was asking to come home. And he didn't know how she'd changed. She wouldn't be a burden. She'd be a help. She'd see to that. But of course Father didn't know her now. Emory had never allowed her to visit, not even when her mother returned to the fort, not even when she died. All Papa knew was the spoiled brat he'd sent away. But surely, Charlotte thought, surely her letters had shown a change.

Faced with yet another day of doubts and possibilities, Charlotte hesitated on her way up the stairs. The thought of another hour alone in her tiny room was unbearable. Will was at school. Garnet had left a little while ago to do the marketing. Mother Bishop and Aunt Daisy had gone to make calls. For what seemed like the fiftieth time, Mother had hinted that it wasn't time yet for Charlotte to make social calls.

"But you wanted me to go to those holiday balls with the Major," Charlotte protested.

"That was different," Mother said, tapping her walking stick as she spoke. "I didn't want to offend the Major. But I never really approved."

Charlotte had retreated from yet another confrontation. Now, as she sat on the stairs thinking, the sun came out from behind a cloud, streaming through the landing window, throwing rainbows of light all around the entry hall as it passed through the prisms set in the leaded glass. In spite of the sunshine, the grand old house seemed small and dark and oppressive.

Succumbing to impulse, Charlotte hurried up the stairs, changed into riding clothes, and was soon in the stables saddling a tall gray thoroughbred named Isaac. When the horse playfully nipped her shoulder, Charlotte shoved his great head away and tapped him on the nose. "Stop that," she said, "I know it's been a while. We've got to hurry. I don't want the Queen Mother to catch me enjoying something." She giggled at the joke and was shocked by the sound. Just how long had it been since she laughed, anyway?

She scrambled aboard Isaac and headed for the distant hills by a familiar trail, inhaling deeply as her horse minced along, eager to be given his head. "All right, old boy, let's *go*." Isaac leaped away, and for a few moments Charlotte was free of all thought of anything but moving in rhythm with the powerful animal.

Her peace of mind was soon shattered by the sight of Major Riley headed toward her, mounted on a dark bay stallion that, unfortunately, reminded Charlotte of Emory's horse.

"Good morning," the Major said. "I was just headed up to the house to inquire about you. I saw Mrs. Bishop a few moments ago and she indicated you hadn't felt up to making calls today. Obviously it was nothing serious." His horse danced sideways. "I hope you won't get a chill riding on such a cold day."

"I feel wonderful," Charlotte said. "I don't mind cold weather at all."

"This fellow's begging for a workout," the Major said. "Would you mind terribly if I joined you?"

"Well . . . I . . ."

"If it means anything, Mother Bishop gave her blessing," Riley said with a sidelong glance at Charlotte. "In fact, she suggested I lure you out-of-doors for a ride." He smiled. "I'd say this is a happy coincidence."

"Thank you, Major," Charlotte said, ignoring the man's outstretched hand and dismounting. "It's kind of you to offer to brush him down, but I prefer to tend to Isaac myself. He's been neglected since my husband's death." She patted the horse's thick neck. "I owe him some attention."

"Well then," the Major said and bowed stiffly. "I'll pay my respects to Mrs. Bishop and be going. Would I be speaking out of turn to request the honor of your company again tomorrow?" He looked up at the blue sky. "This kind of weather is a gift this time of year. It's a shame to waste any of these lovely winter days indoors."

Charlotte ducked her head, working at an imaginary knot in Isaac's mane. "I don't know," she said. "I'm not certain what time I'll be riding. Or if I will at all," she said. "It's Saturday, and Will—"

"Ah, yes," the Major said nodding. "I remember. The boy isn't fond of horses, is he? Pity."

"Actually," Charlotte said, "I promised Will we'd spend some time together in the stables. He just needs someone with the patience not to hurry him. He had a bad fall when he was little. It's difficult to overcome your fears when you've been forced into something before you're ready."

"Quite," the Major said. He bowed again, thanked Charlotte for her company, and headed for the house.

Charlotte turned to the work of brushing Isaac and was soon humming to herself while she braided the gelding's long white mane.

Charlotte was still humming to herself when she stepped inside the back door of the manse and heard Mother Bishop's angry voice sounding down the hall and all the way to the back of the house. Oblivious to the filth caked on her riding boots, she hurried into the back hall.

"What on earth were you thinking?!" Mother Bishop was practically shouting.

"I was making something for Mother," Will replied.

Charlotte hurried up the hall and to the doorway of her mother-in-law's private parlor. Mother Bishop had Will by the collar with one hand while the other hand held a catalog of some kind. Major Riley was standing in the corner by the small fireplace, staring disapprovingly at Will.

"What's the matter?" Charlotte asked.

Mother Bishop held up the catalog without releasing Will. "THIS is what's the matter," she said.

For the first time, Charlotte noticed the neat holes cut in the top page.

Will blustered, "I didn't know it was important. I was making something for you." He tried to twist away from his grandmother's clutch.

"Stop that," the older woman ordered, shaking him by the collar.

"Please, Mother Bishop," Charlotte said. "Please let him go. He didn't know."

"He didn't know? How could he *not* know? Has he not been in this house every spring of his life? Has he not seen my rose catalogs before? Has he not been told not to bother them?"

"I thought it was an old one," Will protested.

"Well, it isn't," Mother Bishop snapped. "It just came and now it's ruined." She glared at Charlotte. "I was just preparing to show Major Riley the new variety of red we're adding to the rose garden this year."

Charlotte looked across the room at Major Riley. "Roses?" she said.

He nodded. "I have an interest. Although not nearly the knowledge Mrs. Bishop enjoys."

"You have a rose garden?" Charlotte asked.

The Major shook his head. "No. But I have plans."

Something in his tone sent a chill through Charlotte. Will squirmed and his grandmother shook him again.

"Please let him go," Charlotte begged. "He didn't know. And . . . and can't you get another catalog?"

With another shake, Mother Bishop released Will, who moved to his mother's side, rubbing his neck and coughing slightly.

Charlotte took his hand. "If you'll excuse us," she said,

"I'll have a talk with Will now." She turned to go.

Mother Bishop spoke up. "Talk is precisely the problem, Charlotte," she said. "You do entirely too much talking to that boy and not nearly enough *doing*. He has no sense of duty, no sense of propriety. What's worse, he doesn't respect authority in the least." She shook her head from side to side. "What's to be done I don't know, but something must be."

Major Riley spoke up. "If it's discipline and respect for authority the boy needs," he said, "I'd recommend the Longview Academy. They excel at instilling both in their charges. And if he does well, Master Will could look forward to a fine career following in his father's footsteps." He smiled. "Many of our finest officers got their start at Longview."

"Absolutely not," Charlotte said. "I won't hear of it."

"*You* won't hear of it?" Mother Bishop said, staring at Charlotte.

"I won't go!" Will shouted. "You can't make me."

"See here, young man," Riley said. He stepped quickly across the room, and before Charlotte could intervene, he had grabbed Will's arm. "You don't talk to the women in this house that way."

Will jerked free. When Riley went to grab him again, Will kicked him and dashed out of the room.

Mother Bishop's face went white. "Major, I am so very sorry."

"It's all right, ma'am," the Major said.

Riley's tone of voice sent chills through Charlotte. She recognized that tone. It was the exact tone Emory would use—when it was anything but all right.

"Obviously the boy needs help," Mother said.

"Quite," the Major agreed.

"Would you make inquiries on our behalf?"

Charlotte protested. "Will is far too young to be sent away to school. He needs me," she said. "We need each other. It's too soon after his father's death. He's still adjusting."

"He isn't adjusting," Mother said. "That's exactly my point. He's always been a handful, but without Emory here, he doesn't even pretend to obey the simplest of rules. And now he's becoming violent. And *I*," she said, mimicking Charlotte's earlier tone, "will not have *that*. No *child* under my roof is going to be allowed to behave in such a way."

"No," Charlotte said, "I can see that. Violence is only allowed if you're an adult in this house." She rubbed her wrist.

"That is quite enough." Mother spat the words out, tapping the floor with today's selection—an ebony walking stick with a carved ivory handle.

The two women stood staring at one another for a brief moment. Charlotte wavered. "I apologize," she said. She looked at the Major. "If you'll excuse me," she said, and turned to go.

"No," Mother Bishop said. "I do not excuse you. Not until you apologize for your son's outrageous behavior toward the Major."

A dozen similar moments from the past flashed in Charlotte's mind. She closed her eyes, fighting a wave of nausea. "I . . . I'm afraid I'm going to be sick," she said. Clamping her hand over her mouth she fled the room, barely making it up the stairs and to her room before her stomach overcame her willpower.

She was lying on her bed when someone knocked softly on the door.

"It's me, Mama," Will called through the keyhole. "May I come in?"

* * *

"See now," Charlotte said, "Isaac *likes* you. When he turns his head to look at you like that, it's his way of saying 'welcome aboard.' He isn't rolling his eyes or snorting—"

"He is too snorting," Will said, his voice tight with fear. He clutched at the rounded edge of the English saddle.

"No he isn't, honey," Charlotte said. She looked up at the horse and, taking the reins in her right hand, touched his soft gray muzzle. "He's just breathing deeply. Getting to know your scent." She jiggled the reins. "Isn't that right, boy?"

As if in answer, Isaac grunted and nodded his head. Charlotte laughed and smiled up at Will. She was glad she had suggested they come out to the stables together. Already, she was shaking off the unpleasant thoughts she'd been harboring about Mother Bishop and the motives behind her treatment of Major Riley.

"Now you just grip with your knees like I told you. I'm going to walk Isaac around a little. *Just walking.*" She headed across the stone courtyard in the direction of the open countryside beyond the Bishop holdings. As they walked along, she told Will the story of Isaac, how he had been prancing around a paddock miles away when the Colonel first saw him and how, when brought to the Bishop stables, he had proven himself an escape artist and kept returning home until Charlotte had discovered the horse's passion for apples and won his heart. "So you see," Charlotte concluded as she reversed directions and headed back to the stables, "that's the secret with Isaac. You give him apples and he'll be your best friend."

"Is he *your* best friend?" Will asked.

Charlotte looked up at the horse, walking along as calm as any plow horse, almost as if he had understood her whispered pleas as she was saddling him earlier to *be good to Will; he needs some self-confidence.* She thought back to all the rides and the thousands of words the horse had heard on those rides, times when she had simply needed to talk about things she could not say to human ears—even Garnet Irvin's. There were times, Charlotte realized, when the horse had seemed to understand her desperate need to talk. Mornings when he'd begun a ride with energetic, playful bucks and then settled down and plodded along, his ears turned toward her voice while she talked and, sometimes, cried. Reaching up to stroke Isaac's sleek neck, Charlotte said, "In some ways, son, yes, he is my best friend."

They came back to the courtyard and walked into the stables and to Isaac's stall. Will slid down and stood back.

"Here," Charlotte said, taking his hand and pulling him forward to stand nearly beneath the horse's neck. "He loves to be patted right there." She guided Will's hand to the broad chest. As Will stroked, Isaac lowered his head and stood very still. "See how his eyes are almost half closed? That means he likes what you're doing."

"Hey there, fella," Will said. "You like that? I'll do it for you every time you let me ride you. How's that?"

Isaac turned his head and eyed the boy. He arched his neck and touched Will's chest with his nose.

"He's looking for more apples," Charlotte explained.

Will pushed the great head away. "No more apples, boy. Maybe tomorrow."

"That's good, son," Charlotte praised him. "You didn't jump away. If you stay calm, Isaac will stay calm."

Will nodded. "Can I help you brush him?"

* * *

"But—" Charlotte's voice caught. "You can't, Mother Bishop. Please. You can't sell Isaac. Not now. Not when Will's just beginning to learn to relax around horses. Surely you've seen how much better he's been." The two women were in the library. Mother Bishop ensconced in her favorite chair, her feet propped up on a small needlepoint footrest, her teacup perched on a tiny mahogany table at her side, while Charlotte tried in vain to untangle a knot in the embroidery floss dangling from the pillow cover Mother wanted for the guest-room bed.

"Will's improved behavior," Mother Bishop said without looking up from her book, "has nothing to do with the horse. He's simply trying to avoid Longview."

"That's not true," Charlotte protested. "He doesn't need Longview. He's feeling more self-confident and he knows he only gets to spend time around Isaac if he behaves himself."

"He is behaving himself," Mother Bishop said, glaring at Charlotte over pince-nez glasses, "because someone finally has had the fortitude to follow through with consequences." She lay her open book in her lap. "And for my part, I thank God for Major Riley's concern."

"Please, Mother," Charlotte pleaded. "Please don't sell Isaac. You'll see. All Will needs is time to grow and adjust. And Isaac can help us with that."

"It's not as if the horse is disappearing from your life," Mother said reasonably. She rattled her teacup. Charlotte jumped up, went to the tea tray for the pot and refilled Mother's cup. "I'm certain Major Riley will be more than happy to have you visit and ride Isaac any time you feel so inclined. In fact," she smiled, "he's already said as much."

Charlotte set the teapot back on its tray with trembling hands. She glanced at Mother, who had once again picked up her book, a sure sign she considered the matter settled. "But he's mine," she said. "The Colonel gave him to me."

"My dear Charlotte," Mother said, her voice laced with a kindness that was not kind, "I should have thought you would be willing to make this one small sacrifice for the good of the family without causing a stir. You have disappointed me."

"You have disappointed me." A chill went up Charlotte's spine at the all-too-familiar phrase, the one uttered over and over again after her wedding day, the one that always ultimately led to the Colonel's taking what he called *corrective measures* to ensure his wife never repeated an infraction.

Charlotte met Mother Bishop's gaze, at once chilled and

repulsed by the absence of compassion in the old woman's dark eyes. She took in a deep breath, fighting back the wave of fear washing over her. *Don't panic. There's nothing left to take from you after this. Once Isaac is gone, there's nothing left.* Except there was. And now, Charlotte realized, Mother was determined to take it. Will would be sent away. It didn't matter how he behaved. Major Riley didn't like him, and that made Will the last obstacle preventing Mother from attaching herself and Aunt Daisy and the Bishop's holdings to a secure future with Major Peyton Riley, as he stepped into Emory's position as head of the household. Charlotte's feelings and desires were, she realized, irrelevant. She was expected to cooperate. She and Will were little more than pawns the Queen Mother would gladly sacrifice.

Finally, Charlotte knew what to do. The idea terrified her, but beneath the fear was the knowledge that it was right. Even wild animals protected their young. What she had not had the courage to do for herself, she would do for Will. And so it was that late one night not long after Mother Bishop appointed Major Riley to "make inquiries" at the Longview Academy regarding a position for Will, Charlotte climbed the narrow stairs to the third-floor garret and knocked on Garnet Irvin's door.

Garnet opened the door a crack and peered out, then quickly motioned Charlotte inside.

Charlotte perched on the edge of Garnet's mattress in a poorly lit room only slightly smaller than hers. The rough board floor was covered with rag rugs. The room smelled of soap and furniture polish and was impeccably clean.

"Do you think you could find a way to get Will's and my things packed and to the railway station without anyone here at the house knowing about it?" Charlotte asked quickly before she lost her nerve.

Garnet nodded her head. "Of course. Old George can muscle a trunk down the back stairs after Mrs. Bishop and Aunt Daisy are asleep."

"What about the rest of the servants?"

"The cook and some of the others were talking today about some doings over at the church on Wednesday night. If Mrs. Bishop gives them leave to go, that would clear the way." She added, "And I don't think anyone else would ask questions. If they do, old George can just say he's putting some of the Colonel's things in storage."

"Will you come with us?" Charlotte asked.

Garnet hesitated. "I've got a little money saved, but it's not near enough for a train ticket."

Charlotte looked down at the enormous opal the Colonel had put on her finger on their wedding day. "Just pack and be ready," she said. "And have George take the things to the station on Wednesday. But make certain he doesn't say a word to anybody."

"You can trust old George, missus," Garnet said.

"So, you'll come?" Charlotte asked, putting her hand on Garnet's arm.

Garnet smiled gently and patted the back of Charlotte's hand. She nodded. "Where exactly is it we're going?"

"Nebraska," Charlotte said. "We're going home to Nebraska."

CHAPTER THREE

The foolishness of man perverteth his way:
and his heart fretteth against the Lord.
PROVERBS 19:3

WHO, LIEUTENANT NATHAN BOONE WONDERED, would have put flowers at his wife's grave. The small bouquet of wilted wild flowers gave off a faint, sweet aroma that took Nathan back to the days when Lily's had been one of only a few scattered graves in the Fort Robinson cemetery. Her tombstone had been the first granite marker. Now there were several neat rows of identical white stones. And a fence. It was a proper cemetery.

Other than Dr. Valentine, Nathan didn't think there was anyone left at Fort Robinson who would even remember Lily Bainbridge Boone. He looked around and spotted another grave with an identical bouquet of flowers. The same red ribbon. He walked over to read the marker. *Clara Maxwell.* That explained it. Laina Jackson had been here. After all these years, Laina still remembered how intent he had always been on keeping flowers at Lily's grave. *I expect I'll be seeing you sometime early in April,* Nathan had written the Jacksons from Texas. Knowing Nathan would pay his respects upon his arrival, Laina must have wanted to make sure he found evidence that someone else remembered, too.

It would have taken hours for her to ride in from the Four Pines Ranch on such an errand. He shouldn't be surprised by the show of friendship, though. Laina Gray Jackson had proven herself to be the kind of woman who would do just about anything for the people she loved. Hadn't she even said exactly that on that January morning ten years ago when he had left Fort Robinson? Hadn't she stood right at the kitchen table in her quarters down on Soapsuds Row and looked up at him with those shining green eyes and said, "Nathan, you know I'd do anything for you"?

"Anything but marry me," he'd replied, letting the regret sound in his voice.

"I can't marry you, Nathan. You've been my rescuer and my good friend. But you are still married to Lily in your heart. And for that and a thousand other reasons, marriage would never work for us. And in your heart of hearts, you know it."

"Yeah, well, I'd have argued with you about that 'til the cows came home if it wasn't for *him*." He'd waved his hand in the general direction of the post hospital where Caleb Jackson had gone to have over two dozen stitches taken out of his arm.

Laina blushed and touched the scar on the left side of her head, as she often did when she was embarrassed or unsettled.

"Don't get riled up," Nathan had said quickly. "I guess a person doesn't always have control over who they love—or don't, as the case may be."

Laina smiled up at him. "I'll always love you, and I'll always pray for you, Nathan." She cleared her throat. "I wish you were going to be here for the wedding."

"Orders are orders."

Laina nodded. "I know." She put her hand on his arm. "I'll never be able to thank you—"

"Don't," Nathan said, and touched her chin lightly. He

pulled the blanket away from the face of the infant sleeping in her arms. "You take care of this little lamb," he said, stroking the baby's cheek, marveling again at the softness of her skin.

"You take care of yourself," Laina had replied, and stood on tiptoe to kiss his cheek. The baby in her arms grunted softly. "Don't let any of those—What do they call them? Buffalo soldiers? Don't let them know about this side of you for a while. Having a soft heart isn't usually seen as an asset in a lieutenant." She'd brushed an imaginary piece of dust off his new bars.

The next moment the bugler had sounded assembly. Boone put his hat back on. "Well, I guess this is it." Seeing the tears gathering in Laina's eyes, he looked away. "Laina—"

"Yes, Nathan."

"I guess I won't mind if you say a prayer now and then."

And Laina had prayed. In fact, Nathan thought as he made his way back to Lily's grave, both of the Jacksons had mentioned praying for him over the past ten years. It didn't seem possible so much time had passed. The infant in Laina's arms was a young girl now; Laina's little miracle, conceived in terrible circumstances, yet greatly loved long before she saw daylight. Laina had named the baby Joy. Clara Joy, for Clara Maxwell, the dear old woman they had all called Granny Max.

As it turned out, the baby girl was even more of a miracle than anyone realized. In the ten years since Laina had married Caleb Jackson, there hadn't been any other children born to them. Nathan could tell from their letters that Laina and Caleb were what people called "crazy in love," and when he had heard from them at Christmas, Caleb had proudly reported the news that they were expecting a baby early this summer. Still, Nathan thought it odd that the God they both believed in so strongly hadn't answered their prayers for children sooner. That, he realized, was just one more thing in a string of things he didn't understand about the way God handled people.

He certainly didn't understand how God had handled him. Ten years ago he'd still been enraged at the supposedly all-powerful God who had let Lily die an agonizing death from a snakebite. Time had apparently grown a thick layer of scar tissue around that particular unanswered question. As he stood emotionless at his wife's grave, Nathan reasoned that leaving Nebraska had been a good thing. The searing pain he'd always felt here was gone.

So many people at Fort Robinson had said things about his need to move on. Some thought he was wallowing in the past. Others just thought new scenery would be good for him. Dr. Valentine said serving with the Ninth would be a good career move. With Granny Max's death and Laina Gray's decision to marry Caleb Jackson, things just fell into place.

Since leaving Nebraska, Nathan had done what he could for the Jacksons by investing in the Four Pines Ranch. Over time, he had become more interested in ranching than he ever expected. He and Caleb wrote back and forth talking about blooded stock and future expansion. Once when on leave back east, Nathan spent some time with a group of horse fanciers, asking questions for Caleb about certain bloodlines and educating himself about thoroughbreds and Morgans.

Lately, the two men had been speculating about a stallion named Banner, wondering if bringing such a renowned animal west would enhance the reputation of the Four Pines—or bankrupt them both. In all the planning, he'd never suspected that when Fort Laramie closed, Fort Robinson would be named regimental headquarters, and he would once again find himself living in Nebraska, where everything was familiar and yet so much had changed.

He hoped the commander would agree that he'd earned an extended leave from the Ninth. There was more to his desire to visit the Four Pines than just seeing the Jacksons. Old Emmet Dorsey, his tobacco-chewing bunky from the old days, had retired and was living there. According to Caleb, Dorsey was slowing down as his arthritic knees stiffened, but he was still an encyclopedia of common sense and good advice, and the Jacksons were happy to have him around.

And then there was Rachel and Jack. Nathan had been stabbed and was a patient in the infirmary when Rachel was brought in, half frozen, nearly starved, and wild with a combination of fear and grief. Back then, she spat out her name, Winter Moon, with a venomous snarl. Nathan couldn't blame her. She and her husband, Grey Foot, had escaped the Fort Robinson barracks along with the rest of the Cheyenne involved in what the whites were calling "the Outbreak." They had eluded the soldiers for weeks before being caught. For Winter Moon, "being caught" meant she and her husband were pursued up a narrow trail to the top of a bluff. Surrounded by soldiers, Grey Foot had pried his wife's hands from around his neck and dumped her in the snow before throwing himself off a cliff. The troops had hauled Winter Moon to the Fort Robinson hospital where a number of Cheyenne were being treated.

It nearly broke Nathan's heart to see the Cheyenne victims. It took a while, but he finally succeeded in getting Winter Moon to talk to him. Little by little, he learned her story. And at the last minute before he was transferred, he put salve on his conscience by locating Grey Foot's younger brother among the captives and then talking Caleb and Laina into taking both Rachel and Jack under their wing. It didn't take much convincing.

In time, Winter Moon changed her name to Rachel. Nathan guessed she was maybe ten years younger than him. That would make her about twenty-seven now. Nathan remembered her as a desperate, dark-haired, wild-eyed scarecrow. But he also remembered that beneath the despair was a beautiful woman. He wondered why she hadn't married Jack. Everyone said the boy was a lot like his older brother. He'd even started using Grey Foot's name as his last name—as had Rachel. It confused some people, but Nathan respected the boy for honoring his brother and for finding a way to make his name live on. It was only logical that people would assume Rachel and Jack would marry someday, but Nathan knew that logic didn't always affect reality.

Oh well, Nathan told himself, it didn't do to obsess about things a person couldn't understand. If he had learned anything in the years since he left Nebraska, it was that letting things you couldn't control occupy your mind was pointless. He had, for example, stopped obsessing not only about Lily, but also about religion. On the rare occasion when he thought or talked about God, it wasn't in terms of a personal being, but rather an unfathomable power that ruled from some remote location. He bore no resentment toward people who believed differently. Laina and Caleb's letters contained frequent references to God and to prayer. Nathan appreciated their faith and could see it had done them both good. On occasion, he even admitted to himself that he liked the idea of devout believers praying for him.

Of his men who could read, several of them had their own Bibles. Nathan still had Lily's. The difference was, Nathan kept Lily's Bible as an artifact from the past, whereas men like Private Carter Blake treated their Bible reading almost as if it was as important as eating. Nathan didn't begrudge them their faith. It was just, as he once told Private Blake, that religion had done precious little for him personally, and therefore he didn't see the point in pursuing it.

"Well, Lily," Nathan said, looking down at the tombstone, "here I am again." He crouched down and ran his finger over the lettering on the stone. It was odd to feel disconnected from his own wife, not to have words come tumbling out. He still thought of Lily often. Fondly. But he hadn't brought any flowers, and for some reason he felt awkward about that. He whispered an apology.

Standing up, he returned to Granny's marker. "I'm back, Granny," he said. "Wish I could come over to Soapsuds Row and get some of your corn bread." He swallowed hard, surprised when tears, which had not come at Lily's grave, clouded his eyes.

"I think you'd be proud of some of what I've done since I left." He laughed nervously. "But not all of it. I got away from the mess with the Cheyenne back in '79. But there was still plenty of similar things to face down in the Southwest with my men." He shifted his weight. "I did my best. The men of the Ninth are some of the best fighting men I've ever seen. I'd trust my life to them any day. Heck, there's one named Carter Blake—well, I wouldn't be standing here today if it weren't for him. You'd like him, Granny. He talks about God like you used to." He chuckled. "Although he doesn't bring it up quite as often as you." He cleared his throat. "The men of the Ninth are something, Granny. They don't get their due respect from Washington. But they stand tall and walk proud. I wish you could see that."

He stopped abruptly, shaking his head at the absurdity of talking to a grave. "Old habits die hard, Granny. I used to come up here to talk to Lily. It seems I've said all I had to say to her. Guess now it's your turn." He stood for a moment with bowed head. He could almost hear Granny's voice booming, *About time you started talking to the LORD again, Nathan Boone. No better place to do it than at my grave.*

Taking a deep breath, Nathan put his hat back on. He turned to go, surprised at the sight of a very pregnant woman and a girl crossing the bridge at the river, clearly headed for the cemetery. The girl ran ahead, bounding up the hill with exaggerated strides until she saw that a soldier was inside the fence. She stopped abruptly and waited for the woman to catch up.

Nathan recognized Laina when she paused to catch her breath and pushed her bonnet back off her head, revealing her auburn hair. The closer she came the more he realized that ten years had done nothing to diminish her beauty. If anything, she was more lovely than ever, her cheeks flushed with the exertion of the walk, her face aglow with unmitigated pleasure as she called his name.

"Nathan Boone, is it really you?" she called out.

At mention of his name, the young girl whirled back around to face him. She whispered something to Laina. They laughed.

Nathan swept his hat off his head. "It's me," he said.

Laina tugged on one of the girl's red braids. "Say hello to Lieutenant Boone," she said. "And yes, he is just about the handsomest man I ever saw—except, of course, for your daddy."

"Moth-*er,*" the girl's face turned scarlet.

Nathan smiled at her. "Last time I saw you," he said, "you were about this long." He held his hands about a foot apart. "Even then you had that beautiful red hair." He thrust out his hand. "I'm pleased to meet you, Clara Joy."

"CJ," the girl corrected him.

"All right, then," he said, and shook her hand. "CJ. Pleased to meet you." He turned to Laina. "I saw the flowers."

"We came in yesterday. Caleb wants me to be near a doctor when the baby comes, and Maude at the trading post offered to put us up in her spare room."

CJ spoke up. "Pa's going to work here this summer. Then we'll have the money to make the ranch bigger."

Laina looked up at Nathan and smiled. "Who would have thought all that repair work he did with Harlan years ago would come in so handy. But CJ is right. With all the building going on here at the fort, Caleb's thinking he'll try to get on with a crew for the summer."

"What about roundup?" Nathan asked. "Isn't it almost time for that?"

"We'll do roundup like always," CJ spoke up. "Then Pa

will come to work here. And then we're buying the Dawson place right next to ours."

Laina touched CJ on the shoulder. "That's enough, CJ. Why don't you go ahead to Granny Max's grave."

CJ headed off. Laina looked up at Nathan. "CJ has never ascribed to the 'be seen and not heard' version of childhood."

"She seems very bright," Nathan said.

"Sometimes too bright for her own good," Laina laughed. "But she's her daddy's right-hand man at home. Would much rather be out in the barn with him than in the kitchen with me. The two of them have talked over this plan about the Dawson place until I think they've talked it to death."

"Is it for sale yet?"

Laina shook her head. "Not yet. But the old man keeps talking about it. And he's promised to give Caleb first chance."

Nathan nodded. "How's Dorsey doing?"

"He still loves his chewing tobacco, and his knees still kill him when the weather changes," Laina said. "But all in all he's doing fine."

"Rachel and Jack?" Nathan asked.

"Rachel rode in with us. She's over at the trading post right now. We decided she could shop for roundup supplies and then head home in the morning. You should come by later and say hello if you have time." Laina added, "And you won't believe how Jack has grown. He's a man now. And the best wrangler a rancher could want." She smiled. "He talks about you like you're a legend in your own time."

Nathan frowned. "Really?"

"He says you saved his life," CJ said. She had wandered back toward Laina and Nathan and was hanging over the top of the iron gate listening.

"I did no such thing," Nathan protested.

"All I know," said CJ, "is Jack says if he'd gone with the

rest of the Cheyenne to the reservation, who knows what would have happened. Anytime we hear news from there, it's bad."

"Well," Laina said, "whether you want to accept the hero worship or not, the fact is Jack and Rachel seem to be happy at the Four Pines, and we're grateful they are. Although," she added, "Jack would be happier if Rachel would take him a little more seriously."

"Oh, puh-*leeze,*" CJ interjected. "Do we have to talk about *that*?"

"About what?" Nathan wanted to know.

CJ took in a deep breath and recited, "Jack keeps asking Rachel to marry him, and Rachel keeps saying no, she's too old for him, and Jack gets mad or hurt or whatever it is and goes down to the barn, and then in a day or two he's back eating with us again like always until it all happens all over again," CJ made a circle in the air with her hand. "Around and around and around. It's so *boring*."

Nathan laughed. "Sounds to me like you're smarter than most grown-ups I know," he said. "At least you know to stay out of other people's love life."

"I hear you, Lieutenant Boone," Laina said. "And I suppose that means I shouldn't warn you."

"About what?"

Laina smiled innocently. "Caleb just heard that Charlotte Valentine is back at Fort Robinson."

Chapter Four

Will the Lord cast off for ever?
and will he be favourable no more? Is his mercy clean gone
for ever? doth his promise fail for evermore?
Psalm 77:7–8

If Charlotte Bishop expected escaping to Nebraska to solve all her problems, she was sorely disappointed. She had arrived in March, both grateful the railroad had finally reached Fort Robinson—precluding the necessity of enduring a frigid stagecoach ride—and angry that Garnet was assigned a "seat" in the baggage car. Her father, whom she had telegraphed from St. Louis, met her with open arms, undisguised joy at finally meeting his only grandson, and not a little surprise.

"But I wrote before Christmas," Charlotte said.

Her father shook his head. "I never got any such letter." He put his arms around her. "I'm so glad you came anyway, but why didn't you telegraph when you didn't hear from me?"

"I didn't want to insist," Charlotte said. She looked away. "I thought you might not want—"

"Not want you? Oh, my dear." He pulled her close. "I've been so lonely since your mother died. I wrote a dozen times begging you to come home. When you didn't answer—"

Charlotte frowned. She pushed herself away from her father and looked up at him. "*You* wrote to ask *me*?"

Her father nodded. "Many times. I thought perhaps . . . well, Mrs. Bishop wrote and mentioned a Major Riley."

Charlotte shuddered. She pressed her lips together. "*That,*" she said, "will never happen."

Her father put his hands on her shoulders. His eyes searched hers. "Well, you're home now."

"There's Garnet," Will said.

Charlotte and her father turned just in time to see Garnet smooth her hair back with both hands and, with a regal toss of her head, come their way.

That had been a few weeks ago. They had finally decided that Edgar, Mother Bishop's faithful butler, must have been "preempting" the mail, allowing only the letters that didn't mention Charlotte's moving home, to reach her. That likelihood birthed a simmering rage in Charlotte that made her short-tempered and suspicious.

Will brought his own emotional baggage from Michigan. The headmaster at the school for the officer's children declared him *incorrigible* and *unmanageable* and expelled him in short order. Will seemed determined to prove him right. And Charlotte felt increasingly incapable of controlling her son and her own emotions.

She had expected to feel better once she was home. Except Fort Robinson felt nothing like home. Reading her father's letters about the changes and living amongst them were two different things. She wanted anonymity and peace and quiet. Unfortunately, Colonel Bishop's military reputation was more widespread than she had realized. She was expected to make calls and become part of the same social structure she had left behind at Fort Wayne. For Will's sake, she reluctantly decided she must maintain the facade of The Grieving Widow of the Military Hero. The effort left her tired and out of sorts and only served to emphasize the lifetime of changes a decade had wrought.

Ten years ago, a young Charlotte Valentine would have taken advantage of a lovely April day by mincing along the picket fence near the fort's parade ground hoping to be noticed by recruits as they marched by. Now she sat in a rocking chair on her father's front porch, fighting back weary tears, hoping to be left alone long enough to decide how to handle her son's latest infraction of his grandfather's rules.

Ten years ago she would have been mentally designing a new gown for the Fourth of July ball, even if it was three months away. She would have thought it unfair that such a young widow had to wear mourning clothes and forego dancing. Now Charlotte wondered if there was any way to get out of the welcome event being given in her honor in a few days. How she dreaded the thought of making small talk with the string of officers who'd feel obliged to show Dr. Valentine's daughter and Colonel Bishop's widow her due respect.

Oh, no. Her father was crossing the parade ground with a tall soldier who would undoubtedly expect to be invited to stay for dinner. Charlotte closed her eyes, reminding herself that hospitality was not an optional part of military housekeeping. Officers' families were expected to welcome guests at a moment's notice and do so with grace and goodwill. She opened her eyes. This unexpected guest was tall, with very dark hair. As he got closer, Charlotte's heart skipped a beat. *Oh, no. Not him. It can't be.*

She would have known him anywhere. Ten years ago, the sight of Nathan Boone would have sent her through a well-rehearsed routine—smooth hair back off face, pull a tendril or two down onto collar, bite lips to redden them, smile, but not too much. Today, all Charlotte felt was a sense of dread not unlike her response when Mother Bishop first hauled Major Riley in the door.

Charlotte scolded herself. *It's not the same thing at all. Major Riley was on a fishing expedition for the Bishop money. Even if Lieutenant Boone's determination to remain alone has changed, he won't have a flicker of interest in you. Too many changes—and not one of them for the better.* Her waist was thicker. Four pregnancies in five years did that to a woman. Her eyes and mouth were outlined with fine wrinkles. Three infant burials did *that* to a woman, whether her husband drank and gambled or not. She'd stopped her various beauty routines years ago, and she knew it showed in the loss of shine in her ash-blond hair. She'd gone riding without gloves so often that freckles peppered the backs of her hands.

Oh, well, Charlotte thought. *What does it matter anyway*? She hadn't come back for the society functions. She'd come back for Will's sake and to take her recently departed mother's place in her father's household. And while she might have been a disappointment to Colonel Emory Bishop, she had no intention of being a disappointment to her father. She would find a way to settle Will down and run the doctor's household well, if it was the last thing she did. Doing the latter required welcoming her father's guests. Taking a deep breath, Charlotte pasted on a smile. She got up and went to the edge of the porch to greet Lieutenant Boone.

He swept his hat off his head with a white-gloved hand and tucked it beneath one arm. "I convinced your father to let me pay my respects before the reception," he said, smiling. "I suppose I'm taking advantage of the privilege of past acquaintance." He removed his glove and extended his hand. "Welcome back to Fort Robinson, Mrs. Colonel Bishop. And please accept my sympathy for your loss."

Being at a loss for words had never been a problem for Charlotte Valentine. But Emory had changed her. Turned her into something besides an empty-headed flirt, as Emory had called her. For her own good, Emory said. Taught her to think before speaking. Eventually taught her it was usually better not to speak at all, because saying the wrong thing in public would be corrected in private places in secret ways no one would ever suspect.

And so, with Emory's lessons still fresh in her mind, Charlotte simply extended her hand and allowed it to be swallowed up in the lieutenant's without saying anything besides "Thank you." When he dropped her hand, she clasped both of hers together behind her back and waited for her father to speak.

"This old reprobate seems to think he's learned enough in all his gallivanting through the Southwest to finally beat me at chess," her father said, pounding the lieutenant on the back. Looking back up at his daughter, the doctor asked, "Where's Will?"

"Garnet sent him to the trading post for some eggs," Charlotte said. She took a step toward the door. "I'll make you gentlemen some coffee."

"Have Garnet do it," her father said. "You keep us company."

"Garnet's gone down to Soapsuds Row for a visit."

"What about supper dishes?"

"I told her I'd take care of it."

"You're too easy on that girl," the doctor protested.

Charlotte put her hand on her father's shoulder. "Doing dishes makes me feel useful. Don't expect me to spend all my evenings doing needlepoint like some high-and-mighty lady." She patted his shoulder. "I came back to Fort Robinson to take care of you, Papa. Let me do it." She turned to the lieutenant. "Do you still like chokecherry pie?"

"You remembered. I'm impressed," Nathan said, as he and the doctor followed Charlotte inside.

"One of the laundresses down on the Row gave Garnet a jar of chokecherries just yesterday." Charlotte looked at her father. "Garnet hurried to get the pie into the oven before she left for her little visit. It's probably still warm. I'll get you some."

While the men headed into the parlor to collect chairs and a chessboard to be moved out onto the porch, Charlotte made her way through the dining room, down the short service hall, and into the kitchen. Once in the kitchen, she took down two white china dessert plates and fired up the stove for coffee. How many times had she dreamed of serving pie to Nathan Boone, picturing how she would put a single flower beside his plate.

While she waited for water to heat, Charlotte ground coffee, thinking back to simpler days when her only problems were figuring out how to convince her mother to let her try a new hairdo or how to catch a soldier's eye at the next dance. The aroma of freshly ground coffee propelled her memories to another time. *"It's too strong, woman!"* An angry voice shouted. *"How many times do I have to tell you to measure it out more carefully!"*

Charlotte's hands began to tremble. Closing her eyes tightly, she took a deep breath, raised her palms to her cheeks and began to softly sing a song she'd learned from Garnet. "Swing low, sweet chariot, comin' for to carry me home. . . ." Opening her eyes wide, Charlotte looked around her, reminding herself, *You ARE home. It is OVER.* By the time the coffee was ready, she was calm again. She poured coffee, took up the heavily-laden serving tray, and headed back toward the front of the house.

The men were already seated on the front porch, the chessboard between them. She could hear their voices and smell the smoke from their evening cigars wafting in the open front-parlor window. She smiled to herself. Cigar smoke was a welcome change from earlier in the day when they had been downwind from the privies.

As she advanced toward the front door, Charlotte's foot landed in a pile of something just slippery enough to throw her off-balance. Two pieces of pie, two cups of hot coffee, the coffeepot, sugar bowl, and creamer went one way, while Charlotte went the other, landing with her left hand immersed up to her wrist in what proved to be a pile of manure. Shrieks of laughter erupted from behind the parlor sofa even as her father and Lieutenant Boone rushed inside.

"Emory William Bishop!" Her father bellowed, swooping behind the sofa and emerging with a wriggling boy in tow. "If this kind of behavior is going to continue . . ."

"Papa," Charlotte pleaded, grimacing with pain. She blinked back tears, almost passing out as she grasped her left forearm with her good right hand and pulled her left hand out of the pile of manure. She closed her eyes and turned her head, even as Boone knelt at her side.

"You'd better let the boy go and come look at her wrist, doc," he said, leaning closer. "Keep your eyes closed, Mrs. Colonel. It's probably not all that bad, but I bet it hurts something fierce."

Charlotte flinched, pulling away when the lieutenant tried to put a comforting hand on her shoulder. Clamping her lips together, she concentrated on breathing evenly. *You will not faint. You will not faint. Swing low . . . carry me home . . . band of angels.* Her head swam.

Her father knelt next to her on the floor. "Dear Lord in heaven," was all he said.

Charlotte spoke. "Is that . . . is that really what I think it is sticking . . . out?" Her stomach roiled.

"Don't think about it," her father said quickly. "Keep your eyes closed and concentrate on breathing. Slow, even breaths, dear. And don't you dare faint on me. I need you to hold still while I get it wrapped. Lieutenant, hand me that napkin."

"I'm not going to faint on you," Charlotte snapped. Her voice broke as she asked, "Where . . . where's Will?"

"Don't you worry about Will. There'll be time enough to deal with him later."

"He'll be scared. Scared that he's hurt me." Charlotte swallowed hard and bit her lip when her father tightened the makeshift bandage around her wrist.

"And well he should be. I'm going to knock some sense

into that boy if it's the last thing I ever do," her father snapped.

"You'll do no such thing," Charlotte begged. She cried out, gasped for air, and clutched her father's arm. "Please, Papa. Promise me you won't."

Her father pulled her head onto his shoulder. "Now, Charlotte. Calm down. You know I won't. I'm just mad. Now, stop worrying about Will. We've got to get you over to the hospital."

Boone stood up. "I'll fetch a steward and get some men headed this way with a litter."

"No," Charlotte gasped. "Just get me to my own bed." She looked up at her father. "Call Garnet back from the Row. She'll know what to do. I'll be fine."

"You're going to need surgery," her father said.

"I'm *not* going to any hospital," Charlotte insisted. "And certainly not on a litter for all the world to see."

"You *are* going to the hospital."

"I'll carry you," Boone offered.

"Don't be ridiculous," Charlotte insisted. She motioned him away. "Stop fussing and let me get up." Taking a deep breath, she bit down hard on her lower lip as she pushed herself up off the floor and leaned against the wall, waiting for the room to stop reeling. She was to remember the irony of this moment for the rest of her life. As Miss Charlotte Valentine she had actually practiced swooning and falling into the arms of a handsome soldier. But it was 1890 now. She was no longer a child, and she didn't swoon. What she did was worse. The last thing she would remember was doubling over and vomiting all over Lieutenant Nathan Boone's polished boots.

CHAPTER FIVE

Depart from evil, and do good; seek peace, and pursue it.

PSALM 34:14

IT WASN'T JUST THE IRON GRIP OF THE MOLASSES-colored hand clamped around his ankle—although that was surely enough to make Will's heart lurch. But once caught in the man's iron grip, he still had to look past the bulging muscles in the soldier's forearm to two scowling ice-blue eyes. He still had to hear the deep voice rumble ominously, "Just *what* do you think you are doing?!"

Usually extremely talented at squirming out of the grasp of whoever was attempting discipline, Will went limp against the straw and looked up, wide-eyed. "N-n-nothin'," he stammered. "I wasn't doin' nothing."

The soldier let go of Will's ankle and straightened up, his hulking outline filling the space at the opposite end of the stall—the space between Will and freedom. Will opted for backing away instead of trying to bolt past the angry private. He crabbed backward in the straw and plastered his back against the rough boards forming the front of one of the several dozen stalls in Company B's stable. The bay gelding Will had untied lowered his head and blew softly into the straw through velvety black nostrils, slowly shaking his head back and forth. *Great,* Will thought, *even the horse is mad at me.*

"Move over, Dutch," the soldier said, leaning against the bay's haunches. When the horse stepped sideways, the soldier reached forward to grab his lead. He looked down at Will. "I'm gonna back my horse out of here so you don't get stepped on. You stay put." The soldier didn't take his eyes off Will as he reached for a huge iron ring and hitched Dutch out in the walkway.

His horse out of the way, the soldier lounged against the side of the stall, hardly seeming to take notice of Will as he talked. "Funny thing about a man like me. You can call him every name in the book of life, and he doesn't get riled. You can refer to his race and his lineage in whatever terms you want, and he just lets it roll off; does his duty and gets on with life. You can order a march across a desert where it's so boiling hot even the rattlesnakes sweat. Order him through a blizzard and expect him to get half frozen, and a man like me, why, he'll salute and say 'Yes, sir.' Obey orders or die trying."

The man paused, reached for a piece of straw and inserted it into his mouth. He chewed on it for so long Will thought he had forgotten what he wanted to say. But then he threw the straw to the ground and crouched down, glaring at Will as he said, "But you mess with that man's horse, sonny—the horse that carried him *across* that desert and *through* that blizzard, the horse that saved his life in a fight with the Apaches down in Arizona Territory, the horse that has been all the family that man's got—you mess with that horse and you've got yourself a fight." He stood up. "So you'd better have a good explanation for why you were messing with one of the best horses the good Lord ever set on four feet, or—"

"Or what?!" Will blurted out. Hearing his own voice gave such welcome release to his emotions that Will mistook the relief for courage. "You can't do anything to me. You're just a private. My grandfather is Dr. Avery Valentine—*Colonel* Valentine to you. You wouldn't dare do anything to me!"

The soldier's eyebrows shot up in mock surprise. "Oh, so it's *you*." He pushed his hat back off his forehead. "I've heard about you."

"Then you know you'd better leave me alone," Will said, his voice wavering only a little. He'd blustered his way out of more than one tight spot with bullies back in Michigan, and it looked like maybe he was going to manage to do it again. The man was, after all, *only* a private. Will inched away from the stall wall, looking for an escape route.

"Aren't you the same boy who tied a pan to Frenchy Dubois's dog's tail the other day and sent him through the quartermaster's herd?"

Will shrugged. "Just having a little fun. Didn't hurt anything."

"And aren't you the same boy who put salt in the punch bowl at the officers' club social last Friday night?"

"So what?" Will sneered, "*You* weren't there. Didn't have anything to do with you." He inched along the back of the stall. The way the horse was standing, he just might be able to duck under its neck and dodge out the door. "And if you know all that about me then you know who my grandfather is and you know you'd better not mess with me or he'll . . . he'll . . ."

"How'd you do it?"

Will stopped short. He looked at the private, who was staring at him solemnly.

Frowning, he hesitated. "What?"

"Well," the soldier said, leaning back against the stall. "I just wondered how you managed to sneak in there and not get caught." He winked. "That was a wondrous prank. Don't know how you managed a whole *sack* of salt. How come they didn't see you do it?"

He wasn't sure, but Will thought the blue eyes might be thawing a little. Was that an almost-grin barely visible beneath the man's bushy moustache? He shrugged.

"Nothing to it. Didn't have to sneak. I just put salt in a sugar sack is all. It was easy. Frenchy didn't even know I made the switch. He's almost blind anyway. A broken-down old soldier like that is easy to fool."

"Hey!" The blue eyes grew cold again. The corners of the mouth turned down. "You don't disrespect a man who's been through what that old soldier's been through, young man. You salute him."

"What do you mean, what he's been through?"

"Oh. So you don't know about Sergeant Charles Dubois?"

"I know he's old. And he married the trader's widow, and now when he's not behind the counter he just sits on the front porch at the store and chews tobacco and spins yarns."

The soldier nodded. "Well, maybe sometime after you apologize for messing with Dutch here—maybe sometime I'll tell you about Sarge. But not now. It's too near time for parade. So you get outta here. And the next time you want to make the acquaintance of a soldier's horse, you ask the soldier first. You could get yourself hurt. Dutch is a good old boy, but some of these hacks in this stable would just as soon eat you for supper as look at you. And they could do it, too. Send you flying with one well-placed kick." The soldier stood up. "And as you've pointed out, since I'm just a lowly private and your grandfather is *Colonel* Valentine, I don't want to be held to blame for his grandson getting sent to glory ahead of schedule."

"He wouldn't care," Will said. He ducked his head, mortified by the blush he could feel creeping up his pale cheeks. "Even if he *is* looking for me, it's just to give me a walloping."

"You think you need wallopin'?" the private asked.

Will shook his head, then looked down at the soldier's boots, embarrassed by the tears filling his eyes. "I didn't mean it. Didn't mean to hurt anybody. Sure didn't mean to hurt Ma." He tried to control his breathing, tried to keep the short jerky sounds from overtaking his voice.

The soldier was quiet again. When he spoke, the ragged edges of anger in his voice had mellowed into something almost kind. "Mothers are a strange breed, son. They forget hurts faster than any creature alive. Whatever you did, if you ran off, I bet she's more worried than she is angry." He picked up a hay rake and stabbed the straw with it. "Either way, running off on a stolen government horse is no way to handle it. If that's what you were thinking of doing, you need to think again. That kind of behavior never solves anything. Just makes a man miserable for longer."

"You don't know what I did," Will said. "It's bad." He rattled off the prank, embarrassed by the tears that began to flow while he talked.

"Are you sure she broke her wrist?" the soldier asked.

"I saw the bone sticking out," the boy murmured, touching his own wrist as if to illustrate the injury.

The soldier set the hay rake aside and crouched back down. "Well your grandpa's a good doctor. I bet your ma will be just fine."

Will looked into the blue eyes. "That's not what he said. He said the manure means it'll get infected as sure as anything. He said she could . . . she could . . ." It was so horrible, he could barely make himself continue. "He said she might *die*!" The last word was said through a mighty sob that erupted from his innards and ended any hope of further speech. He crumpled back down into the straw, hid his face against his arms and let the sobs come.

"No such thing," the soldier said.

Feeling a giant hand on his shoulder, Will's first inclination was to jerk away. He went with his second inclination, though. He threw himself against the stranger's chest and for the first time in a long, long while became the frightened little boy he was. Will had learned to hide that boy beneath pranks and bluster and anger. He'd learned to keep that boy hidden all day, every day. Only once in a while had he let that boy out—and only *after* his mother had tucked him in and left him alone. Sometimes then, in the dark, Will had covered his head with a goose-down pillow so no one could hear. Because when he came out, that boy inside always had to holler and cry. Now, feeling the warmth of strong arms around him, Will let that frightened little boy cry his tears.

"You know better than that," Carter said when Will begged him to go home with him. "An enlisted man doesn't just stroll up to a Colonel's front door and knock. And besides that, first call for retreat will sound soon. I've got to get Dutch saddled and get myself ready for parade."

"Then I won't go back," Will said, the rebellion returning to his voice. "I'll hike up onto the butte."

"And do what?"

"Maybe I'll just take a run at one of 'em and be done with it," Will blurted out. "Like that Cheyenne warrior I heard about."

Carter didn't question the plan. He nodded slowly. "That's one answer. Sure would make it hard on your ma, though. She'd blame herself. Mothers are like that, you know. Whatever bad their young'uns do, they seem to take it on themselves."

"That's crazy. If I run off it's not her fault."

"She'd think it was. And she'd grieve until the day she died, wondering what she did wrong." Carter tilted his head to one side. "But the other option is for you to stand up like a man. Take the blame on yourself for what you did. Tell her you're sorry."

"She wouldn't believe me."

"She would," Blake said. "*I* believe you're sorry, and I just met you."

"Aw," Will said, kicking at the straw. "That's because I acted like a baby, crying on your shoulder and all."

"There's nothing wrong with a man crying when he's done wrong, Will Bishop," Carter said. "The fact is, it takes a better man to apologize and shed a few tears than to lock it all up inside and go out and do harm to someone else—or himself."

"You're just saying that 'cause you want me to go home," Will said.

The soldier's blue eyes narrowed. "I never lie, Will Bishop. Never. And I'm telling you the best thing is to admit your wrongs, and go see your ma. Your grandpa was angry when he said those things, and he'll be as glad as your ma to see you. Or my name isn't Carter Blake."

Looking up at the man, Will swallowed hard.

A few minutes later the looming shadow of the giant behind him gave Will courage as he stood at his grandfather's back door, doing his best not to tremble while he waited for Garnet to answer his hesitant knock.

Chapter Six

Let us therefore come boldly unto the throne of grace, that we may obtain mercy, and find grace to help in time of need.

Hebrews 4:16

Whatever Garnet Irvin had expected when she agreed to accompany her widowed employer west, it did not include the sight of a hulking black soldier with muddy boots appearing at her back door with Will Bishop in tow. Of course Garnet realized that when it came right down to it, it was not *her* back door. It wasn't even Doctor Valentine's. The United States Army owned both the back door and the house attached to it. Still, Garnet Irvin had a way of sweetly, yet completely, reigning over whatever territory ended up being assigned to her by the white people who thought they were in charge. Thus, in the Year of our Lord 1890, Garnet Irvin's newest kingdom was comprised of a surgeon's residence at Fort Robinson, Nebraska—including the back door.

Reigning over the surgeon's residence meant many things. For instance, it meant that you sweetly accepted whatever your employers suggested and then quietly did what you pleased. And as long as they had clean linens and an immaculate house, they usually didn't notice. On the rare occasions when Dr. Valentine did notice and try to take issue with Garnet's rule, a freshly baked pie provided a satisfactory distraction.

Reigning over the surgeon's residence also meant doing what one could to keep young Will Bishop from completely destroying his mother's peace of mind—what little of it Mrs. Bishop had left. And so, however Garnet felt about the man in the muddy boots, she was relieved to have him haul Will home so she could send the little rascal over to the hospital. Maybe then his mother would stop worrying about Will and listen a little better to what the doctors were saying, which was that they needed to do surgery right away.

But Mrs. Bishop wasn't even considering surgery. Not until she saw Will. "I won't have him coming in here later tonight and thinking I'm almost dead. I want to see him before you do it," she had insisted.

"Then I'll find him," that nice Lieutenant Boone had said. And he'd gone looking. Now here was Will, but no sign of Lieutenant Boone.

The private who had Will in tow seemed to have been rendered speechless. Garnet waited for him to speak, but the soldier just stared at her with eyes so blue it would be impossible not to notice them. Just as it was impossible for Garnet not to notice his physical size. Will's entire shoulder was hidden by one of the man's hands. Garnet observed it all without a word and then met the private's gaze, hoping to encourage him to say something. When Will was dragged home there was usually a lot more to it than someone just bringing Will home. People usually had complaints. Something was usually broken. Garnet waited for the telling of Will Bishop's most recent sin.

But this time there was no complaint, no tale of a broken treasure. When the giant man finally cleared his throat, all he did was introduce himself as "Private Blake, ma'am" and add "Found the boy over in the stables. He's worried about his mama."

Garnet nodded and turned to Will. "Your mama needs surgery right away to mend that wrist," she said. "But she won't hear of it until she sees you. So you need to get yourself over to the hospital. Right now."

"Is she gonna be all right?"

Garnet heard the terror in the boy's voice. When she noticed Private Blake patting his shoulder, her voice mellowed. "Your grandpa said he saw a Dr. Reed work on a homesteader who had a much worse break a few years ago. Said the man's ankle was almost crushed. He says he learned a lot from Dr. Reed, and he thinks it will be all right. But since it's been broken once before, that might make it a little harder."

At mention of the other time his ma broke her wrist, Will squeezed his eyes shut. He tried not to ever think about that night, but now it all came back. Father had been angry and shouting and then there was a loud thump against the wall separating Will's room from his parents. The next morning when Ma appeared at the breakfast table with her arm in a sling and a story about falling in the dark, Will realized that what had hit the wall the night before was not a *thing*. Not long after that Will was moved to a bedroom farther away from his parents. As time went on, he realized he had begun to hate Emory Bishop and would do whatever it took to be as unlike the man as possible. But Grandfather Valentine said he looked just like his father. And now, as he stood at his grandfather's back door looking up at Garnet, all Will could think about was how not only did he *look* like the man he hated—he was starting to act like him, too. He'd even broken his mother's wrist. He squeezed his eyes shut trying to keep the tears from flowing. When he was unsuccessful, Garnet's voice gentled even more.

"Don't cry, Will. Everyone knows you didn't mean to hurt your mama. She's more worried about you than she is about herself. So you just go on over there and ease her mind. I'll be along directly when I get this beef tea clarified."

Will looked up at Garnet's smile.

"Nothing like my beef tea to bring a body back to health."

Lieutenant Boone came around the corner of the house. Private Blake straightened up, saluted, and stepped back. "Found him in the stables, sir. In Dutch's stall."

Boone returned Blake's salute, thanked him for seeing the boy home, and dismissed him. Then he turned to Will. "Your mother won't let your grandfather do a thing until she talks to you. Let's get over to the hospital."

He hadn't expected this. Hadn't expected that Grandfather would be gone, called out to check on some fool soldier who'd shot himself cleaning a rifle. Hadn't expected Ma to be left in the hands of a hospital steward while Garnet made beef tea. Hadn't expected her hospital bed to be at the far end of a row of empty cots, surrounded by upright screens so a person couldn't even see who was there. And when he finally did walk the interminable distance to those upright screens and peer around them, Will hadn't expected his mother's face to be as pale as death.

Look what you did. It was the same voice that had so often warned Will he'd better watch himself and be ready to duck. The voice wasn't audible this evening, but Will could still hear the words as clearly as if it were Father and not Lieutenant Boone standing beside him. He startled when a hand touched his shoulder. Realizing it was Boone, he resisted the urge to twist away.

"She's just sleeping," Boone said, and crouched down beside him. "Look carefully, son. She's breathing low and even. Your grandfather likely gave her something for the pain."

Boone was right. The sheet covering his mother's still form was rising and falling with her even, deep breaths. Will felt the spring wound tight inside him relax a little.

"There you are."

It was his grandfather's voice sounding from the doorway. The spring wound tight again, and Will stepped closer to Boone while his grandfather strode up the aisle between the two rows of empty cots.

"One of my men found him in the stables," Boone said.

Will pressed his lips together to keep his chin from trembling.

Grandfather's voice was stern. "Do you have any idea how serious this is, young man? Do you know how many limbs I've amputated after injuries like this?"

Now look what you've done. They'll cut off her arm and it's your fault.

"Answer me."

Yeah. Go ahead. Tell the old man you're sorry. Whine and squeeze out a tear or two. Give the old man what he wants. You know you're too soft to be a soldier so just go ahead and cry.

Will swallowed hard. He wanted to answer, but somewhere between the spring wound up inside and the voice in his head, he lost the words. His mother's foot moved beneath the sheet next to him. Will jumped and looked back up toward the head of the bed. "Is she . . . is she . . ."

"She'll have surgery to repair the break," Grandfather said. "We'll have to put some drains in the incision to try to control the infection."

"D-drains?"

"Little glass tubes. Over the next few days they'll likely be dripping with pus." The doctor clasped his hands behind his back and shook his head from side to side. "What were you thinking, Will? *Manure,* for goodness' sake."

"Is she going to die?" Will blurted the words out past the tightly wound spring, past the voice in his head.

"Of course she isn't going to die. I won't let that happen."

The words gave no comfort. Will knew soldier-talk when he heard it. The kind of talk that made it sound like nothing was impossible. Will's father had told him battlefield stories of unbelievable things like soldiers running on broken legs to get to safety or lifting loaded wagons to free comrades pinned beneath the wheels. Even miracles seemed to be possible on the battlefield.

But not for you, Will Bishop, the voice in his head whispered. *The old man is just blustering soldier-talk. He'll have to cut off her arm in a few days. He knows she's going to die. He's just being a good soldier. She's going to die. You've killed your mother.* Will closed his eyes. A shudder passed the entire length of his body. He felt a flood of tears threatening and scrubbed his cheeks with the palms of his hands.

"Garnet went home to make some beef tea," Grandfather was saying. "You run tell her I'll sit with your mother tonight. She was talking about bringing a bedroll up here. Tell her that won't be necessary—but the beef tea is a good idea and she should bring that early in the morning. I'll keep the night watch." He leaned down and put a hand on Will's shoulder. "We need to operate soon, but I'll wait for you to get back before I take her into surgery. If she's awake at all, you can talk to her then."

Will shuddered again.

"You hear me, boy?" His grandfather's hand shoved him toward the door. "Run, now, and tell Garnet what I told you. Lieutenant Boone has evening parade to worry about. Don't be wasting any more of his time."

As he headed for the door, Will felt the spring inside him unwind a little. There was something he could do to help his mother. He might be a bad person, but here was something good he could do.

"Will," his grandfather called out.

Will stopped at the door and turned around.

"You didn't mean to hurt her. I know that. But this is serious. We still need to have a talk about your behavior."

Will nodded. "Yes, sir," he said, saluted, spun around on his heel and charged out the door, across the trail and one corner of the parade ground, and up the row of officers' quarters toward the one occupied by the Valentines.

"Run faster, you little runt. Can't you run any faster? You'll never be a good soldier. Too small for the infantry. Unfit for the cavalry. I can't believe a son of mine would turn out to fear horses. Maybe that's it. Maybe you aren't really my son after all. That would explain a lot. Run faster, you little runt. Can't you run any faster?"

"Grandfather said you don't need to come tonight," Will repeated when Garnet told him to wait a minute and then emerged from her room behind the kitchen with a pillow and a bedroll.

"I heard you," Garnet replied. She poured the beef tea into a glass jar and settled it into a basket along with some other things, including Charlotte's hairbrush and comb. Handing the bedroll to Will, Garnet headed for the back door. "Let's go," she said.

In the time it had taken Will to carry the message to Garnet and for Garnet to pack up, the evening retreat formations and drills had been conducted on the parade ground. Garnet and Will were rounding the commanding officer's headquarters building at the end of Officers Row and crossing the trail toward the hospital when the retreat formation was dismissed. Two soldiers, mounted on bays, broke away from their company and rode up.

Lieutenant Boone and Private Blake dismounted. Boone asked, "Are they going to operate tonight?"

"That's what Grandfather said," Will replied.

"Do you mind if we wait with you?" Boone asked. He nodded at Blake, "Private Blake here is something of an unofficial chaplain for the Ninth. It can't hurt to have a praying man on your side."

Will stared up at the two men. He looked at Garnet, who lifted her free hand to her mouth as she said, "It's not my place to say."

Will spoke up. "A prayer can't hurt, can it? Ma won't mind."

"Then we'll come," Lieutenant Boone said. He called on another soldier to take the two horses to the stables, and he and Private Blake fell in behind Garnet and Will.

By the time they all filed into the hospital, the sun had set and an orderly had lighted the oil lamps hanging from the ceiling. Nathan and Blake lingered at the door. "We don't want to intrude," Nathan said. "You go on. We'll wait here."

"If you think it will settle her mind," Blake said to Garnet, "tell the missus I'll be praying for her."

Nathan saw the smile Garnet flashed at the private. "Thank you, sir."

Blake nodded and perched on a narrow bench outside the hospital ward door.

Garnet took Will's hand and led him toward the corner of the empty ward, to where the portable screens shielded Charlotte's bed from view. Nathan lingered in the doorway and saw Will stop at the foot of the bed and grab one of the iron rails and hang on.

"There's my boy," he heard Charlotte say. "Where'd you run off to? I've been worried about you."

Will's breath came in little jerks. Nathan could tell the boy was trying hard not to cry as he asked, "Does it hurt terrible?" He realized he was rubbing his own wrist as he listened.

"It hurts, baby," Charlotte said. "But not as much as it hurts to think you were afraid to come to Mama. We agreed you'd never be afraid to come to me. About anything. No matter what. You remember that?"

Will inhaled again and let out a raggedy moan. "I'm sor-sorry, Mama. I didn't mean—"

"Of course you didn't mean to hurt me, baby. Come here and hold my hand."

Will moved from the foot of the bed to his mother's side and out of sight. Nathan imagined him taking his mother's good hand. Remembering his own mother's last illness, he could imagine Will laying his head on his mother's shoulder, could almost feel her warm breath as she kissed the boy on his forehead or cheek. Feeling guilty for eavesdropping on the moment, he stepped away from the door and settled on the bench beside Private Blake.

The doctor's surgical assistant must have arrived then, as there were other voices, and finally he heard Will approach, his younger footsteps echoing on the hospital's bare board floor. Will appeared in the doorway, with Garnet at his side. From behind the screens, Charlotte called, "Make him eat, Garnet. I can hear his stomach rumbling from way over here."

When Will refused to go home to eat, no one fought him. He supposed they thought he'd eventually grow weary of waiting on the bench at the hospital. But sitting still was nothing new for Will Bishop. He'd spent so many hours being disciplined with "sit still," he'd practically made a study of chairs. There was the Windsor chair in Grandmother Bishop's formal dining room back in Michigan. It had a tilted slippery seat that made a boy feel like he was going to slide right onto the floor beneath the dining room table, something Will often wished he could do when he'd been told to "sit there until you eat every last pea on that plate."

His own bedroom at Grandmother Bishop's had a plain oak chair that he liked to draw up to the window overlooking the apple orchard. After being sent to his room for spilling his milk at dinner, Will could sit in that chair for hours, watching Shep, the groundkeeper's dog, snuffle in the grass and bark at garter snakes. In spite of the reason he knew the oak chair so well, Will liked it. Being in the chair meant he wasn't going to have to face his father's belt.

The kitchen at Grandmother's held a variety of chairs. Will's favorite had once been painted blue. It was scarred and nicked and a little wobbly, but it was higher than most chairs and sometimes Garnet let Will pull it up to the counter when she made pie crust. If there was any crust left over, she'd let him dust the pieces with cinnamon and sugar, and when they came out of the oven she gave them to Will along with a glass of milk. Those were the times when that old blue chair was Will's favorite place in the world.

There were other chairs in Will's life, too. The one he hated most was red mahogany. Its back was almost a semicircle, and when he sat on that chair in the entryway of Grandmother's grand old home he felt swallowed up, not only by the chair but also by life, because being ordered to wait in that chair meant facing Father the minute he came in the door. Waiting in that chair meant admitting to disobedience of one kind or another and having Father mete out punishment. For most children, waiting for their father was probably the worst part of the punishment. For Will, the waiting was only the beginning of sorrows.

Will's thoughts were brought back to the present situation when he heard Lieutenant Boone ask Private Blake to pray for his ma. Will had never heard anything like the big man's simple prayer. It was, Will decided later, as if God were a special kind of doctor and Private Blake's good friend; as if God stopped by and was right there with them, ready and able to help the minute the private asked. Will had never heard anyone address God the way Private Blake did. He thought people were supposed to grovel at God's feet and beg for what they wanted, and that sometimes God gave it but most of the time He didn't just to remind people that He was in charge. Will wasn't sure, but he thought Blake just might be making God angry, treating Him like he was a friend or something. He hoped God wouldn't hold it against his mother and mess up her surgery.

"Do you know how to play chess, son?" Lieutenant

Boone asked as soon as they all said *amen*. When Will shook his head, Boone declared that to be a shame. He left for a few minutes, and when he returned he had a leather-covered box tucked under his arm that, when opened, proved to be a portable chess set that he positioned on another chair between himself and Will. As the night wore on, Boone explained the arrangement of the pieces to Will. When he came to the figure called a knight, Will looked up at him and asked abruptly, "How'd you get to be a soldier?"

Boone continued placing chess pieces on the board. "Well, I was a little older than you when my Uncle Billy visited my parents' farm in Missouri. He was on leave from his regiment in the War Between the States." Boone shook his head back and forth. "And the stories that man could tell. I thought every soldier in the army was a hero. It all seemed so grand. And when Uncle Billy walked down the street in our little town . . ." Boone chuckled. "Well, all the women noticed. I decided being in the army was the best thing a boy could do. We were poor, and when my pa died, my ma married a man I didn't like much. So I begged and begged until Uncle Billy got me signed on as drummer boy for his regiment." Boone sat back in his chair. "And I've been in the army ever since. Never wanted to do anything else." He moved the knight on the chessboard. "What about you, son? You plan to be a soldier when you grow up?"

Will shook his head from side to side. "Father told me I couldn't."

"Why not?"

"I'm too small. Too slow. I wouldn't be a good soldier."

"So what did your father think you should be?"

Will shrugged. "He never said. Just said I wouldn't be a good soldier. It made him mad sometimes." Picking up a pawn, he murmured, "He was a cavalry officer. Like you. First thing I remember about my father is him lifting me up on Buster. Buster was a really tall horse, and he didn't like me one bit. I remember him looking around at me and rolling his eyes and snorting. Then he bucked and I fell off. It scared me when he picked up one of his big feet. I thought he was going to step on me. Or bite me. Father laughed. When he went to put me back up on Buster, I cried. It made him mad." Will bit his lower lip. "I've sort of been afraid of horses since then."

Will pointed at the rook. "What's this one do?"

Boone went back to explaining how each piece could or could not move across the chessboard.

Will interrupted him. "You ever fight any Indians?"

Boone nodded.

Will drew his legs up and wrapped his arms around them, resting his chin on his knee. "Tell me about it."

CHAPTER SEVEN

A foolish son is a grief to his father,
and bitterness to her that bare him.
PROVERBS 17:25

HAMMERS POUNDING, VOICES SHOUTING, MULES braying, wagon wheels grinding—the noise of construction at Fort Robinson reached Laina's ears long before she was ready to get up. Barely awake she snuggled against her husband and moaned, "What *is* that infernal noise?!"

Caleb spooned up behind her and kissed the back of her neck. "Progress, Mrs. Jackson. The sound of progress." He slid out of bed. "You stay put. I'll get you some coffee."

Laina closed her eyes, hoping for a few more minutes of sleep. But the baby was awake, too, rolling and kicking inside her, gleefully pummeling until she sat up to catch her breath.

Caleb came in with coffee. He reached over and covered her belly with his hand. "Whoa, in there," he said, leaning down to talk. "Give your Mama a rest, son. There's plenty of time to learn bull riding and wrestling later." He winked at his wife. "Want to take a walk with me?"

Laina nodded. "As soon as the coffee takes hold."

"I'll be in the kitchen," he said. "Mrs. Dubois made flapjacks!"

In the ten years since she and Caleb had married and started ranching, Laina had visited Fort Robinson often. She'd witnessed the beginnings of an entirely new collection of buildings around a larger parade ground to the west of the original fort. This morning, as she and Caleb and CJ made their way around the West End, they paused before one of the newly constructed barracks, a frame L-shaped building with a main living area across the front and a kitchen and dining room at the back. Caleb pointed east toward the old log barracks on the opposite side of the original parade ground. "It sure is a far cry from where I lived. Can you imagine . . . running water in the kitchen!"

"Why didn't they just tear down that awful old place?" CJ asked, nodding toward the old barracks.

Laina agreed. "It has to be filthy . . . and flea infested."

"Apparently several families claimed it right away," Caleb said. "They call it the Bee Hive now. You know how the army does things. If they haul their wife and children along, enlisted men are on their own to provide shelter."

CJ spoke up. "I'm glad *we* don't have to live any place like that!"

"Well, as a matter of fact," Caleb said, "that's where you'll be going to school."

"There better not be any *fleas,*" CJ retorted.

"You just see to it you pay attention in class and learn a lot," her father said.

Caleb pointed toward what he said was the administration building. "They have hundreds of library books in the post library," Caleb said, "and some of the companies even have their own reading rooms now." He shook his head. "Quite a change since I was a new recruit." He pointed south toward Soapsuds Row where Laina had once lived. "Not much has changed over there though."

"Except the view out the back door," Laina pointed out. "Stables and corrals instead of wide open country."

They walked by a huge pile of adobe bricks. "I can see

why they needed ten adobe mills," Laina commented.

Caleb nodded. "Frenchy's watched them plow up the clay. Says they found a good source about four miles away, and before all the building is finished, they will have made hundreds of thousands of bricks right here on the site. Their biggest problem—other than delays in shipping—has been finding enough labor." He nodded toward the east. "Crawford's booming, too. Once I get on a work crew here at the fort, maybe I'll be able to make connections in both places. Between the ready cash from working here *and* the future market for Four Pines beef here and in town, the Jackson family should do very well."

He leaned over and spoke to Laina's belly, "You hear that, son? And it's all for you and your brothers." They walked between a maze of barns and corrals and headed east toward where the post trader's store still occupied the northwest corner of the old fort grounds, now known as the "East End."

CJ grumbled. "It's going to drive us crazy having to listen to hammering all day every day."

"I knew things were going to change, but my goodness," Laina said, nodding toward the swarms of enlisted men and civilians clustered around the work sites, some laying foundation, others hammering siding or installing windows. Dust hung in the air from the continual passing of supply and water wagons. More dust was being kicked up on the new parade ground, where a company of black soldiers performed a mounted exercise to the shouted orders of a white sergeant. "It just doesn't look like the same place," she wondered aloud.

Frenchy Dubois, the soldier who had married a widowed Maude Gruber five years ago, appeared in the doorway to the trading post. He motioned to CJ, teasing, "Ooh-la-la, *ma petite,* I will keep ze rifle close by." When CJ looked confused, Frenchy raised an imaginary rifle to his shoulder and took aim. "To keep ze soldier boys away from the lovely young woman you are to become."

CJ made a face. "Boys? UGH!"

Frenchy shrugged. "You don' like boys? Is good! Soon enough you will be changing ze tune, *non*?" He motioned everyone inside, where Maude was piling flapjacks onto a platter.

"Come in," she said and pointed Caleb to the chair at the head of the table.

"Thanks very much, Mrs. Dubois," Caleb said, patting his stomach, "but I already ate more than my fill." He leaned down and kissed Laina on the cheek. "Enjoy the girl talk. I'll be back when I have a job." He left with Frenchy.

"How are you feeling dear?" Maude asked, patting Laina's shoulder.

"Like a spring cow ready to burst." Laina settled heavily into a chair. "Or at least how I imagine a spring cow feels right before the calf makes his appearance."

"Might be a she-calf," Maude observed.

"Oh, it's a boy," Laina said quickly.

"It had *better* be a boy," CJ agreed.

"Really?"

"Caleb ordered a boy," Laina said, grinning. She patted her belly. "And I think he'll get his wish. Carrying this one has been nothing like CJ. This little guy is three times as active and he's just settled in differently. Rachel says her mother always believed that if you carry the baby lower, it's a boy. I definitely think it's a boy."

Maude arched one eyebrow. "Well, Rachel can predict and Caleb Jackson can order up all the boys he wants, but I expect the good Lord will send what the good Lord will send, and Mr. Jackson will just have to adjust."

"Speaking of Rachel," Laina said, "where is she?"

"Already up front, filling her order. I told her to help herself and just leave me a list of what goes into the wagon headed for the ranch." Maude settled into a chair and stacked five flapjacks on the plate in front of her. "Now, ladies, let's thank the Lord and get down to business!"

• • • ◆ • • •

Nathan Boone groaned when reveille sounded the morning after Charlotte Bishop's surgery. He'd fallen into bed three hours ago, but it felt like only ten minutes. He had sent Private Blake to his quarters shortly after the private offered up his prayer for Charlotte's welfare and young Will's peace of mind. Nathan found Blake's concern for the latter quite touching, and evidently Garnet Irvin did, too. Nathan had noticed the admiring glance she had cast in Blake's direction as the private exited the hospital and headed for the barracks.

Nathan had stayed on through the night, playing chess and telling stories until fatigue finally threatened to send Will Bishop face first into the chessboard. "Settle here beside me," Nathan had said, patting the place next to him on the bench. "I'll tell you about the first time Private Blake saved my hide." Will had come to sit next to him and was asleep and snoring softly in less than five minutes, his head lolling against Boone's shoulder.

Not long after Will fell asleep, Doctor Valentine came through the door to report that Charlotte's surgery was finished.

"We'll be bringing her into the ward in a few minutes," he said.

"Is she going to be all right?" Will had asked, rubbing his eyes as he spoke.

"How long ago was it that she broke her wrist the first time?" the doctor had asked his grandson.

Will pressed his lips together. "I was little," he said, looking down at the floor. "I don't remember exactly."

"Well," the doctor said, "bone has a good blood supply. It should heal up just fine. I was just curious."

"But you said it'll get infected," Will said.

"Maybe not," Garnet interrupted. "The Good Book says 'the effectual fervent prayer of a righteous man availeth much.'"

"You talking about Private Blake?" Will asked.

Garnet nodded, and then Nathan noticed how quickly she changed the subject. "I've got some beef tea for tomorrow. And I brought my bedroll over."

"I told Will to tell you I'd stay with her tonight," the doctor said.

"He told me," Garnet said. She turned toward the hospital ward door. "If you men will excuse me, I'll be unrolling my pallet." She looked up at the doctor. "You let me know if there's anything special I need to watch for." She interrupted the doctor's protest. "I can't answer this boy's questions. You can. As soon as the orderly comes by in the morning I'll go home and start breakfast for you two." She'd hurried away before the doctor could protest further.

"Well," he said, shaking his head and shrugging his shoulders. "I guess she told me." He looked down at Nathan and Will. "You wait here with Lieutenant Boone, and as soon as your mother is settled you can have a look, so you know she's all right. Then we'll go get some sleep." He rumpled Will's hair as he said, "One thing I've learned these past weeks is that Garnet Irvin's gentle and quiet facade camouflages a will of steel. It does no good to argue with her."

And so it was. The men retired, leaving Garnet to tend Charlotte through the night.

•••◆•••

Nathan checked in at the hospital after assembly. Garnet reported the patient had slept well, then told Nathan that her main concern was for Will Bishop and how to keep him occupied and out of trouble until his mother was allowed to leave the hospital. "Doctor says it'll be a few days," Garnet worried aloud.

"I could take him over and introduce him to the Jacksons," Nathan offered. Quickly, he told Garnet about Laina and Caleb and their plans. "CJ is going to school while Mrs. Jackson stays here at the fort."

"Doc said he was going to see to it that Will goes to that school. They won't have him at the other one. Doc said he'd be taking Will over this morning to meet the teacher," Garnet explained.

Nathan nodded. "I'll just head over to the trading post and talk to the Jacksons. Laina would want to know about Charlotte's being in the hospital anyway."

Here I am again, Nathan thought as he headed for the trading post, *taking up my old ways of trying to fix things for everybody around me.* He smiled to himself, remembering how Granny Max used to scold him. *"Never saw a man so set on helping others and so set against helping himself,"* Granny used to say. *"You'll never be happy until you spend a little time on your own troubles. Get yourself right with God. Then you'll be even better at helping the rest of the world."* Granny had told him he was a good man . . . and then reminded him that the good he did would go to the grave with him until he joined what Granny called God's family.

As the sun tipped the distant bluffs with gold, Nathan remembered Granny's talk about gold. *"You need to think less about making it better for a little while here below and more about making things better for time and all eternity, Nathan Boone. All the good you do is only so much wood and hay and stubble unless it is done for the glory of God. And you can guess what happens to wood, hay, and stubble when the refining fire of the Lord God descends upon it. You're a good man, Nathan Boone. I want to see you build with gold and precious stones . . . send things on ahead and know it will last for eternity."*

Nathan paused beside the trading post and looked toward the new West End. He could almost hear Granny Max calling him back to the same questions, the same answers, the same God. As he headed for the front door, he shook his head. Returning to Fort Robinson was surely bringing things to mind he had not thought about for a long, long time.

"Sorry to be so early, Mrs. Dubois." Nathan removed his hat just inside the trading post and called out. From the sounds of things, she was packing canned goods into a crate. He could hear the *thunk* of the cans being stacked, one on top of the other. "I was hoping to talk to—" In one instant Nathan saw the woman, took in the river of dark hair flowing over her shoulders, the huge dark brown eyes and flawless skin. In the next he recognized her.

"Hello there, Rachel," he said.

"Lieutenant Boone," Rachel Greyfoot replied. "You were looking for Mrs. Dubois." She turned sideways and pointed through the doorway. "In the kitchen. With Mrs. Jackson and CJ."

"Who's there?" Maude's voice called from the back of the trading post.

Rachel stepped to the doorway and called out Nathan's name.

"Come on back, Lieutenant," Maude called.

Rachel stepped aside. She smiled up at him.

Nathan smiled back. "Mrs. Jackson told me you were here when I saw her up at the cemetery yesterday. She said you're headed back to the ranch?"

"This morning," Rachel said. "As soon as we get supplies loaded up."

"For roundup," Nathan said.

Rachel nodded.

"You drive the chuck wagon, as I recall."

"Not this year."

"Oh, right . . . I forgot. Mrs. Jackson told me. You and Jack . . ." Nathan paused. "How *is* Jack?"

"Taller than his brother was. Healthy as a horse, as they say." She smiled up at him. "Thanks to you."

Nathan shrugged, "You both deserved a chance."

"You went to a lot of work to see that we had that chance," Rachel said. "We owe you much. Jack feels the same way."

"Well, you tell Jack that next time I visit the ranch, I'll consider the debt paid if he refrains from making fun of my attempts to be a cowboy."

Rachel laughed softly. "I'll tell him." She turned back toward the storeroom.

Nathan headed up the hall. He joined Laina, Maude, and CJ in the kitchen. He told them about Charlotte's accident, then left for target practice out on the firing range. He was halfway through the morning before he realized he had been thinking entirely too much about Rachel Greyfoot. He had, in fact, forgotten to tell the ladies that Will Bishop would probably be going to the same school as CJ.

Early that same Monday afternoon, a teary Laina clung to Caleb just before he climbed aboard the wagon that would take Rachel and him back to the ranch for roundup. "Now, don't cry, sweetheart," he whispered. "I won't be gone that long and you know this is for the best." He patted her belly. "I don't want us taking any chances—with you or our baby boy."

"There's a perfectly good midwife up on Hat Creek," Laina said, sniffing.

"And there's an even better doctor right here at Fort Robinson."

"I know, I know," Laina said. She closed her eyes and put her cheek next to Caleb's, inhaling deeply. She rubbed her cheek against his beard and fought back tears. "I'm sorry. But I'll miss you."

Caleb lifted her chin and looked down into her eyes. "I'll miss you, too, honey-lamb. It won't be long and you'll be in my arms again. Now give me a kiss and let me go before CJ throws up. She's watching."

Laina glanced over Caleb's shoulder to where CJ stood beside the wagon, trying not to watch her parents' display of affection. "She's really not very happy with you."

Caleb sighed. "She'll get over it." He tipped his head so he could see around Laina. "Hey, girl. Cheer up. You might like school."

"And those horses just might sprout wings and fly home," was the answer.

"Watch your tone, young lady," Caleb said, a little more sternly.

"Yes, sir. I'm sorry."

Caleb nodded. He tapped the tip of Laina's nose and winked at her. "It's going to be all right, honey-lamb. I'll miss you. Shoot, I already miss you."

"Go," Laina said. She pulled away. "I'm being silly. Go." She called to Rachel, "Thank you in advance for everything you are doing for us. I don't know how we'd manage without you."

"You are welcome, Mrs. Jackson," Rachel replied.

Laina watched the wagon until it disappeared in the distance.

The next thing she knew, Maude Dubois was leading her back inside the trading post for tea. Once the two women were settled at the table, Maude smiled and said, "I know it's hard to watch him go, dear, but be thankful you have such a hard-working husband. Many women aren't so blessed."

"You're right," Laina said. She sighed. "He has such dreams. He's even been talking about changing the name of the Four Pines. Drawing up a new brand."

"Really?"

Laina nodded. "Wants something that says Jackson & *Sons*."

"*Sons*—plural?" Maude asked.

Laina nodded.

"A little ahead of himself, ain't he?" Maude asked. "Or do you expect this is twins?"

Laina shook her head. Her expression softened. "All I expect is the Lord's blessing on a precious new life. Ten years is a long time to wait for a baby."

"Don't I know it, child." Maude raised her teacup in a mock toast. "One of my friends waited *eleven* and then had one a year for five years. So you just watch out, Laina Jackson. The Lord may be fixin' to rain babies on that ranch of yours!"

"Showers of blessings," Laina said and laughed, raising her open palms toward the ceiling. "Let it rain!"

"Amen," Maude agreed. She set her teacup down and lowered her voice. "You know, dear, you're not the only woman at Fort Robinson needing the Lord's blessing on her child. The news about Charlotte Valentine doesn't bode well for her son." Maude clucked her tongue and shook her head from side to side.

"What do you mean?"

"Well, the Widow Bishop is an odd bird to begin with." Maude seemed to anticipate Laina's response. "I know, I know, dear. You're not one to gossip. I'm not carrying tales. And I'm not holding grudges from the past, either. Charlotte's been back at Fort Robinson for nearly a month, and she hasn't made a single call. She's declined three invitations to tea. And although she's apparently quite the horsewoman, she doesn't go riding with the ladies. And I can tell you her reclusive behavior hasn't set well with the women here. And that boy of hers!"

"What about him?"

"The most mischievous troublemaker I've ever had the displeasure to know. Tormenting dogs, pouring salt in punch. I've never seen the like of such pranks." She shook her head from side to side. "No wonder Charlotte came back here to stay with her father." Maude lowered her voice, "In fact, although Lieutenant Boone didn't say so, I wouldn't be surprised if the little rascal didn't have something to do with his mother's broken wrist."

CHAPTER EIGHT

A man that hath friends must shew himself friendly.

PROVERBS 18:24

MISS JACKSON."

CJ closed her eyes and pressed her lips firmly together, barely avoiding making a face. "Yes, *Mr.* Phelps," she replied, exactly copying the teacher's exasperated tone. The boy behind her uttered a half cough, half laugh of approval.

Mr. Phelps took a deep breath and put on a disapproving expression. "I realize, Miss Jackson, that you have come late to school—"

"I wasn't late," CJ interrupted. "I was here before you today. Remember? I was waiting outside the door when—"

"That's *not* what I meant," the teacher snapped. "I was referring to your being *unschooled*."

CJ frowned. "I haven't been unschooled. My ma's been teaching me at home. She's a good teacher and don't you say she isn't!"

"There's no reason for you to be impertinent, young lady," the schoolteacher said.

"And there's no reason for you to say my ma isn't a good teacher," CJ replied.

Mr. Phelps sighed deeply and pointed to the corner. "You may occupy the seat of honor until you have learned to respect your elders," he said.

CJ stood up slowly. Head held high, she marched to the corner, climbed onto the waiting stool, and sat facing the class.

Mr. Phelps smirked, lifting his right hand and making a circling motion with his index finger. CJ turned around, relieved to be facing away from the class full of strangers.

Since CJ's arrival at school, every last one of the fifteen students seemed to have entered into the game of "Make the New Girl Miserable." Even Will Bishop, who wasn't even supposed to *be* at this school and was new himself, seemed to enjoy tormenting her. Ma had said there was a separate school for the officers' children. But CJ had also heard Mrs. Dubois telling Ma how Mrs. Bishop's son had been kicked out of that school. The teacher wouldn't teach Will, even though, as far as CJ could tell, he was plenty smart. Well, she could wonder about that while she stared at the corner. Time might go more slowly, but at least no one would see her cheeks flaming red with embarrassment. And no one would see her eyes fill with tears. They might think she was sad when really she was mad. CJ tended to cry when she got really, really mad. Ma was going to be angry when she heard about this. Ma didn't take disobedience lightly. And she'd been cross ever since Pa had gone back to the ranch to get things ready for spring roundup.

After an hour of sitting on the backless stool in the schoolroom corner, CJ's legs began to feel all tingly. Her back hurt. Mr. Phelps was lecturing in a droning monotone. CJ dozed off and jerked herself awake just in time to keep from falling off the stool. Several of the girls tittered with laughter. Mr. Phelps put his hand on her shoulder, pressing on a spot with his thumb until pain shot up the back of her neck. He said something about "helping her to stay awake." She mentally transported herself to the ranch, counting off the horses by name, wondering if Jack had convinced the gelding she called Rebel to eat grain out of his hand yet, if he had managed to saddle him yet, and if Rebel would really be ready to be ridden when CJ finally got to go home.

CJ tore off a piece of beef jerky and chewed it slowly, trying to shut out the sound of laughter wafting through the schoolroom window. Of course, she told herself, the girls weren't laughing at *her*. She hadn't dozed off again all morning. The girls were just having fun while they ate their lunches. They were probably talking about something else besides her. And even if she *was* allowed off this stool, it's not like they would have included her in the fun anyway.

At least half the day was gone. Maybe Mr. Phelps would let her out of the corner. Maybe, she thought, he'd sprout wings and fly back east where he belonged. It sure was obvious to Clara Joy Jackson that Phineas Phelps (she took silent pleasure in refusing to call him "Mr. Phelps" in her mind) didn't know much about teaching. And he thought he was so much better than Ma. CJ bet Phineas Phelps couldn't say one word if Frenchy Dubois started talking French. But her Ma could. She'd heard her. So who was Phineas Phelps to call her *unschooled*? Who did he think he was, anyway.

CJ could read as well as any student in the class. And what if her ciphering was a little behind? What did a girl need with ciphering anyway? It wasn't like she was going to run a ranch someday like her pa and have to keep track of market prices and such. All the ciphering she would ever need would be for shopping at the trading post, and didn't she already know how to do that? Calico was eight cents a yard, and she knew her times tables just fine. No shopkeeper would ever be able to cheat her.

CJ had closed her eyes and was gesturing in a mock argument with some future store owner who'd just overcharged her for calico when she heard the school door creak. She opened her eyes in time to see one of her classmates walking toward her with a dipper full of water. She held up her hands, "Don't you dare think you can throw that on me and not get pounded," she said, and held up her fists.

"I don't think any such thing," the boy said. "I'm bringing you a drink."

"*You* drink it!" CJ said. "I don't need Mr. Phelps trying to be nice, sending you in here after he made fun of my ma."

"Mr. Phelps doesn't know anything about this. He went over to the canteen for something," the boy said. He held out the dipper. "I spent plenty of hours on stools and chairs. A body gets thirsty. Phelps doesn't care."

CJ narrowed her gaze and sized up the boy. "Why do you want to be nice to me? Nobody else does. I've heard what they say about me. Like they're better'n me." She looked at the dipper full of water. "Well they aren't."

"You gonna drink this or not?" he said.

"You afraid you'll have to sit in the corner with the ranch girl if you get caught?"

"I'm not afraid of anything," the boy said. "If you don't want a drink then say so, and I'll go back outside." He shrugged. "It's not like they want to have anything to do with me, either. I'm supposed to be in school with the *officers'* brats."

CJ grabbed the dipper and drank the water down. It was lukewarm, but it slaked her tremendous thirst.

"Why don't you go to that other school? When my pa tells stories about the army he always says the officers and their families don't have much to do with the enlisted men and the civilians."

"It doesn't matter who my father was. They don't want me at that school anymore," the boy said, grinning wickedly. "They can't handle me."

"Exactly *what* do you think you are *doing,* Master Bishop?" Mr. Phelps must have been lurking in the narrow space just inside the door where they hung their coats. Looking over the boy's shoulder to where Phelps was standing made CJ dread what was coming. She didn't need to hear his voice to know the teacher was angry. His closed mouth was pinched shut so tightly it looked like he had deep wrinkles turned downward from the corners. It had taken CJ exactly one hour in the schoolroom to learn to fear that expression. She gripped the edges of the stool with both hands and waited.

The boy looked around. "It's not right to make her sit up there all during lunch. And it's not right for her to go thirsty. My grandfather says a man can go without food, but you take away water and he'll die. Fast."

"Miss Jackson is in no danger of dying for lack of water," the teacher sneered. "But since you are so concerned for her well-being, you may sit next to her this afternoon. You'll be much more able to monitor her condition. Be certain you inform me if you think she needs medical attention. After all, with your grandfather being a *doctor,* I imagine that qualifies you much more than the adults around you to judge these matters."

* * *

At the end of the day, schoolmaster Phelps delivered his well-practiced sermonette on the dangers of showing disrespect to your elders. While his teacher droned on, Will let his eyes wander to the corner of a window where a leggy white spider was scurrying up and down a slender thread, attaching more and more threads, weaving them all together in a busy dance. While Phelps talked, Will inched closer to the window. He might have learned his lesson about pranks that made adults fall down, but that didn't mean he wasn't still Will Bishop.

"Do I make myself clear, Master Bishop?" Phelps cleared his throat loudly. His arms were crossed in front of him, his toe tapping the floor.

"Yes, sir," Will said quickly. "Very clear, sir."

"Very well, then." He turned to CJ. "In light of the fact that you are in a new situation, Miss Jackson, I shall refrain from speaking to your parents about today's difficulties. But let us agree that such a display of disrespect will not happen again, shall we?"

"Oh, yes, sir," CJ said. "I won't hold it against you. You haven't even *met* my ma."

Phelps's eyes opened wide along with his mouth. With a sound of exasperation he scooped the geography book up off his desk and turned to go. He paused at the door. "Before you two leave today, I want the floor swept and the stove polished." He sniffed. "I'd stay to be certain you do it correctly, but I have an appointment. If it isn't done to my satisfaction," he said, looking back at the two children, "you'll both be taken *to your mothers* first thing in the morning." He swept out of the room, like a dictator who held life and death in his hands.

As soon as Phelps was gone, Will turned around and destroyed the spider web.

"What'd you do *that* for?" CJ said. She looked down at the window ledge where the spider had landed. "Now she has to start her web all over again."

Will looked at the girl in disbelief. He had been watching that spider all day and had devised a plan involving the brown-eyed girl who had crossed her eyes and stuck out her tongue at him. Her name was Molly Plummer, and Will hated the way she smirked when he pretended he didn't know an answer to one of Mr. Phelps's stupid questions. Of *course* he knew when the Battle of Vicksburg was fought. Of *course* he could name the states on the eastern seaboard. But right answers were boring because they were too easy. Will loved the entertainment of confounding the teacher. But snobbish Molly Plummer didn't get it, and Will had decided the spider was just the thing to get her attention. Everybody knew girls were afraid of spiders.

"I said," CJ was repeating, "What'd you do *that* for?" She

was standing at the door with a broom in hand. When Will didn't answer, she shrugged. "I'll sweep. You polish the stove."

"I'm not polishing any stove," Will said.

CJ held out the broom.

"I'm not doing *anything* for Phelps."

"I'm not doing it for *him*," CJ said. "I'm doing it so he won't bother my ma." She began to sweep.

"You're afraid of your *ma*?"

"No," Clara Joy shook her head. "She's going to have a baby soon. My pa made her stay here at the fort so she'd have a doctor. She's homesick. I don't want to make her any sadder." She shrugged. "Some things just aren't worth getting into more trouble for." She sneezed and rubbed her nose with the back of her hand. "Besides, this floor *does* need to be swept!"

Will watched the girl for a minute. She kept working. Going to the the back of the room, he took a rag from a bucket on the teacher's supply shelf and began rubbing the stove top.

"You wanna come with me to the stables?" Will asked CJ as he put the finishing touches on the once filthy stove. "Lieutenant Boone is going to let me groom his horse. He's been showing me things about horses."

"What's there to show? Everybody knows about horses."

"Well I don't," Will snapped. "We had servants who did everything back home. Ma was going to let me ride Isaac—that was her horse—but then my grandmother decided to sell him. My Father's horses were half-wild stallions and they liked to eat people for breakfast. My father was the only one who could handle them, but he didn't have time to show me and then he died."

CJ frowned. "I don't know what kind of army your father was in," she said matter-of-factly. "But the United States Army doesn't let their soldiers ride wild stallions. And horses don't eat people—although we have a horse at home that has a nasty habit of biting. Jack's going to cure him of that. And when I get back home, I'm going to ride him."

"You can't ride any horse that likes to bite people," Will said.

"Well, when I ride Rebel all the way back here and come up to your back door, I'll guess you'll know I can! Just because *you're* afraid of horses doesn't mean I am!"

"Who told you I'm afraid?"

CJ pointed to Will's clenched fists. Her voice gentled. "It's all right. If your father's horses were mean, I bet you just haven't had a chance to know any good ones. You should meet my horse back at home. Pappy doesn't have a wild bone in his raggedy old body." She smiled. "I bet Lieutenant Boone has a great horse, too." She added, "*I* don't care if you're a little afraid of horses. Even if you are, it's just 'cause you haven't learned. Like you said, you didn't have a chance to learn before your pa died." She saw Will's fists relax a little. "It's funny," she said.

"What's funny?"

"Well, your pa was mad because you were afraid of horses, and my pa gets mad because I'm not. He caught me in Rebel's stall once and nearly tanned my hide good."

"Lieutenant Boone says it's dangerous to get in a stall with a half-wild horse."

"Well of course it is," CJ agreed. "But Rebel isn't half-wild. He's just afraid."

"Afraid or wild, I don't see it makes any difference. They can still smash you good."

"Rebel doesn't want to smash anybody," CJ said. "He just has to learn to trust people." Her face brightened. "And Jack's going to teach him that."

"Who's Jack?"

"He's a Cheyenne Indian who lives on the ranch. He came there with Rachel. Rachel was married to Jack's brother, but he got killed. Jack and Rachel have been there ever since I can remember." CJ leaned close. "You want to know a secret?"

Will looked at her from beneath furrowed brows. "What secret?"

CJ moved closer to him and whispered, "I'm going to marry Jack."

Will jerked his head back and looked at her in disbelief. "Go on," he said. "You're not going to do any such thing."

"I am, too."

"Why'd you want to go and marry an *Indian*?" Will went on to expound his vast knowledge of Indians gleaned from stories told by a father who'd never met one he didn't want to shoot.

"I don't know what Indians you're talking about," CJ said, "but Jack and Rachel aren't anything like that. Rachel cooks the best flapjacks ever and Jack knows everything about horses." She smiled. "Maybe you can come visit. And we could go riding together."

"My ma won't hardly let me go across the parade ground by myself," Will said. "She's not gonna let me go off to some ranch where there's Indians." He stuffed his hands in his pockets. "I gotta go. Lieutenant Boone's probably wondering where I am. You coming or not?"

CHAPTER NINE

Use hospitality one to another without grudging.

I PETER 4:9

FOR A LONG WHILE CHARLOTTE WASN'T SURE WHICH of the flashes in her mind were reality and which were dreams. Eventually she realized she was drifting in and out of consciousness. The hospital ward was real, as were the screens around her bed . . . Will's terrified eyes . . . her father's voice. She wasn't certain about *all* the voices. She recognized Garnet's. And Lieutenant Boone's. But there was another one she didn't know. The other surgeon, probably. Did she really hear praying? She was too tired to open her eyes, too tired to be polite to strangers, too tired to care. The only constants in all the swirling of impressions to Charlotte's brain were the throbbing pain on the left side of her body and Garnet Irvin's voice. Sometimes she would wake and Garnet would be sitting next to the bed in the simple pine chair, her head bowed over a book.

When Charlotte finally jerked awake to full consciousness and looked around, she wondered exactly how much time had passed. It was a sunny day outside. Garnet was seated beside the hospital bed, her hair bound up in a bright yellow kerchief, her head tilted back against the wall. She was napping with her mouth slightly open.

Charlotte lay still for a few moments, remembering and reciting to herself. She'd been taking coffee and pie out onto the porch to her father and Lieutenant Boone . . . and then Will . . .

Looking out the window, Charlotte wondered about Will. Where was he? She hoped her father had forgiven the boy this infraction. She hoped he had talked Mr. Phelps into taking Will into the school that met over at the Bee Hive. If only that teacher could handle him. She was almost glad Will had been evicted from the school attended by the officers' children. Perhaps seeing how hard life could be for the enlisted men and civilians would be a good thing. She did not want her son to become a soldier.

It must be afternoon. There were no orders being barked, no drills ongoing at the parade ground—at least not as far as she could tell. In the short time since she had been at the fort, she'd grown accustomed to the incessant noise of construction and could ignore it, just as she'd learned to ignore the passing of a carriage or a stagecoach in Michigan.

She lifted her head to look down at her wrist. It was so heavily bandaged it looked nearly twice its normal size. Glass tubes protruded from the bandage. She knew those were meant to drain pus away from the wound, but there was no sign of infection or drainage and the bandage was clean. That was good—surprising, given the circumstances of her accident, but good. Maybe she could talk Garnet into taking her home. She tried to sit up. Her head swam only a little. Then pain shot up her arm, across her shoulder and up the back of her neck. She gasped and Garnet sprang awake.

"What day is it?" Charlotte wanted to know.

"It's Saturday, missus," Garnet said, rising to help Charlotte sit up.

"And I fell on Monday." She frowned. "I've been unconscious all that time?"

Garnet nodded. "Mostly. But you're doing so fine you're nearly a miracle. That's what the doctor says, anyhow."

Charlotte looked down at the bandage. She pointed at one of the glass tubes. "There's no drainage."

"There was a little at first. But nothing like what you'd expect. It's going to be a while healing, and you might have some trouble with stiffness, but they say you'll be fine." Garnet plumped a pillow and tucked it behind Charlotte's head. "No infection, missus. There's no explanation for it except the good Lord took a hand in the healing." Garnet poured Charlotte a glass of water from the white pitcher at her bedside. As she handed over the glass, she said, "Private Blake came that first night. He said a fine prayer."

"Private Blake?"

Garnet nodded. She covered her mouth with her hand, but Charlotte could see the smile in her eyes. "Yes, ma'am. A big hulk of a soldier that came hauling Will home the night you got hurt. He found Will over in Troop F stables. Scared him silly, I guess, before hauling him home. Will seems to have taken to him." Garnet turned aside and rummaged in a basket while she talked. "Then there was a preacher stopped by. You remember him at all?"

Charlotte shook her head.

"He asked the Lord to heal you. Spent a good while praying over it. Dr. Valentine knew him. Said he's been riding the circuit out this way for as long as anyone can remember." Garnet nodded. "I'd say between Private Blake and the Reverend, the Almighty just had to answer *yes*."

"How is Will?"

"The day after you fell, doctor took him over to the barracks school and handed him over to Mr. Phelps, just like you wanted. Lieutenant Boone and Private Blake have had him with them in the stables every day after school. He's keeping busy and out of mischief for the most part. He seems to be getting acquainted with one of the older horses. Name of Bones. Will talks about Bones like he was almost as important as his new best friend, CJ."

Before Charlotte could ask who CJ was, Garnet leaned close, hairbrush in hand. "You got company," she whispered, nodding toward the door.

"I don't want—" Charlotte started to protest, but then she heard a woman's voice from halfway down the hospital ward.

"I promise not to stay but a few minutes." Laina Jackson stepped between the screens at the foot of the bed. "We rode in from the ranch the same day you fell," she explained. "Nathan Boone told us about your accident the morning after it happened. But you've been too sick for visitors."

"I . . . I didn't think you were living here at Fort Robinson," Charlotte said. *No, that's not right. She told you. Something about a ranch.* She rubbed her forehead with the back of her good hand and tried to focus on what Laina Jackson was saying.

Laina talked more slowly. "We've got a ranch up on Soldier Creek." She turned sideways, emphasizing her pregnant belly. "Caleb got it in his head I should be here where your father could take care of me when the baby comes. So CJ and I are staying over at the trading post with Maude and Frenchy."

"CJ?" Charlotte feigned interest, all the while thinking how tired she was and how she wished Garnet would step in and make Laina leave.

"Clara Joy has decided she'd rather be called CJ." Laina smiled. "She's quite put out with God for making her a girl. Much prefers the open range to the kitchen. Chooses riding over stitching every time."

Invite her to sit down. Charlotte knew it was only polite, but she was having trouble staying awake. She should introduce Garnet.

Laina raised her hand to the left side of her head and tucked a ringlet of auburn hair behind her ear. "It's good to see you doing so well," she said. "I'm sorry about your husband. And your mother. Goodness but you've had to deal with a lot since we parted ways all those years ago. I know your father must be so pleased to have you back under his roof. And having Will around will keep him young."

Charlotte nodded, wearied by the litany of condolences.

"I don't want to wear you out, Charlotte. I just wanted you to know I'm praying for quick healing. And I'm grateful for your son, Will."

Charlotte roused. "Will?"

Laina nodded. "You've raised a good boy."

"Will?" Charlotte repeated, inwardly telling herself not to sound so surprised.

"Yes, *Will,*" Laina nodded, emphasizing the name. "Of course we put CJ in school. We both agreed she should take advantage of the opportunity, even if I'm only here at Fort Rob for a few weeks." She paused. "At any rate, she can be quite a handful—as the young schoolmaster has discovered. And she doesn't have the gift of . . . tact. Mr. Phelps took things a bit far in the discipline department the other day, but . . . well . . ." Laina smiled. "Will was very sweet. Stood up for CJ. You should be very proud of him." She patted Charlotte's hand. "And now I really do need to let you rest. As I said, I'll be praying for quick healing."

Charlotte listened to Laina's departing footsteps echo through the empty hospital ward. She had been in the hospital for five days. How quickly life could change.

Laina and Caleb Jackson were staying at Fort Robinson. *Caleb Jackson.* Memories of a morning long ago when a young and foolish girl named Charlotte Valentine had nearly been compromised by an even more foolish Caleb Jackson flashed in her mind. *The last person on earth I want to see again is Caleb Jackson.* If she was lucky, Laina would feel she'd done her duty with this one visit.

But Will was apparently becoming friends with the Jacksons' daughter. *Laina Jackson thinks my son is sweet?* Charlotte wondered what kind of miracle that had taken.

And Garnet had mentioned that Will was spending time with Nathan Boone. Charlotte didn't know how she felt about that. She'd hoped that getting away from Bishop House would provide a positive male influence for Will. But she'd only thought in terms of her father. What would people think about Lieutenant Boone's calling at the surgeon's residence? *I am so tired of ordering my life to please other people.*

Most puzzling of all was that Garnet Irvin obviously thought more of Private Carter Blake than she was letting on. Charlotte planned to look into that. As soon as she felt better.

* * *

"Ma! Guess what! Lieutenant Boone is going to let me *ride* Bones tomorrow."

Will had been walking at the lieutenant's side as the two crossed the parade ground in the direction of the house, but as soon as he caught sight of her in the rocking chair on the porch, he ran the rest of the distance between them and blurted out the announcement.

When Boone caught up, he leaned toward Charlotte and muttered under his breath, "Bones is ancient and half lame. Don't worry."

"So will you come watch me?" Will asked as he stopped to catch his breath.

"Perhaps you can ride over here from the stables and show off to your mother," her father interrupted. He leaned back in his chair next to Charlotte's and drew on his pipe. "She's just out of hospital, and she really shouldn't—"

"Please, Papa," Charlotte said wearily, "I feel fine."

"You need your rest," the doctor insisted.

Charlotte grumbled, "It's been two weeks, Papa. If I rest any more I am going to *decompose*!" She smiled at Will. "Of *course* I'll come watch you."

"We'll be in the corral behind the first set of barracks to the east," Lieutenant Boone said. "What if I send one of the men over to pick you up?"

" . . . and then I'll walk home," Charlotte said. She looked at her father. "You said walking would be good for me. You've been talking about a 'daily constitutional' of fresh air."

"All right," the doctor grumbled. "But you take Garnet along. And use your sling."

◆

"Hey," Will said. "You didn't have to come."

CJ climbed onto the lower rung of the corral and rested her chin on her arms. "Wouldn't miss it," she said. "Where's your ma?"

"Coming directly. Lieutenant Boone sent Private Blake to fetch her in a carriage. My Grandfather thought it was too far for her to walk both ways. How's *your* ma?"

"Grumpy," CJ replied, shrugging.

"They get that way right before a baby," Will said. "At least my ma always did." He kept brushing Bones while he talked. "She had three babies after me. I was little, but I remember enough to know Ma was real short-tempered. Every time." Before CJ could ask, he said quickly, "They died."

"*All* of 'em?" CJ wanted to know.

Will nodded, picking at an imaginary tangle in the horse's mane.

"That's awful," CJ said. She frowned. "She must have been *real* sad."

Will shrugged. "She was sad a lot when we lived with Grandmother. But she only got the 'angries' when her belly got big like your Ma's." He pondered. "Grandmother made her sit in the parlor with her feet up and do needlework."

"What's so bad about that?" CJ wanted to know.

"My ma *hates* to sew," Will said.

"My ma seems to hate just about everything right now," CJ said. "She's got what you call the 'angries' most of the time."

"That probably means the baby will be here soon," Will commiserated. "Things will get better."

"I'll say," CJ agreed. "We'll get to go *home*." She stared off into the distance. "I can't believe I'm missing roundup for *school*. With *Phineas Phelps*."

"What's so bad about missing roundup?" Will wanted to know.

"You're kidding, right?"

Will shook his head. For the next few minutes, CJ regaled him with stories about spring roundup, ending with, "And if you want a different horse from Bones, then you should get your ma to let you come out to the ranch, 'cause there'll be all kinds of Indian ponies out there. You could have your pick. Most of our horses only cost thirty-five or forty dollars."

"I wouldn't know the first thing about picking out a horse," Will said. "And we don't have that kind of money anyway. Not since my pa died. And besides that my ma would never let me go. The only time she ever let me go anywhere without her was the first time she broke her wrist. My pa sent me to stay with some friends while he took care of her himself. He said she needed peace and quiet. Wouldn't let anybody else near her—except Garnet—for a long time." Will pondered, "Since then Ma's kept me real close. Like she's always worried something awful is going to happen."

"Mothers are just like that," CJ said.

"Yeah. That's what Private Blake says, too. Mothers are like that." He chewed on his lower lip. "But I sure would like to see roundup on a real ranch."

•••◆•••

"So," CJ explained to Laina over dinner. "Will did great today. Even his ma said he's getting good at riding. And when school gets out in June, he won't have anything to do. And since Pa's coming to work at the fort after roundup, I was thinking maybe Will could come to the ranch and help us out. He said he'd really like to."

Laina closed her eyes and sighed wearily. "I don't know, CJ. You'll need to talk that over with your father. I don't know how Jack and Mr. Dorsey would feel about having a boy to keep track of. Especially one who grew up in town. And I don't know that Mrs. Bishop would be at all eager to let her only son go off with strangers."

"We *aren't* strangers," CJ said. "Will's my best friend. And you and Will's mother aren't strangers, either."

"Don't argue with me, young lady," Laina snapped. "I said you will have to talk to your father about it."

"He won't care. He wants a passel of boys. Will's a boy."

"It's not the same thing."

"But—"

"I said you will have to talk to your father. Mrs. Bishop and I are not strangers, but neither are we friends. And as I said, I doubt she will be enthusiastic about being separated from her only child."

"We could invite her to the ranch, too," CJ said.

Laina closed her eyes and shook her head from side to side.

"Well," CJ repeated. "We could. Will says his mother loves to ride. Will says she's been sad since she came to Fort Robinson. Maybe she'd feel better if she visited us for a while. She could ride and—"

"*No,*" Laina said. "Not now. Maybe later in the summer. There's just too much going on right now with a baby on the way and your father planning to come back to the fort to work all summer. It's just not a good time for us to have guests."

"I thought you said God wants us to take care of whoever

comes to our door," CJ protested. "At least that's what you said when the preacher started showing up and staying for a week every spring and again in the winter. You said God gave us a nice home and we should share it with people. You said that's how Rachel and Jack and Mr. Dorsey came to stay with us. And that we should never turn people away from our door. That God expected us to show kindness to strangers 'cause they might be angels."

"Mrs. Bishop and her son have a good home here at Fort Robinson," Laina said.

"They *don't.* Will *hates* it here. And he says his ma is sad all the time. The other kids treat him awful, and he—"

"That's enough, young lady," Laina said. She shook a finger at CJ. "I've told you to talk to your father about this. And I don't want to hear any more about it."

"You don't want to hear anything about anything," CJ said, and huffed out the door. When she heard her mother call her name, she ignored it, darted across the trail, around the corner of the commanding officer's headquarters, and thus out of sight in case her mother should come to the door and call for her . . . which, CJ grumbled to herself, she doubted her mother would have the energy to do.

"Babies!" she huffed to herself. "If having 'em makes everybody so miserable, I don't know why they bother."

CHAPTER TEN

And be ye kind one to another, tenderhearted, forgiving one another, even as God for Christ's sake hath forgiven you.

EPHESIANS 4:32

LAND SAKES, CJ," LAINA FUMED. "DOES EVERY OTHER word out of your mouth have to be *Will Bishop*? You didn't even know the boy two weeks ago, and now you can't seem to take a breath without him." Laina pushed herself upright with a grunt and scooted back against the headboard of the bed where she had been trying to take a nap.

"I thought you'd be *glad* I have a friend," CJ said. "You said you wanted me to make friends at school."

"I was hoping you'd meet a young lady."

CJ made a face. "Can I go or not?"

"Tell me again where you're going."

CJ sighed deeply. "For a *ride*. Lieutenant Boone is going to take Mrs. Bishop for a carriage ride, and he said Will and me can ride Bones alongside the carriage." She added, "Will doesn't believe I can ride as good as I can." She smiled hopefully, "Maybe you could come, too."

Laina shook her head. "I wasn't invited. And besides, a bumpy carriage ride is the last thing in the world I need right now," she said. "Do you have any schoolwork to do?"

"I'll do it later. It's not much. *Please,* Ma. I haven't gotten to ride since we've been at Fort Robinson. *Please.*" CJ went on to expound on Charlotte Bishop's recovery and Will's newfound interest in horses with more details than Laina's weary brain wanted to process.

Laina held up her hand. "All right, CJ, all right. Go. But be careful and—"

CJ disappeared, calling out a thank-you from the trading post kitchen. The door slammed, and with Maude Dubois working up front in the trading post, a welcome silence reigned. Laina closed her eyes. She tried to settle back into her nap, but could not get comfortable.

My back hurts, my knees hurt, I can hardly breathe, I'm sick of making trips to the outhouse in the middle of the night, I'm tired of waiting for the baby, and . . . Laina's eyes teared up. *I miss Caleb.* She sniffed. The walls in the tiny room seemed to move in closer. The baby rolled up against her midsection, pushing so hard she gasped for breath.

Get hold of yourself, Laina. Maybe you should have followed CJ's suggestion about that carriage ride. You know Nathan won't mind.

But the last thing Laina wanted to do was try to befriend Charlotte Bishop. *I've done my duty, Lord. I visited her in the hospital. She's doing fine. Good heavens, she's out for a carriage ride. And Maude said she doesn't socialize much, anyway. She probably wouldn't even want a visit from a ranch wife. I'm hardly the kind of person she is used to associating with.*

Remembering how a young Charlotte Valentine had ordered her around years ago when Laina worked as the Valentine's housekeeper convinced Laina she was right. It didn't matter how many years had gone by, the widow of a colonel would definitely not be interested in having tea with a former servant.

She went to the bedroom window and raised the sash. Someone down on Soapsuds Row was screaming obscenities. A wagon rumbled by, the driver lashing the team of mules to a faster pace, the mules braying in protest as they pulled. The spring breeze was blowing from the direction of the stables. Grimacing, Laina closed the window. How she longed for the peace and quiet and fresh air of the ranch, the methodical routine, the sound of Caleb's voice as he came in for supper and called to CJ to come in lest supper get cold. *He'll be back right after roundup,* Laina reminded herself. *It won't be long now.*

It almost hurt to walk, and yet she could not bear the thought of being cooped up inside the trading post for one more moment. Snatching up her shawl and bonnet, Laina decided to head for the fort cemetery—the one place she could be assured of being left alone, the one place there might be a respite from the sound of construction. *Land sakes, if I have to listen to very much more hammering and hollering, I am going to go stark raving mad.*

I'm waddling, she thought as she ducked outside and headed toward the East End. *I can't even walk right.* Once at the cemetery, Laina opened the gate and went inside, plopping down in the shade at Granny Max's grave and raking her hand through the short grass. "I miss Caleb, Granny." She spread her hand over her abdomen. "I didn't expect to miss him so much. And if it's this hard now, how am I ever going to get through the summer when he's working here at the fort and I'm back home at Four Pines?" The baby landed a kick against her bladder.

Once again, she thought of Charlotte Bishop, convalescing alone at the surgeon's residence. *She has Garnet to talk to. And I'm not fit company for anyone, Lord.* She held back a sob. "I'm a mess," she murmured aloud, and looked at the tombstone engraved with Clara Maxwell's name. "Would you believe it, Granny? *CJ* is preaching me sermons about hospitality and friendship." She swiped a tear away. Another followed. And another. Several minutes later, Laina was still crying, albeit more quietly.

"Well," she murmured. "Let's hope I got *that* out of my

system." She scooted across the grass and leaned against the tombstone. She felt tears surging again. "I just want to go home, Granny. I never wanted to come back to Fort Robinson, and I certainly don't want to *stay* here without Caleb. I need his arms around me. Nothing is right when I'm lonesome for Caleb."

Think of what it would be like without him at all. What if you were going to have to raise this baby all alone? Like Charlotte.

The baby pushed against her belly. Laina put her hand over the place and pressed down. The baby pushed back. *It's high time you made your appearance, you stubborn little boy. Just like your father, the man who knows what is best for his family and won't consider any other way. The two of you are going to lock horns some day, and I hope I don't have to be there to witness it.* When the baby kicked as if to answer her, Laina laughed and said aloud, "You *are* a stubborn little thing, aren't you. That's just what we need at Four Pines. Another child to question our decisions and be forever asking 'why.' You know, little boy, your sister already has that job pretty well in hand."

And what about you, Mrs. Jackson? a voice in her mind asked. *You're just as stubborn as CJ. Questioning why. Complaining about Fort Robinson. Pining for home. When are you going to stop grumbling and start paying attention? Maybe you are here for a reason other than the obvious ones.*

Long ago, she had read something in Granny Max's Bible about God not liking it when His children grumbled. When she really thought about it, Laina realized she had been spending a lot of time lately telling God what she didn't like and what she didn't want. Like not wanting to pay Charlotte Bishop a visit.

It's not about you. The circuit-riding preacher who visited the ranch on occasion had once given a sermon on that very subject. He'd talked about how the Lord didn't expect folks to handle their troubles on their own and how He often ministered to people through one another. "God puts on skin," he'd said, "by working through his children to love others." The preacher had encouraged people to be available to God. Laina had congratulated herself during that sermon, thinking how she and Caleb had welcomed Rachel and Jack into their lives and made a place for Corporal Dorsey to spend his retirement years.

Caleb had been affected by the preacher's teaching, too. Ranchers all around the Sandhills were up in arms over the influx of grangers into the area. The grangers wanted to farm. They put up fences and plowed fields and disrupted the open-range days that many of the big ranching operations depended on. Troops from Fort Robinson had even been sent out to quell range wars between ranchers and farmers. While he would never participate in the violent conflicts, Caleb had done his share of grumbling against grangers. But after hearing Preacher Barton talk about eternity and loving your fellow man, Caleb had said, "The folks coming in around us seem like a good bunch. I'll let them live in peace." He'd decided to look on the good that could come of the changes. "When they want cattle or a good stallion to breed with their mares, they'll come to the Four Pines. I fought enough battles back in the war. I don't want to fight any more."

It's not about you. Laina realized she hadn't thought about anyone else but herself for quite a while. She sighed. "I've had all these years to read your Bible and hear the preacher's sermons, but I'm still nothing like you, Granny. You always welcomed whatever lambs God brought to your door. I remember you saying that. Goodness, I owe just about everything I've become to the fact you loved me when I didn't deserve to be loved."

She had refused God's urgings to visit Charlotte again and again. At first, she had used Charlotte and Caleb's past flirtation as an excuse. She had even mentioned it to Caleb. But when she hinted that things would be "awkward" between the two families, Caleb just shook his head. "Don't be ridiculous," he said. "We were both young fools.

Completely different people. What's past is past and I, for one, wish Charlotte the best, and I'll be sure she knows it if you think I should tell her." And he had one evening before he left for the ranch, walking over to the surgeon's residence with CJ under the guise of meeting Will. One part of Laina admired him for it, while another part—the selfish one, she admitted to herself—wished she could hide behind that imaginary barrier and stay away from the surgeon's residence. When CJ expressed concern for the Bishops and wanted to help, she had brushed it off. She had reminded God of how, in her youth, Charlotte Valentine had looked down her nose at people. She had assured God repeatedly that, grown up or not, Charlotte Valentine would have no interest in a visit from lowly Laina Jackson. She had reminded God that in the military economy, officers' families just didn't mix with lower-class civilians. *She was married to a COLONEL, for goodness' sake. She's probably more high-toned than ever. I did visit. And she wasn't exactly happy to see me.*

But God, in the guise of Granny Max's voice, was relentless. *It's not about whether or not she was happy to see you. She was hurting. Her boy is hurting. He's acting it out right before everyone's eyes. Don't you wonder about what's behind Will Bishop's reputation for pranks? What's he so angry about?*

Some of the things CJ had said in recent days all tumbled together.

"Will says his ma was always sad when they lived in Michigan."

Charlotte's marriage must have been less than happy.

"Will says his pa was usually mad about something."

What would it be like, Laina wondered, if Caleb were perpetually angry with her. The thought brought a knot to her stomach.

"Will didn't like his pa."

What would it take for a boy to grow to dislike his own father?

"Will had three baby brothers, but they all died."

With a grunt, Laina stood up, arching her stiff back and lifting first one foot, then the other, making little circles in the air with each one in an attempt to limber up. She would call on Charlotte Bishop tomorrow.

A voice sounded behind her. "You all right, ma'am?"

She turned around. The circuit-riding preacher was standing at the cemetery fence, hat in hand, his long white hair especially snowy as the evening sun bathed his profile in light.

"Why, it's Mrs. Jackson," the preacher said. "Just the person I've come to find."

"Is . . . is something wrong . . . at the ranch?" Laina asked, her heart pounding.

"Everything's just fine." The preacher reached into his breast pocket and pulled out a small package wrapped in brown paper. "When I told Mr. Jackson I was coming this way, he asked me to bring you this."

Laina walked to the fence and took the package, chuckling when the preacher's ancient white mare, Elvira, stepped forward, stretching her neck over the cemetery fence, and nuzzled Laina's pocket. "Sorry, old girl, I didn't know you were coming. There's no sugar for you today." She patted the mare's soft muzzle and asked, "What brings you to Fort Robinson? Caleb was counting on your usual prayer before roundup."

"Oh, I expect to get back in plenty of time for that," the preacher said. He looked toward the fort. "I was just impressed to check on a little gal I prayed for some days ago. Didn't really want to make the ride, but the Lord just wouldn't let it go. Kept bringing her to mind. The doctor was mightily worried over her. You wouldn't happen to know how she's doing, would you?" The preacher tapped his wrist. "She had just had surgery for a broken—"

"—wrist," Laina finished his sentence. "As a matter of fact, I do know she's left the hospital. Word has it she's enjoying a nearly miraculous and trouble-free recovery." She looked at the preacher, who only smiled. "If you'll come with me, I'll show you to her house. Mrs. Bishop has a son—"

"Will," the preacher said. "I remember him from the hospital. Troubled boy. So unhappy."

Really, Laina thought. *He could tell that from just the one encounter?*

"He and CJ have become good friends. As a matter of fact, they're on a ride together now. One of the soldiers apparently took Mrs. Bishop for a carriage ride."

"That would be Lieutenant Boone, I suppose," the preacher said.

"Yes. You know him?"

"We met the night of Mrs. Bishop's surgery. He was waiting with young Will." The preacher put his hat back on his head. "You take a minute to open that message from your husband. Elvira and I will wait at the gate yonder, and then, if it's all right with you, you can show me to Mrs. Bishop's."

Laina opened the box and removed the piece of paper on which Caleb had written, *Gave you this years ago. Hope you still want to keep it.*

Frowning slightly, Laina looked at the smooth, flat rock in the box. Caleb had never given her a rock. What could he be talking about? She looked at the note again. Lifting the rock from the box, she put it in the palm of her hand and ran her finger around the edge. Smiling, Laina closed her hand around the *heart-shaped* rock as understanding dawned on her. *Gave you this years ago. Hope you want to keep it.* She headed for the cemetery gate. She would stop grumbling to God about being at Fort Robinson. Her presence here was, after all, testimony to Caleb's love for her. She would have to consider the possibility that perhaps, it *really* wasn't about her.

•••◆•••

When the Reverend Barton concluded his brief visit at the Valentines' house, he asked to pray a blessing. Being the well-bred woman she was, Charlotte Valentine Bishop thanked him and bowed her head. Having been trapped into staying during the visit by the preacher's assumption of a friendship where none existed, and not wanting to appear rude, Laina Gray Jackson bowed her head. The two women sat opposite one another in the Valentine parlor. The preacher stood up, held his hat in his hands, and lifted his face toward the ceiling, smiling as he prayed.

"Thank you, heavenly Father, for answering my prayers for this young lady's wrist in a positive way. And now for this friendship, Lord, I pray your blessing."

Friendship? Laina thought. *I'd hardly call it a friendship. All right, Lord. I'll keep an open mind about it.*

"You know it is hard to be a rancher's wife . . ."

Amen to that, Lord, Laina agreed. *But then I suppose it was harder for Charlotte, being married to a man who was so difficult he alienated his own son.*

" . . . and you know it is hard to be a widow."

Especially when you are supposed to be brokenhearted but you are not, Charlotte thought. *God forgive me . . . it's such a relief not to be so afraid all the time . . .*

"But you have given these women one another . . ."

Granny would call Charlotte one of her lambs, Laina admitted to herself. *I know she is one of yours, Lord. But I can't see friendship happening. We're too different.*

I doubt Laina Jackson is going to want to be my friend, mused Charlotte. *She'll never believe I've changed.*

" . . . and similar life experience . . ."

Preacher, you have no idea, Charlotte thought.

" . . . and may they shore one another up . . ."

Laina doubted.

Charlotte rebelled. *The last thing I need is another self-righteous Christian telling me what to do with my life.*

"In the name of our dear Savior, I pray. Amen."

In your name, Lord, I'll try to do what you want, Laina prayed. *I know you love Charlotte and you care what happens to her. If you want me to help, I guess I should be willing to try.*

I tried praying, God, Charlotte thought. *My babies still died and Emory still hit me. Where were you?*

The preacher put on his hat. He beamed at the two young women before him. "I don't mind telling you two ladies that I was somewhat put out with the good Lord when He insisted I make the ride to Fort Robinson. But He just would not give me peace." He turned to Laina. "And then Caleb gave me that little package and I knew I must come." He stepped toward the door.

"Surely you'll not be heading back to the ranch tonight," Laina said.

"Please stay for supper," Charlotte urged.

The preacher hesitated. "I wouldn't want to impose."

"If there's one thing I've learned from living in an officer's household," Charlotte said, "it's hospitality. One never knows when visiting dignitaries will need a place to stay. There's always extra food ready at our table, and I would never turn a man out into the night without offering him shelter, even if it's just a pallet on the floor." Charlotte smiled warmly. "Garnet's made a huge pot of beef stew. And she makes the lightest biscuits you've ever eaten." She turned to Laina. "You and CJ would both be welcome. I believe Father said something about Lieutenant Boone and a chess game this evening." She turned back toward the preacher. "So you see, we've already been expecting company. Please stay."

The preacher accepted and then left to bed down Elvira in the doctor's stable.

Laina and Charlotte proceeded to set the table for dinner.

"I remember these dishes," Laina said, setting a blue-and-white plate on the table. "Your mother was so excited when we took the top off the crate. She'd been waiting for the freighters for weeks." She set a soup bowl on the matching plate. "The folks who lived at Camp Robinson back in the seventies would be amazed at the changes now that the railroad's come."

"Mother would be so much happier," Charlotte agreed. "How she used to fuss over how long it took to get things shipped. And Father was always unhappy over the cost." She leaned down and reached toward the back of the sideboard, pulling a stack of soup bowls toward the edge. "Do you mind?" she asked Laina. "I don't think I can handle them one-handed."

Laina took the bowls while Charlotte counted out soup spoons.

"Your mother was so horrified when I didn't know the difference between a soup spoon and a teaspoon," Laina said.

"Yes," Charlotte said. "I remember." Without looking up she added, "I'm sorry."

"Don't apologize," Laina said quickly. "Just being around the people who came and went through this house did a lot for my self-confidence. It helped me stop being afraid."

"You were afraid? At our house?" Charlotte didn't try to hide her surprise.

Laina nodded.

"What on earth did you have to be afraid of?"

"Failing," Laina said. "Disappointing all the people who believed in me. All the people who'd done so much to help me." She smiled. "And I will admit I was a little afraid of you."

"Of *me*?!" Charlotte's eyebrows shot up. "Why, for goodness' sake?"

"You and your mother were real ladies," Laina said. "The kind of women who wouldn't want to be seen with someone like me."

Charlotte stopped counting knives. She looked at her own reflection in the sideboard mirror. "For whatever it's worth, Laina, that girl who treated you so poorly has had a great deal of that kind of foolishness knocked out of her . . .

and hopefully some maturity knocked *in.*" She turned to look at Laina. "And the woman standing here humbly apologizes for the foolish girl and anything she might have done or said to hurt you."

Laina refolded a napkin. "Oh, goodness, Charlotte—I wasn't fishing for an apology. You said it. You were a girl, that's all. As far as I'm concerned that's all part of the past. It's forgotten." *Liar. You haven't forgotten a thing. You've been holding the past against Charlotte since you first heard she was back at Fort Robinson.*

Charlotte reached up to finger the lace at her throat. "Well, whatever our differences, we can certainly agree about wanting to forget the past." She absentmindedly ran her hand over her bandaged wrist. Footsteps sounded on the front porch. Charlotte headed for the kitchen, calling out over her shoulder, "Tell them dinner will be served shortly."

•••◆•••

"And how are those riding lessons coming along, young man?" the preacher asked Will.

"He's a natural," Nathan Boone said. He buttered a biscuit and then pointed the tip of his knife at Will. "He'll be an expert just like his mother in no time."

When the lieutenant turned and smiled at her, Charlotte felt color creeping into her cheeks.

"Don't worry, Mrs. Colonel," he added, "we'll start with old Bones hopping logs. I think even Bones can manage that."

"By the time you're riding again, I'll be able to come along!" Will said.

"I'll look forward to it." Charlotte wondered if she sounded too eager and worried that Lieutenant Boone might misunderstand.

"Will tells me you've become quite the horsewoman since you left Fort Robinson," Boone said.

"I took it up to please the Colonel," she explained. "Even I was surprised at how much I loved it.

"Ma had a big gray thoroughbred. His name was Isaac. He could jump *high*." Will demonstrated by raising his hand above his head. "She had a whole bunch of ribbons she won. And a trophy." Will sighed. "But we didn't have room to bring them when we left Grandmother's. We had to hurry."

Charlotte shifted in her chair. "Does anyone want more coffee?"

"Caleb's plotting to buy an entire herd of thoroughbreds from back east. Maybe you'll want to check over them if it works out. You could replace Isaac," the lieutenant said.

Charlotte was relieved that Boone seemed to understand her desire to change the subject. She shook her head. "I could never afford another horse like Isaac. He was an angel—just the right combination of power and good temperament."

"You sound like you really did take an interest in the horses," Laina said.

Charlotte shrugged. "It was something to do. I used to accompany the Colonel to sales from time to time. He bought Isaac after hearing me go on and on about Banner/Jesse Belle bloodlines." She looked down at her plate, remembering how any reference to stallions and mares and their "behaviors," as Mother Bishop had worded it in true Victorian code, had been forbidden at the Bishop table.

"Banner, did you say?" Boone asked. When Charlotte nodded, he continued, "Caleb's been trying to get me to go in with him on a stallion named Banner. I told him the price was ridiculous."

"Well, if it's the same Banner I know about, and if his owners are considering selling, I don't think you'd ever be sorry. He's magnificent," Charlotte said. "Isaac definitely took after the sire's side of his ancestry, and he was some animal."

"It really is a shame you couldn't bring him with you," Boone said.

"Grandmother said she was going to sell Isaac to Major Riley," Will blurted out. "She said she couldn't afford him anymore. And she sold the team. And she wanted Ma to marry Major Riley."

Charlotte jumped up from the table and hurried into the kitchen from where she called, "Will, I need some help out here."

CHAPTER ELEVEN

My little children, let us not love in word,
neither in tongue; but in deed and in truth.

I JOHN 3:18

NATHAN BOONE DIDN'T SPEND MUCH TIME ASKING himself why he cared about Will Bishop. He just knew he did. Ever since Nathan could remember, it had been in his nature to care about wounded things, and Will Bishop had been wounded. Nathan didn't know all the details, but he could see the current of fear running just beneath the boy's surface. He saw the same thing in Charlotte Bishop. The things Will had blurted out at dinner the night before said a lot about where the fear and self-doubt had originated. He didn't think it was his place to help Charlotte Bishop, but fate seemed to be making a way between Will and him.

"I don't know as either one of us will really be a help to Caleb," Nathan explained to Will's mother as they stood on the front porch of the doctor's residence, "but I need to see the Dawson place before I decide about investing in more land out here, and I think Will would have a good time seeing real cowboys in action. I have plenty of leave coming, and the colonel doesn't have a problem with my being gone.

Is it all right with you if Will comes with me on the roundup?"

"I don't know," she hesitated. "Do you think he can ride well enough yet?"

"Bones is as reliable as they come," Nathan said. "And from what Will tells me, I'm thinking it would do him good to get away from school for a few days. I think he's bored—and just about ready to plot some new torture for Mr. Phelps."

"Really?"

"Really," Nathan said. "Look Mrs. Colonel—"

"Would you please call me Charlotte?" she surprised him by asking. She rubbed the back of her bandaged hand. "I really hate that Mrs. Colonel title."

"Why?" Nathan asked. "You earned it."

"Yes," was the reply. "I did. In more ways than you care to know." She stared up at him and repeated, "And I'm asking you to please call me Charlotte."

Nathan nodded. "All right, then. Charlotte. And you must call me Nathan." He took a deep breath. "The thing is, Will is just too smart for Mr. Phelps. He's bored. And he's got so much energy he doesn't know what to do with it. I realize you don't want to reward his pranks. But maybe, just maybe, if Will has some time away, maybe he'll be able to come back and settle down and finish out the school year without any more incidents."

"That," Charlotte said, "would be a miracle."

* * *

Getting away from the fort seemed to unwind something deep inside Will Bishop, and while he didn't gush about the past during the half-day ride to the Four Pines Ranch with Nathan, he was less guarded about it. With his guard down, he said things that revealed a lot about Colonel Emory Bishop and how he had interacted with his wife and son.

What Will said birthed a seething anger in Nathan against the man, not unlike the helpless rage he had felt years ago against the worthless piece of flesh who had kept Laina Gray locked in a cellar.

As Nathan recalled the day he and Emmet Dorsey found Laina Gray, something about Charlotte clicked. He thought back to Will's prank and his mother's fall. When he'd put his hand on Charlotte's shoulder to help her up, she had reacted by pulling away. In fact, Nathan realized, she held herself apart in just about every setting he'd observed. She was slow to say much of anything. He'd chalked it up to her being physically hurt. Now he realized it was probably more than that. Living with Emory Bishop had apparently taught Charlotte to be on her guard. *No wonder she doesn't want to be called Mrs. Colonel.*

Nathan found himself wondering if Laina Jackson had any idea what was behind some of the more radical changes in Charlotte's personality. He wondered if Laina might be able to help. Maybe he'd talk to her about it when he got back to the fort. He couldn't think of anyone better to understand Charlotte's experience with Colonel Bishop. Maybe fate would bring those two together.

The boy riding alongside him this morning was really starting to come around. Nathan smiled to himself, remembering the look on Will's face a few days ago when he had finally succeeded in making old Bones trot all the way around the corral. That smile was worth a lot. Now, as they rode up the canyon in the sunshine, Will began to whistle, and Nathan was doubly glad he had talked Charlotte into letting the boy come. She seemed to trust him with Will. She'd been so pleased that morning when the boy rode Bones for the first time. Even her eyes had smiled.

"How much farther?" Will squirmed in his saddle.

"Your backside starting to ache?" Nathan teased.

Will nodded. "Yeah. And I'm hungry."

"We can take a rest if you like," Nathan offered. "I'm

sure Bones wouldn't mind a chance to do some grazing."

"Naw," Will said. "I was just wondering. We can keep going." He stood up in the stirrups. "I'm a tenderfoot," he said, grinning.

"Doesn't look to me like it's your feet that's tender," Nathan said. He laughed and urged his horse into a lope.

Will finally got Bones to follow suit. Before long, they were coming up over a ridge. Nathan pulled his horse up and waited for Will and Bones. "There it is," he said, motioning down into the valley where a half dozen log and board buildings of various sizes were nestled against a low rise. "The biggest building over there is the barn, of course. The corral's out back. You can't tell from here, but it's a good strong one. Caleb wrote me about how he hauled in cedar logs for it. I think he already had a breeding operation in mind when he put it up."

"The house is big," Will said.

Nathan nodded. "They've added on. Started out with just two big rooms. Next came two more off the back. There's a huge loft. Room for his boys, Caleb said." He motioned to a small cabin next to the barn. "We'll likely sleep there tonight. That's the start of a bunkhouse for the future wranglers. You'll get to meet Jack Greyfoot."

"The Indian?"

Nathan looked at the boy. "Yes. He's Cheyenne. Why?"

Will shrugged. "I never met any before. That's all. My pa said—" He hesitated. "Never mind." He sucked in a deep breath.

"Jack was about your age when the Outbreak happened. Did your pa ever tell you anything about that?"

Will shook his head.

"Jack and his brother Grey Foot and Grey Foot's wife, Rachel, had been at Fort Robinson since October when, in January they were locked up in the old barracks south of the East End parade ground. A hundred and thirty Cheyenne in all."

"In there? But there isn't room."

"Well, that's where they had to stay. Until they said they would go back down to Kansas where they had been sick and dying."

"That's not fair," Will said.

"They didn't think so, either. And I doubt they thought it was very fair when the army quit giving them food and water."

"They didn't!" Will protested. He turned in the saddle and stared at Nathan. "You wouldn't . . . do that . . ." He frowned.

"I was in the hospital when that happened," he said, and went on to describe how he'd been stabbed by a Cheyenne named Wild Hog inside the commander's office, hours before the Outbreak. "One night the Cheyenne decided to break out and run for freedom." He went on to tell Will about the following weeks, sparing the boy the worst details, yet hoping what he said would overcome the prejudice Will had been taught. "So now you know a little bit about Jack and Rachel," he finally said. "It's been ten years since all that happened. The Jacksons are happy to have them on the ranch, and they seem happy to be there. If you want to learn how to break and train a horse, Jack is the man to get to know. Caleb says sometimes it seems like Jack can whisper in a horse's ear and get it to do anything he wants."

Nathan waited for the information about Jack to sink in a little before he went on. "You'll also meet an old friend of mine named Emmet Dorsey." Nathan added, "Now, just like you shouldn't let any of the Indian nonsense you heard back east stop you from getting to know Jack, you shouldn't let Dorsey's cranky exterior fool you. Emmet's a good man. Just don't get between him and a spittoon and you'll do fine. If you want to know how to train a horse, you ask Jack. And if you want to hear war stories, you ask Dorsey." He urged his horse forward. "Let's go. I can hear your stomach growling from all the way over here."

They rode directly to the house and dismounted, tying their horses to the hitching post that also served as uprights for a wide front porch. Just as Nathan was showing Will how to tie Bones, the front door opened and Caleb Jackson emerged, followed by two old men. And Rachel. She was smiling at him. He took off his hat. Smiled back.

"I don't believe it," Caleb said, turning to the white-haired man next to him. "Preacher Barton, meet Lieutenant Nathan Boone, who, as I told you, knows more about me than any human being has a right to know . . . and did his best to steal Laina Gray right out from under me."

"Well now," the preacher said, pumping Nathan's hand and smiling. "That wasn't exactly mentioned over Mrs. Colonel Bishop's dinner table the other night, was it, Lieutenant?"

Nathan smiled and shrugged. Rachel turned away and headed back inside. "Guilty as charged," he said, shaking the preacher's hand. "Except there wasn't a prayer in . . . uh . . . excuse me, Reverend . . . there wasn't a chance she was going to have a thing to do with me after that moonlight sleigh ride." Nathan clapped Caleb on the back. "Let me introduce my young friend here. The reverend has already met him. This is Emory William Bishop, Jr., Charlotte's son. I talked him into coming up here to the ranch with me so I wouldn't be the only greenhorn on the roundup. That is, if you'll have us."

Caleb shook Will's proffered hand. "The boy is welcome. But I don't know about you," he teased Nathan. "Don't imagine you know a branding iron from a cattle prod."

"As a matter of fact," Nathan said, "I believe I do. But I'll try not to get in your way."

Caleb nodded. "You still good with that?" He pointed at Nathan's rifle.

"I've been known to hit a target or two."

"Well, maybe you'll bring in some game for the outfit," Caleb said.

Nathan looked at Will. "We'll do our best. Right, partner?"

Caleb nodded toward the barn. "You two men take your horses—that *is* a horse, isn't it, Nathan?" he said, peering at Bones. "Take your horses down to the barn. Jack's down there trying to convince a gelding CJ has taken a shine to that people aren't rattlesnakes." He grinned. "He's already eaten once tonight, but I bet he'll be easy to convince to come back up to the house with you for some more. Tell him Rachel is heating up the stew." He looked down at Will. "You *are* hungry, aren't you?"

"The boy's been hungry since we left Fort Robinson," Nathan said. He untied the horses, and he and Will made their way down to the barn.

Nathan was proud of Will. He might be trembling with fear and uncertainty, but the boy stuck out his hand and shook Jack Greyfoot's and looked the man in the eye.

"I told this young man you're the one to pay attention to if he wants to learn how to break and train a horse," Nathan said.

Jack shrugged. He nodded over his shoulder to where the gelding stood, his rear pressed into a corner, his front feet splayed. "Tell *him* that."

"That the horse CJ has her heart set on?"

Jack nodded. "I promised her she'd be able to ride him when she gets back."

"That must be Rebel," Will said.

"And a rebel he is," Jack said, turning around and walking to the stall. The horse snorted and tossed his head. Jack smiled. "At least he wants me to think that." He lifted his chin and directed his next words to the horse. "But I don't believe it. It's all an act."

Will's stomach rumbled. The two men laughed.

"Guess we'll put breaking Rebel on hold so you don't starve," Jack said. He reached for Bones's reins.

"Caleb said to invite you back up to the house for seconds," Nathan said.

Jack grinned. He patted his stomach and winked at Will. "Wait until you taste Rachel's fry bread."

* * *

"He's going to explode. That's all there is to it." Nathan looked across the room to where Rachel stood at the stove. "You'd better stop," he called out. "You're going to kill the young man with good cooking." He nudged Will, who was sitting next to him at the table, still eating after all the grown men had stopped.

Will took one last huge bite, then sat back and belched loudly. "Excuse me," he apologized, smothering a giggle.

"Good eats, ma'am," Nathan agreed, holding out his coffee mug for a refill as Rachel approached the table, coffeepot in hand. "We're going to wish we had some of that bread on roundup."

"I'll make you some," Rachel said. "You can take it in your saddlebags." She touched his shoulder lightly.

Jack pushed himself back from the table and stood up. "I have some work to get done before sundown," he said, and left abruptly.

The rest of the men sat at the table until long after sundown. Caleb wanted to know about Nathan's escapades in the Southwest. With a glance in Rachel's direction, Nathan changed the subject to ranching and the future for western Nebraska in the scheme of things. When Caleb mentioned importing a good quality thoroughbred stallion, Nathan turned to Will. "Tell Mr. Jackson what you know about Banner."

"My ma's horse Isaac was from Banner's line," he said. "I remember my father talking about Banner."

"Really?" Caleb said. "Tell me what you remember."

Will yawned. "Ma said Isaac took after Banner. He could

jump higher than any horse I ever saw. Ma had a whole bunch of ribbons and trophies. She really liked Isaac. But Grandmother said we couldn't afford to keep him. It made Ma really sad. The day Major Riley came to get him, she cried."

***

The morning after Will left with Nathan, Charlotte stood on her father's back porch gazing at the bluffs in the distance.

"Don't worry, missus." Garnet's voice sounded behind her. "Lieutenant Boone won't let anything happen to Will."

"I'm not so much worried as lonely." Charlotte turned back around and headed inside. "After all of Will's mischief, who would have thought I'd be complaining about being bored the minute he's out of sight?"

Garnet poured a cup of steaming water into a china cup, measured loose tea into a silver tea ball, and plopped it in the water. While the tea brewed, she took a tray of fresh biscuits out of the oven and slid them into a basket. "Don't fret so. It won't be all that long and you'll be taking rides with Will up into the hills on a high-stepping horse. I know how you miss your rides."

Charlotte ran her hand over her bandaged wrist. "Of all the things I anticipated about coming back to Fort Robinson, missing Isaac wasn't one of them," she said wistfully. "I hope the Major is treating the old boy well."

Garnet added a lump of sugar to Charlotte's tea. "Doctor's already gone over to the hospital to make his rounds," she said. "The ladies will be making their calls soon."

"I think they've finally given up on me," Charlotte said, and sat down at the table to sip her tea.

"If the ladies aren't calling on you anymore, maybe *you* could call on *them,*" Garnet suggested. "I expect that nice Mrs. Jackson could use some company."

* * *

The idea of calling on Charlotte would not go away. Climbing out of bed, Laina looked at herself in the mirror. *Haven't I done enough, Lord? I had dinner with her just two nights ago. And you saw—she was doing all right.*

Of course, Laina had to admit, the woman was probably a bit lonely with Will gone. Maybe even worried. Especially if CJ was right and Charlotte hadn't let the boy do much on his own.

She headed into the kitchen where CJ sat staring glumly at a bowl of steaming oatmeal.

"Are you ready to do that recitation for Mr. Phelps today?" Laina asked.

CJ shrugged.

Laina sat down next to her. "I know you miss Will, honey-lamb," she said. "But maybe you'll make a new friend in school today."

"I don't see why it was all right for Will to leave school but not me," CJ grumbled.

"Neither your father nor I are about to let you be the only female on a roundup," Laina said. "You can go this fall when things are back to normal and Rachel is riding with the chuck wagon again."

"Why does *everything* have to be different just because there's a baby coming?" CJ whined. She scooped up a dollop of oatmeal and watched it slide off the spoon and plop back into the bowl. She slumped in her chair. "And when's the baby coming, anyway? We've been here *forever*."

Laina willed her temper away. Hoping she sounded confident and not just irritated she said, "This is the way your father wants things. He would have been very unhappy with me if you showed up with Lieutenant Boone and Will without any notice. And besides that, we both want you in school, not gallivanting all over the countryside with a bunch of cowboys."

CJ's mouth turned down at the corners. She put the spoon down and dropped her hands into her lap.

"Listen to me, Clara Joy." Laina was glad to see the girl's expression in response to hearing her full name. *Good. That got her attention.* She continued, "Obedience is easy until we have to do something we don't want to do. I know you aren't very happy with things right now. The truth is, neither am I. I'm homesick for the ranch the same as you. But your pa's got enough on his mind without having to worry about you and me. So we're both just going to have to obey what he says and stay here at Fort Robinson for a while longer. That's what God would want us to do—trust that Pa knows what's best and obey him *and* God, who tells us to do everything without grumbling."

Yes, Laina. Exactly. No grumbling. So are you going to visit Charlotte today?

Laina ignored the thought. She lifted CJ's chin and turned the girl's face toward her own, insisting CJ meet her gaze. "I want to go home, too. But we can't. You have to go to school and . . ." Laina sighed. "I have to—"

"Take a nap," CJ interrupted. She turned away and stabbed at the oatmeal again, sighing dramatically. "I *know*, Ma. You're *tired*. You're always tired."

"Actually," Laina said, tugging on one of CJ's red braids, "I was going to say that I have to call on Mrs. Bishop today."

CJ perked up. She glanced up at her mother hopefully. "Really? Do you think you can get her to let Will stay at the ranch this summer?"

"I think," Laina said, "that you need to do your job, which is eating breakfast and going to school and trying not to drive Mr. Phelps crazy, and let me do mine—which includes taking care of things at the ranch." She forced a smile, and the edges of CJ's mouth turned up. "That's what I like to see." Laina stood up. "And for your information, I'm feeling quite well today. I don't need a nap. What I need is some female company. I'm thinking Mrs. Bishop is missing

Will about now. She may even be a little worried. Maybe having second thoughts about turning him loose in the Wild West. So if you'll gather your school things, we'll leave together."

◆

Charlotte was standing on the back porch watching Private Carter Blake sink a spade in the lumpy earth that would soon be Garnet's kitchen garden when Laina Jackson rounded the corner of the house, her sewing basket over her arm, a smile on her face.

"It doesn't seem so long ago that Frenchy Dubois was out here digging," she said.

"Yes," Charlotte agreed. "Frenchy had quite the garden in his day."

Private Blake swiped his hat off his head and bobbed a greeting to Laina. "Miss Irvin's got her heart set on a big garden." He smiled. "I told her that between the good Lord and me, we'd do what we could to make it happen."

Garnet stepped out on the porch, holding a tray with two steaming mugs of coffee and a plate of biscuits. "Breakfast, Private," she called and then nodded at Laina. "Morning, ma'am." She set the tray on an upturned barrel at the edge of the porch and handed Blake one mug of coffee before handing the shawl she had draped over her arm to Charlotte.

"You two enjoy your breakfast," Charlotte said. "Mrs. Jackson and I will just go on inside and have ourselves a cup of coffee." She turned to Laina. "If you have time?"

Laina nodded. "Actually, I was coming to see you. I thought you might be missing Will," she said and followed Charlotte inside. "The first time CJ went on roundup, I nearly worried myself sick. And all she did was ride in the chuck wagon with Rachel."

"Oh, I'm not really worried," Charlotte said. "I've no

doubt Lieutenant Boone will keep an eye on him. But I do miss him." She took her shawl off and draped it across a kitchen chair.

Laina nodded at Carter and Garnet, visible through the kitchen window. "What's going on with those two?"

"I don't know," Charlotte said. "I didn't think Father asked for a striker. But I haven't been keeping track of things like I should. Garnet hasn't had a lot to say, other than that Private Blake is a 'powerful pray-er,' whatever that means. But then Garnet has always been a woman of few words." She nodded at the basket over Laina's arm. "You brought your knitting."

Garnet appeared at the back door. "I'll be right in to make you ladies some coffee," she said.

Charlotte waved her away. "We can make our own coffee. We're going to be in the parlor for a little while. Enjoy yourself." She winked at Garnet, who grinned, covered her crooked teeth with her hand, and went back to where Carter Blake was sitting eating a biscuit.

"Well," Charlotte said, looking at Laina. "I guess that answers our question." She took down two coffee mugs. "You go on and get settled in the parlor. I'll be right there with some coffee."

Once she had served up two cups of coffee, Charlotte was at a loss for what to say next. She didn't want to talk about Michigan, and she knew nothing about ranching. After a few false starts, the two women settled on the one thing they knew they had in common—their children.

"I'm so glad you decided to put CJ in school," Charlotte said. "I swear, Will thinks she hung the moon."

"I believe, given a chance, she'd try to prove she could," Laina joked. "Especially if climbing were involved." She sighed and shook her head from side to side. "That girl. Sometimes I wonder where she came from. She hates the kitchen, doesn't care about cooking. Refuses to sew. Wants to spend every spare minute she can with her father riding, hunting, herding—whatever he's doing."

"How wonderful," Charlotte murmured, staring off into the distance, "for a child to have that kind of connection with her father." She rubbed her bandaged wrist with her open palm.

"Oh, Charlotte. I am so sorry," Laina said. "That was very thoughtless of me. Will must miss his father terribly."

"Actually," Charlotte said, "they weren't all that close." She cleared her throat. "The Colonel had very definite ideas about what his son should be like. When Will didn't love horses right away and didn't want to 'play war,' the Colonel saw it as a weakness. He didn't take very well to the notion that his son didn't 'measure up.'"

"What do you mean, Will didn't measure up?" Laina said. "I know he's had his moments—but who wouldn't love Will?"

Charlotte shrugged. "I don't think it was a matter of love . . ."

"Of course not. I didn't mean it that way," Laina said.

"Of course, Will wanted to please the Colonel. Every boy seeks his father's approval. It just never seemed like Will could get it. The Colonel was always in such a hurry for him to grow up. I lost three babies after Will—"

"Oh, Charlotte," Laina said. "Will told CJ . . . and she told me, but I just didn't know what to say." She paused. "I am so very sorry."

"There's nothing else to be said," Charlotte answered. "Thank you." She took a sip of coffee to steady her voice. "They were all boys.

"It seemed like the Colonel's expectations for Will got more intense with each loss. Of course, the Colonel assumed Will would follow in his footsteps. West Point. Cavalry. When Will was only eight months old, the Colonel taught him to walk by planting Will's feet on the tops of his shoes and walking backward. Will was only two when the Colonel decided it was time he learned to ride. He took him out to the barn and set him up on one of the plow horses. The horse was gentle, of course, but Will got excited and let go of the mane and tumbled off. He broke his collarbone. After that, he didn't want to go near a horse." Charlotte looked down. "I'm afraid the Colonel didn't handle that disappointment very well."

"What do you mean?"

"Oh, he kept insisting on repeating the process. Said Will would finally get over being afraid. Except that Will didn't get over it. Finally, one day the Colonel was carrying Will out to the barn, and Will was screeching for me—" Charlotte closed her eyes, trembling with emotion at the memory. "I intervened. I just couldn't listen to my baby screaming like that."

"Of course not," Laina said quickly. "What mother could."

"Exactly," Charlotte said. "So I put a stop to the 'riding lessons.'"

"Good for you," Laina said. "I hope the Colonel learned his lesson."

Charlotte was quiet for a long time. "The Colonel wasn't very open to learning lessons. He was more the kind of man who *taught* lessons." She looked down at the clenched hands in her lap. When she finally looked up, Laina was watching her carefully.

"But that's all done with." Charlotte forced a smile and shrugged. "Things are better now. Between Lieutenant Boone and Private Blake and my father, Will's finally getting to be around men who can set a good example. I'm thrilled he's finally learning to ride. I'm hoping that will help focus some of his boundless energy. He's a strong-willed child. Unfortunately, after the Colonel died, I didn't have the emotional strength to discipline Will. The Colonel's mother tended to be too strict. Will's been bouncing between my leniency and Mother Bishop's unreasonable demands for so long. . . . Sometimes I worry he's been ruined."

"Don't be so hard on yourself," Laina said. "It takes time to heal after loss. Especially a sudden loss like you've had. Will's going to be all right. You'll see. The older I get, the more I am convinced it's just part of parenting to worry over our children and to feel guilty about decisions we've made. I worry about CJ all the time."

"Why?" Charlotte asked. "She's terrific. Bright and funny and sweet."

"Sweet?" Laina said. "No one's ever called CJ *sweet*."

"Well, she is," Charlotte said. "She's taken time with Will. She's looked past the pranks and the streak of mischief—"

"Oh, I don't think she's looking past it as much as looking *for* it and *participating* in it," Laina quipped.

Charlotte laughed. "They *are* quite a pair. Maybe we should just arrange a betrothal now."

Laina worried aloud. "That'd be fine. Because I don't personally know any boys who are particularly attracted to a woman who wants to wear pants most of the time and can ride and rope with the best of the cowboys. CJ's still pouting that I didn't let her go on roundup with the men. It didn't help any when she overheard Nathan offering to keep an eye on her if I wanted to change my mind." She shook her head from side to side.

"I'm so grateful Lieutenant Boone has taken an interest in Will," Charlotte said. "The Colonel was all barking orders and discipline. I don't want my son to grow up like that. He needs to learn that a man can be gentle and still be a man. Will is lucky the lieutenant makes the effort he does to spend time with him."

"I don't think he sees it as a terrible sacrifice," Laina said gently. "After all, getting to know Will has put him in the company of Will's mother."

Charlotte spoke up. "I came back to Fort Robinson with one thing in mind, and that is to raise my son. All I care about is doing what's best for Will. And I'm quite certain that's all Lieutenant Boone has in mind, as well. I'm grateful he's in our lives—for Will's sake. But I am also quite certain that his spending time with me is just an unavoidable part of the package that comes with Will Bishop."

"Yes," Laina said quietly. "I'm sure you're right. It was Will he was thinking of at dinner the other night when he mentioned escorting you to the officers' ball next month."

Charlotte got up and went to the parlor window. She closed her eyes, absentmindedly running the palm of her good hand back and forth across the strap of her sling. "I'd appreciate it if you'd not tease me about that. Lieutenant Boone was being polite. That's his way."

"I'm not teasing. It would be good for both of you to be friends. I've been praying for Nathan since he left Fort Robinson ten years ago. Praying that God would heal his heart and draw him closer. Praying that maybe, just maybe, Nathan would someday open that great heart of his to friendship with someone—maybe to more than friendship."

"Well," Charlotte said, "I empathize with your concern for Lieutenant Boone. I know he was deeply hurt when his wife died so young. I was too self-centered to see it then, but on this side of grief, I do feel for those who experience tragedy." She turned around and looked at Laina. "And I can also tell you from this side of grief, that the last thing Lieutenant Boone needs is for well-meaning friends to meddle in his personal affairs. When I think back to the way I behaved toward him in those days, I could cry with shame. It's a tribute to his character that he will come near us at all. I don't intend to do or say anything that would risk Will's benefiting from Lieutenant Boone's investment in his life."

Laina focused on her knitting. Silence reigned for a few minutes. Finally, Laina lay aside her needles and stood up. She arched her back and grimaced. "Your father keeps insisting that walking is the best thing I can do for myself and the baby. I've been promising myself I'd take another bouquet of flowers to Lily Boone's and Granny Max's graves. Care to join me?"

Grateful for something to do besides wonder how Laina felt about her impromptu sermonizing, Charlotte jumped up. "I've been lax about tending my mother's grave. I'll get some ribbon." Rummaging in the sideboard drawer, she pulled out a length of yellow ribbon and cut three pieces before tucking it into her sling.

Together, the two young women went out the front door and headed across the parade ground, past the barracks and stables, and finally across the bridge spanning the White River and into the field beside the cemetery. They picked wild flowers for several minutes, then made three bouquets and entered the cemetery.

"You know," Charlotte said as she bent to place the first bouquet at Granny Max's grave, "I have a lot of regrets about things that happened here at Fort Robinson when I was a girl. But one of the greatest is that Mother and I let *where* Granny Max lived keep us from getting to know her." She sighed. "That was yet another mistake I made in the old days."

"I learned a lot from Granny," Laina said.

Charlotte pulled her shawl around her. "I suppose I owe Granny Max a thanks, if she's the reason you came to visit today. And the reason you put up with my paranoia about Lieutenant Boone."

"It isn't paranoia," Laina said. "And you're right. I should mind my own business." She smiled. "You said it very tactfully—and from experience—and I appreciate that."

"Thank you for trying to understand," Charlotte said. "I do appreciate your company." She sighed. "I fear time is going to pass very slowly while Will is gone." When Laina was silent, Charlotte walked to her own mother's grave and placed a bouquet there.

"I was sorry I didn't know about your mother's death until after the funeral," Laina said. "I would have come."

Charlotte shrugged. "I wasn't here, either. The Colonel wouldn't allow it."

"Why on earth not?"

Charlotte sighed. "We weren't getting along very well. The Colonel was very unhappy with me."

"So he took revenge by preventing you from coming to your own mother's funeral?"

Charlotte stared down at the grave. "I think he knew that if he let me come, I might never return to Michigan."

Laina put her hand on Charlotte's arm.

Charlotte took in a deep breath. She blinked back tears. But she couldn't stop the trembling. "We should go," she said. "I don't want to wear you out."

"Let's go over and sit in the shade awhile," Laina said. "If you don't mind."

The two women made their way to a place just inside the fence where a cottonwood tree was throwing its shadow. They settled on the grass. Finally, Laina spoke up. "You know, Charlotte, one thing I learned from Granny Max is that humans aren't meant to handle all their troubles alone. God puts people in our path to help us. Sometimes He sends people who've had experiences that enable them to understand us in a way no one else could." She paused. "Granny was able to help me first of all because she loved God. He gave her supernatural love for me long before I was anything near loveable. So it was definitely God at work that enabled Granny Max. But from a human perspective, it surely didn't hurt that she had once had an experience like mine." Laina briefly told Charlotte about Granny's nightmare experience as a girl. "Knowing she had been through that really helped me trust her." Laina put her hand on Charlotte's arm. "I don't know how much of my story you heard when you were here before. I always imagined it was common knowledge."

Charlotte answered, "I don't know about common knowledge. But Mother, God rest her soul, wasn't exactly the best person about keeping confidences. And there was a time she thought you were competition for Lieutenant Boone's affections—which, as you will recall, she was intent on turning toward me." She sighed. "I probably know more than I should."

"It's all right," Laina said. "The thing is, Granny Max used to tell me that someday I would see the reason behind that awful time. That I would actually be able to see God using what happened in that dugout with the monster who kidnapped me." She put her hand on Charlotte's shoulder. "I have to admit, that as much as I loved and respected Granny, I never really believed her." She squeezed Charlotte's shoulder before letting go. "But I'm thinking now I do."

Charlotte looked down at her sling where she had tucked the last bouquet of flowers. She pulled it out. Together, they walked to Lily Boone's grave.

"Do you think . . .do you think it's possible Will won't be . . . damaged . . . permanently?" Charlotte fought for control, determined not to break down. "The Colonel tended to be . . . strict. Demanding. Sometimes he lashed out." She sucked in a wobbly breath.

"You mean he hit you," Laina said.

Charlotte pressed her lips together. She shrugged. "Not so often." She murmured, "What matters is Will. Do you think Will can get past it?"

"I think," Laina said gently, "that God promises to make all things new. And, unlike we humans, He keeps His promises."

"I don't have much confidence in God," Charlotte said.

"I understand how you could feel that way," Laina said. "I did, too. For a long time." She took Charlotte's hand.

Charlotte didn't pull away.

It was late afternoon before Laina Jackson and Charlotte Bishop stepped out onto the back porch of the doctor's residence together.

"Look at that," Charlotte said, pointing to the tips of the distant bluffs, still brilliantly illuminated by the setting sun. "Nebraska can be a beautiful place." She surprised even herself by hugging Laina. "Thank you for what you did for me today. I'll never forget it."

Laina protested. "All I did was listen."

"Well," Charlotte said, "you're a good listener."

Laina stepped down off the porch. She had only gone a short distance when she turned around and called Charlotte's name.

Charlotte came back to the edge of the porch. "Yes?"

"If he enjoys roundup, maybe you'd consider letting Will spend some time at the ranch this summer."

Charlotte nodded. "I imagine he'd love it."

"And," Laina added, "I'd like it even more if you'd consider coming with him. I think you'd enjoy it, too." She smiled. "Who knows. Maybe God brought you west to turn you into a cowgirl."

CHAPTER TWELVE

A man's heart deviseth his way:
but the Lord directeth his steps.

PROVERBS 16:9

IT HAD BEEN TEN YEARS SINCE WINTER MOON AND her husband, Grey Foot, fled the barracks at Fort Robinson as part of what would be called the Cheyenne Outbreak; ten years since Winter Moon had taken the name Rachel Greyfoot and come to live at the Four Pines Ranch with Laina and Caleb Jackson; ten years of internal struggle to come to terms with the contradictions that were her life. On the one hand, if it were not for the soldiers pursuing her husband, he might still be alive. On the other hand, if it were not for soldiers like Caleb Jackson and Nathan Boone, *she* might not be alive. If it were not for greedy white gold diggers and homesteaders and ranchers, Rachel's people might still be free to live in the old way. But if it were not for white ranchers like the Jacksons, she might be living in poverty on the reservation. Some whites she hated. Others she loved. Some whites talked about God all the time and then stole from their own the minute they had the chance. Others who rarely said the name of God were honorable and trustworthy.

It had taken most of the past ten years, but Rachel had

finally learned to live in the place of tension between two opposing forces. She had found a measure of internal peace and was determined to see each person as an individual and to do her best not to judge them for either their skin color or their name for God. Most of the time, she was content with her life on the Four Pines Ranch. She worked hard for the Jacksons, who had proven themselves to be both kind and fair, and she grew to be genuinely fond of CJ.

On days when living suspended between two colliding worlds threatened her inner peace, Rachel found solace in climbing alone to the summit of a hill. Sometimes she watched clouds or stars cross the ancient sky and let her mind wander into the past. Sometimes she closed her eyes and listened. She heard the rustle of the grass when a rabbit poked its nose out of a clump of wild sage along with the buzzing of grasshopper wings. She heard the wind in the pines. Sometimes there was the far-off cry of an eagle or the less noble cawing of a crow. Most of the time, her moments up on the hill watching or listening helped her recapture herself and re-create the feelings of enforced contentment. She worked hard, was never hungry or without shelter, and was almost at peace.

Lately, Rachel had even begun to think maybe Jack was right, that they should be married. Everyone agreed that Jack was, like his brother before him, a good man. Even if he was four years younger than Rachel, he loved her with a desperate, youthful emotion that, even if she could not return it, Rachel at least appreciated. A woman could do much worse than being loved by Jack Greyfoot. She wasn't getting any younger, and she did not want to grow old alone.

But then Rachel accompanied the Jacksons to Fort Robinson and saw Lieutenant Nathan Boone. For the past ten years she had thought of him only as the hero who saved her life. He was one of the good soldiers, a tall, handsome white man with dark hair. He had been wounded before the Outbreak, and when they brought her to the fort hospital, he made sure she got good care for her frozen feet. Before he left, he arranged for her to stay with the Jacksons instead of being taken to the reservation. He even found Jack, Grey Foot's younger brother, and convinced Caleb Jackson to give him a home, too. Boone left Fort Robinson before Rachel was well enough to thank him.

She heard news of him from time to time. Sometimes the Jacksons talked about him over dinner. He had helped Caleb buy the ranch. He wrote about cattle and horses. Sometimes Mr. Jackson read one of his letters aloud after dinner while she and Mrs. Jackson worked in the kitchen. Boone wrote of the army and the buffalo soldiers. He was promoted to lieutenant. He described the land he was in. It sounded barren and lonely. He wrote of other native people. Sometimes, Rachel thought, there was a cloud of sadness over his words. Time blurred her memory of him, but it did not erase her sense of a debt owed.

And now he was back. In the few moments she'd seen him at the fort trading post, she had noticed that time had aged the lieutenant more than she would have expected. There was white in the hair at his temples. She also noticed that, to any woman's eyes, Lieutenant Nathan Boone was still a handsome man. When he arrived at the ranch with a boy in tow, something stirred inside Rachel. She didn't know if the lieutenant sensed it, but it did seem to her that as she moved about the kitchen, his brown eyes were on her every time she looked up. When she offered to make fry bread for Boone to take on the roundup, Jack reacted. He must have sensed something, too—something that made him jealous. At least it wasn't her imagination. That night, Rachel's nightmare returned.

Grey Foot was dragging her bodily up the face of the impossibly high butte. Rachel wanted to help, but her frozen feet would not obey. "Leave me," she begged him over and over again, but he would not. Pretending he didn't hear, he kept moving, scrambling up the same narrow crevice their people had used for generations, dragging her with him between vertical walls of earth jutting up out of a broad valley toward the icy gray sky.

The sound of approaching hoofbeats from behind fueled his ascent. He grasped her around the waist more firmly. She tried to help, tried to push off from the rocks, to be something less than dead weight. The blue coats from the fort were hesitating. As she watched, a soldier mounted on a huge buckskin charged the cliff. The horse scrambled valiantly before sliding backward. The soldier shouted an order, and all his men dismounted and began climbing on foot, their boots sending a shower of rocks behind them.

A blast of cold wind shot up the crevice and Rachel shivered. Her best beloved loosened his grip momentarily, pausing on a thin ledge to suck air into his lungs.

"Leave me," she repeated, trying to pull away.

Grey Foot's dark eyes stopped watching the pursuers. They focused on hers. "I will never leave you," he said. He bent low, putting his windburned cheek next to hers for just an instant before once again encircling her waist and resuming the desperate climb.

She clung to him, focusing on the great bird soaring above them, wishing the two of them could leap off the cliff and ride on the wind like the bird that seemed suspended in the air above them. Another blast of icy wind pelted them. The bird screeched, flapped its wings, and disappeared over the ridge.

With a grunt, her husband surged upward, over the edge, onto the summit. Together they fell to the earth, shuddering when their thinly clad bodies made contact with the snow. He got up onto his knees with his back to her. She knew what to do. How many hundreds of times had he knelt just like that when the two of them were children. How many times had she dreamed of the day when a son of theirs would clamber onto his father's back so the two of them could gallop through the tall grass, the father trumpeting like a wild horse. She fell forward, clasping his shoulders even as he pinned her thighs against his waist and staggered to his feet.

Grey Foot had gone only a few feet when mounted soldiers emerged from the pine trees ahead of them. He darted to the left. More soldiers. He spun around to look behind them. Soldiers poured from the crevice, their breath rising like plumes of smoke in the frigid air.

"Our family is dead. We should go to them," she whispered in his ear. Her right thigh tensed against his waist, signaling him as she would a horse, knowing that even as they had always seemed to think as one, he would read her thoughts now. She felt him take in a breath, felt his elbows press against her knees, sensed his message of love even as he lunged to the right and ran straight for the edge of the cliff. She clutched his shoulders, closed her eyes, waited for the soaring through the air, wanting what would come next. Just as she thought her heart would burst with love, he ripped her hands from his neck and flipped her off his back and into the snow.

Soldiers shouted. A gun went off. She screamed. Everything seemed to slow down. Grey Foot turned around and put his clenched fist to his chest, even as his dark eyes sought her face. He smiled. Nodded. And then, as the blue coats launched themselves toward him, he spun away, spread his arms, and jumped.

She gasped as someone grabbed her shoulder. She tried to fling the hand away, to struggle up from the cold, but the soldier was strong and wouldn't let go. She screamed and started kicking, but the giant man with dirty blond hair wrapped his arms around her and held tight. The smell of him made her gag.

Rachel woke with a start. She raked her hands through her long dark hair and swiped at the tears she had cried in her sleep. She lay awake for a few moments, staring at the ceiling. Her breathing returned to normal. Still, she could not shake the sense of terror in her heart. Finally, she got up, dressed, and went outside.

She was headed for the hill, the way so familiar she needed no daylight for the journey, when Jack's voice sounded in the night. He must have been leaning against the barn, just out of sight of the house.

"Are you all right?" he called, barely loud enough for her to hear. He came to her side and touched her shoulder. "You tremble," he said.

Rachel shook her hair back over her shoulder. "A dream.

It's nothing. I was going to take a walk."

"*The* dream?" Jack asked. "I thought you said it had left you."

"I thought it had," she said. She shivered a little and crossed her arms, hugging herself.

"Seeing Lieutenant Boone has brought it all back for me, too," Jack said. "You had the dream. I couldn't sleep at all." He pointed toward the distant hill. "I just kept remembering what it was like trying to run with frozen feet. And the hunger. I remember the hunger."

"Don't." Rachel put her hand to his chest. "Don't go to that place. We are here. Safe."

"Safe." Jack seemed to taste the word. He looked around him. "Is that all you want, Rachel? To be safe?"

She didn't answer. She waited, dreading the next words, which she knew would come.

"I want more."

"I know you do," Rachel said. She moistened her lips. Swallowed. "And you should have more. But—"

He smothered her words with his lips, and she answered, refusing to shrink away and yet unable to respond with the same unspoken longing he displayed. When he released her, a breeze blew her hair across her face. She didn't try to push it away. She didn't want him to see her face in the moonlight. He started to apologize, but Rachel put her fingertips to his mouth. "Don't," she said. "Don't." She leaned toward him, resting her forehead against his chest. "I'm sorry, Jack. It isn't you. You're a beautiful man. A good man." She stood away and looked up at the sky. "It isn't you."

"Yes. I know." The words he said next wrenched her heart, for he turned them to their real meaning—the truth that he had always refused to acknowledge. "It isn't me." He walked away toward the bunkhouse. Rachel stood and watched him go, saw the sliver of golden light pour into the night from the open door, saw it disappear, heard him latch the door. The wind rustled her hair again. She went back to the house, back to her bed, but not back to sleep. Lying awake in the dark she argued with herself. *Brown eyes and a uniform are NOT what you have been waiting for. They are NOT.*

• • • ◆ • • •

"Where's your war bag, sonny?" Emmet Dorsey asked. He sent a stream of tobacco juice into the dirt at Will's feet.

"What?" Will asked, looking at Nathan Boone for help. Nathan raised his eyebrows and shrugged. Apparently he didn't know what a war bag was, either.

Dorsey retreated to the barn, emerging with two empty feed sacks. "Your war bag," he said, handing one to Will and one to Lieutenant Boone. "You put a change of clothes in there. A towel. Your toothbrush and your hairbrush." He winked at Will. "Not as if you'll use 'em, but it'll please your ma if you can tell her you took 'em along."

Will and Nathan went to the bunkhouse and stuffed the required items into the sack. When they came back out, Dorsey was waiting. "Toss 'em in the big wagon along with the others," he said.

Rachel came walking down the path from the house carrying a sugar sack. "Pemmican," she said, handing the sack to Lieutenant Boone. She flashed a smile at him and then turned to Will. "You'll like it," she said.

"Thanks," Nathan said. His cheeks turned a curious color of red.

As Rachel turned to go, Dorsey chuckled and spit a stream of tobacco.

Nathan glowered. "Don't say a word," he muttered. "Come on, Will. I'll show you how to tie your bedroll on behind your saddle." He put his hand on the boy's shoulder. "You'll look like you grew up on a horse before we're finished with you." He glanced back at Dorsey. "And Rachel's right. You'll like her pemmican. It's like jerky, only better."

Dorsey called after them. "You think that sorry excuse

for a horse you got this boy riding can keep up with Jack's outfit?"

"Bones isn't much to look at," Nathan said, "but he and Will have an understanding. They'll do fine."

Just as they arrived at the barn, a dozen or more Cheyenne rode in. Will inched closer to Nathan Boone, who put his hand on the boy's shoulder while he called out to get himself and Will hooked up with Jack's outfit.

Will saddled Bones with shaking hands. He'd never felt so excited and yet so frightened at the same time. It was one thing to get to know Rachel and Jack, but another thing entirely to be in the middle of what seemed to him to be an entire tribe of Cheyenne. The forty or so men milling around the ranch house were a diverse lot. Some were quiet, almost sullen. Others laughed and joked as they went about the task of lassoing their mounts and saddling up. All of them had an air of bravado and confidence that made Will want to be like them—except, of course, for the fact that they cursed a lot, which would displease his mother.

"You go ahead and get mounted up," Lieutenant Boone instructed Will. "We're greenhorns enough. No need for the rest of these men to have to wait for us." He took his horse's reins and headed for the house.

"Where you going?" Will wanted to know.

"I forgot something," Boone said. "I'll catch up."

Dorsey chuckled. He looked up at Will and winked. "Forgot his sugar."

Nathan hesitated just inside the front door of the ranch house. Rachel was nowhere in sight. He looked around, scratched his beard, then turned to go.

"Is that you, Mr. Jackson?" Rachel called from the loft. Nathan looked up in time to see her look down. He was pleased to see the smile light up her face when she saw it was him. "Mr. Jackson wanted me to sneak another blanket in the chuck wagon for Dorsey."

Nathan grinned. "I take it the old coot still won't admit to needing a little extra attention for his knees."

She shook her head. "We all just go behind his back to try and take care of him. Did you need something?"

"Uh . . . no." Blast it. He felt as awkward as a schoolboy. "I'll . . . uh . . . take the blanket down to the chuck wagon if you like. Dorsey will think it's for the boy."

Rachel nodded. "I'll be right down."

He heard her footsteps scurrying across the loft and back to the ladder. She tossed a blanket down to him. He caught it *and* a glimpse of Rachel's bare legs as she descended the ladder and lighted so close he could smell the freshly washed scent of her hair. "Thanks. I'll . . . uh . . . I wanted to thank you. For being so nice to the boy. He's a good boy." *You sound like an idiot.*

"He is," Rachel agreed. "A sad boy. But a good one." She smiled up at him. "Not unlike a certain man I know." Without warning, she reached up and touched the crease between his eyebrows. "This is new in these ten years." She touched the gray hair at his temples. "And this."

He shrugged. "The years catch up to a man. We can't always hide the things we've done that we aren't proud of." He looked down at her and swallowed the lump in his throat before saying, "I always wanted to tell you how sorry I was."

She shook her head. "That's for others to say. Not you. You gave us a life. You know what it would be like for Jack if you hadn't found him. You know where I would be." She gestured. "Look around you, Nathan Boone. It is not for you to say you are sorry. It is for us to say *thank you*." She stood on tiptoe and brushed his cheek with a kiss.

"Hey, Lieutenant," Will called from the door. "Everybody's leaving!"

Nathan spun around. "Then let's get going," he said. With a nod toward Rachel, he headed outside.

The men rode north, away from Four Pines Ranch, up into the buttes. Before long they had broken off into several groups of four or five, each group heading in a different direction. Will followed Nathan Boone, Jack Greyfoot, and three other Cheyenne cowboys, riding north and west.

Gradually the landscape began to change. Verdant pastureland gave way to splotches of white chalklike stone jutting up from the earth. Little by little, the grass disappeared completely and the men were riding single file through outcroppings of strangely formed rock. The horse's hooves echoed loudly as they rode along. For all the strangeness of the landscape, Will noticed masses of blooming plants clinging to the tops of some of the rock formations. He thought about how his mother would smile if he brought her some of those flowers, then looked around him guiltily, as if the men might read his mind and call him a "mama's boy" for the thought.

"Your mama would like those," Lieutenant Boone said, nodding toward a clump of orange flowers. "Too bad you can't take her some." He grinned at Will's look of surprise. "You give her flowers, and she might not worry so much about what you're learning from this bunch of cowboys."

Will peered at Boone from beneath the brim of his oversized hat. "Thank you for talking her into letting me come. I never thought she would."

"As I recall," Boone said, "mothers sometimes have a bit of trouble letting their boys do what boys got to do. Mine certainly did." He smiled. "She threw a fit when I left home."

Will commiserated. "Yeah, mothers are like that." He added, "Mine said to make sure I didn't try to rope any cows. She was afraid I'd forget to put on my gloves and get rope burns on my hands." Will looked down at the soft hands holding Bones's reins.

Boone burst out laughing. He leaned over the saddle horn toward Will. "I'm thinking you'd better learn to rope while we're out here or you'll feel like you've missed the perfect opportunity to rebel." He urged his horse forward. "Let's see if we can't find ourselves a couple of strays. I can't rope worth a darn, but maybe we can manage to at least herd them this way."

Will flapped his boots against the old gelding's sides, and Bones galumphed forward with a sound of protest. By the end of the day, Will and Lieutenant Boone had ridden until Will could no longer feel his backside. Jack and the others, with only a little help from the two greenhorns, had managed to round up a dozen cattle. Will thought they were ornery critters, bawling and protesting and not wanting to go toward the ranch at all. He watched the men drive the recalcitrant animals with growing respect for both the men's riding ability and their horses.

"It's like the horses know what the cow's thinking," Will said at one point while he rode alongside Jack.

"Well, in a way, they do," Jack said. "A good cow horse does, anyway." He patted his horse's withers. "Wait until you see this one cut."

While he was certain whatever Jack was talking about had nothing to do with a knife or scissors, Will had no idea what a horse could do that would be called *cutting*. But he nodded as if he understood. As the cowboys drove the cattle ahead of them, Will and Lieutenant Boone enjoyed the scenery and mostly tried to stay out of the way.

One day Lieutenant Boone shot an antelope and that night they all had steak for dinner. More than once Boone gave chase after a bolting cow at the same time Jack did. Boone's army horse was strongly built and the lieutenant was an expert rider, but it was always Jack's tightly muscled little gelding that made the final move that turned the old cow and her calf back into the herd. Will watched such things from his safe seat aboard old Bones, his own muscles tensing, his arms reining left and right as he pretended to be Jack Greyfoot.

• • • ◆ • • •

Will and Nathan rode with the Four Pines outfit for over a week. They gathered up strays until, when they finally headed for the ranch, they were herding nearly a hundred cattle ahead of them. Will thought he would never be able to describe it all to his mother. He wouldn't have words for the smell of dust and manure and leather, the sounds of hoofbeats and yelling men and ropes whistling through the air. When the outfit neared the ranch, and they were greeted by the sight of nearly a thousand cattle milling around in the valley below, Will's mouth fell open.

Boone nodded. "We've only been working the north. There have been other outfits doing the same thing west, east, and south. Now the real work begins."

"Cutting?" Will said.

"Cutting, branding, heading for market," Boone said.

"And now you'll see what I meant when I bragged on this fella," Jack said, urging his horse down into the valley. "At least two hundred of those beeves belong to the Four Pines. Let's go get 'em."

For this part of the roundup, a frustrated Will Bishop was ordered to watch from the relative safety of the chuck wagon seat. Over the next few days, he saw horsemanship like he had never imagined. It was nothing like the fancy stepping of his father's horses in a military parade, nor was it anything like the steeplechasing his mother liked. To Will, it was better because it wasn't just for show. Just as Jack had said, the cutting horses were amazing. Will was on his feet for most of the day, standing on top of the wagon seat, watching as the horses bobbed and wove their way through the herd, turning this way and that, singling out a cow and her calf and giving chase until both were separated from the herd.

Now that they were camped near the ranch house, Rachel came down every day to help the chuck wagon cook. Will noticed that Lieutenant Boone showed up at the wagon more often. One day when he was standing nearby, Will said, "Oh, I *wish* I knew how to do that!"

Boone looked up at him, squinting into the bright morning sun.. "You'll be riding as good as any of them soon."

"No, I won't," Will said, slumping down onto the wagon seat. "Bones is a good old horse, but he's too slow."

"You won't be riding Bones forever," Boone said. He nodded toward the string of horses belonging to the wranglers. "You'll have a good pony like one of those."

"Mother would never let me have a wild ranch pony. She'd be afraid I'd get hurt."

"Well now," the Lieutenant said, "I think the word you have to avoid with your mother is 'wild.' Mr. Jackson has plenty of fine working ponies that don't have a wild bone in their body. That's the kind you'll need first."

Will just shook his head.

"Don't get discouraged before you even get started," Boone said. "And don't let anybody tell you that you can't. Because you can."

"I can what?"

"Just about anything you set your mind to. Think about it. A boy who was afraid of horses just spent the last two weeks on a roundup. And he handled his horse just fine. And tomorrow—"

Caleb Jackson rode up. "Tomorrow is branding," he said. "And you can help."

Will hardly slept. Lieutenant Boone didn't spend much time in his bedroll, either. Will suspected it had something to do with Rachel Greyfoot.

Branding lasted only a day. Will was up early, watching Jack and a few other men build a large fire in the predawn light, and helping them plunge several branding irons into the hot coals until they glowed red hot.

When the lassoing began, Will once again admired Jack's and Caleb Jackson's abilities with a twirling rope. Once again, he admired the cow ponies, who seemed to know what to do without any signal from their rider. As soon as the ropes hit their mark, the ponies began to back up, straining against the struggling cow until the bellowing creature was stretched full out.

Will winced when the first brand was applied. After the cows were all branded, the men began to work with the calves—roping them only around the hind legs while cowboys wrestled them to the ground. Lieutenant Boone waded right in, laughing and joking while he sweated and strained with the other cowboys. At one point, Rachel came down and perched on the top board of the corral and watched for a while. Will sat next to her, surprised when she was able to explain as well as anyone what was going on and why.

"It's your turn," Lieutenant Boone finally said. He moved toward where Will and Rachel sat, taking off his leather gloves as he walked and slapping the dust out of them against his thigh. "You want to brand or wrestle?"

"Neither," Rachel teased.

Lieutenant Boone laughed.

"Both," Will said. "I want to do both."

Boone nodded and tapped the brim of Will's hat. "Well then, cowboy. Let's get you out there." He winked at Rachel.

Rachel had long since gone back to the chuck wagon to start cooking supper when Will finally succeeded in wrestling a calf to the earth without help. He held it down with all his might until the branding was done, then leaped up, extending both hands to the sky and yelping with joy. The men around the corral burst out laughing. Will felt himself starting to blush, but then Caleb Jackson came forward with a red-hot branding iron and said, "Brand the next one, and you're a real cowboy, Will Bishop."

Will worked alongside Lieutenant Boone this time, applying the brand as soon as Boone threw the calf. He winced in sympathy as the smell of burned flesh filled the air, but then the same men who'd laughed when he wrestled the calf to the ground cheered. The feeling that he was being laughed at was replaced by a sense of camaraderie the boy had never experienced before.

By the end of the week, Will Bishop had heard more swearing than in all his life put together. He'd overheard jokes that would have made his mother gasp, been offered his first chaw of tobacco, and been teased until his cheeks were flaming red. He had also been rescued from an angry bull, taught to lasso a pole, and allowed to ride one of Jack's horses—a pretty little mare with more energy than old Bones had probably ever had in his entire life. He had decided that while he couldn't speak for the entire Indian nation, the Cheyenne certainly were nothing like the Indians his father had told him about. He had learned that men who swore could also be generous and kindhearted and brave. And he had decided that no matter how long it took to convince his mother, he was never going to be in the army. Will Bishop was going to be a cowboy.

• • • ◆ • • •

Roundup was over, the calves all branded, the herd culled, the various outfits scattered to the half dozen Sandhills ranches around Fort Robinson. Will stood in the dark with his arms crossed atop one of the corral boards, admiring a gray pony.

"You look almost like a ghost," he said aloud. "In the dark I can hardly see your black legs or your mane or tail. It's like you're floating above the ground." He extended his hand inside the corral. "You hear me, Spirit?" He was amazed when the filly stopped milling around with the other horses and looked at him. "Is that your name, then? Are you Spirit?" Will said, his heart pounding.

The horse snorted and tossed her head.

"Oh, yeah, you're something," Will said. He wiggled his

fingers. "Afraid of a little boy. What's that about, huh? You afraid of me? I'm not going to hurt you."

The horse pawed the dust with one black hoof. She shifted her weight from one foot to the other and back again before taking a step toward him.

"Come along, then," Will said, thinking surely the pony could hear his heart pounding. Surely she would be afraid of the unusual sound and whirl away. Any minute now.

But she didn't. As Will talked, the little horse inched her way across the corral until Will could feel her warm breath on his open palm.

Afraid to move, Will kept talking. "My name's Will." Just as he said the name, the filly thrust her muzzle into his palm. When he didn't snatch it away, she took his fingers between her velvety lips and nibbled gently. "Hey," Will said quietly. "That's not food. That's my hand." She let go and stood, looking at him.

Bones rambled up to the corral fence, thrust his big head over the top rung and shoved Will playfully. "Hey, now," Will protested. "I'm talking to Spirit. You go on."

As Bones stood at the fence, the gray horse edged closer until she had sidled alongside him, and the two horses stood side by side, listening to Will talk.

From the darkness behind him, Lieutenant Boone's voice sounded. "What'd I tell you? She doesn't have a mean bone in her body. She just needed the right person to pay her some attention. And a little courage borrowed from old Bones."

"What should I do now?" Will asked.

"I don't think you need any advice from me," Boone said. "Seems to me you're doing just fine. That little gal won't come near me, and here you've got her nibbling on your fingers. I'm thinking she's picked you out to be the one she trusts."

"Why'd she do that?" Will wanted to know.

"Guess she's the only one that knows that," was the

answer. "But one thing's for sure, she trusts you and Bones. You think you've got the patience to break her in? She's going to take a little extra time. But I've got a feeling she'd be a good horse for you."

"F-f-for me?" Will stuttered at the idea.

"That's right," Boone said. "For you."

"Ma wouldn't let me," he said.

"Your ma's a first-rate horsewoman," Boone said. "She'll take one look at this little gal and know she'd make a good ride for you. Maybe we could ride out here with your ma next week and show her."

"I don't have money to pay for a horse," Will said.

"Can you haul hay and clean out stalls?"

"Sure."

"Then I imagine we'll be able to work something out with Mr. Jackson," Boone said. "You've been talking about wanting to be a cowboy. Maybe you can start this summer."

"I'd work hard," Will said.

"Tomorrow at breakfast I'll give you some sugar cubes so you can give her a treat." It was Rachel Greyfoot. Will hadn't realized she was with the lieutenant.

Boone spoke up. "See to it you stay *outside* the corral, you hear? She likes you, but she doesn't know you well enough yet. Getting kicked in the head is no way to start your career as a cowboy."

Will nodded. "Yes, sir," he said. "I'll stay here. I'll just talk to her. Get her used to my voice."

"That's good. She likes listening to you. Look at her now. Those little ears are taking in every word."

Boone's and Rachel's footsteps retreated toward the house.

"That's Lieutenant Boone," Will said to the horse. "He's nice. Maybe you'll let him help me put a halter on you tomorrow. I met him because he came to see my ma." He pondered for a moment. "But I think he really likes Rachel."

* * *

"First we rounded 'em up and then we lassoed 'em—I can lasso a pole but not a calf yet—and then we branded 'em, and I branded one, and everybody cheered and even the Indians were nice, Ma. And there's something I got to ask you, Ma. . . ." Will, who had wrapped both arms around his mother's waist, leaned back and looked up at her, his face flushed with joy.

"Hold on, Will," Charlotte said, gasping for breath.

Will jumped back and let go. "Did I hurt your arm? Oh, gosh, Ma—I'm sorry."

Charlotte put her open palm on the boy's cheek. "No, you didn't hurt me," she said, smiling. "I just can't take it all in. You've rounded up and lassoed and branded and met nice Indians—and I want to hear more." She stepped to the edge of the porch and smiled at Nathan who was waiting, still mounted on his horse, holding the reins to Bones. With his free hand he reached up and raked his fingers through his scruffy beard.

"I'll take Bones on over to the stables, Will," he called out.

"No," Will protested. "Wait!" He looked up at his mother. "I should take care of my own horse, Ma. You understand. Right?" He was already scampering off the porch and climbing into the saddle. "We're starved," he called from the saddle. "Does Garnet have any pie? "

Nathan spoke up. "Never mind the pie for me."

"Just because it isn't chokecherry," Charlotte said, "doesn't mean you won't like it." She interrupted before he could object. "It's the least I can do to say thank-you."

"Thank-you for what?" Nathan asked.

Charlotte pointed at Will, who had already turned Bones around and started to ride toward the stables.

Nathan shrugged and tugged on the brim of his hat.

"Ranch life agrees with him." He headed for the stables. Halfway across the parade ground he looked back over his shoulder. Charlotte was still standing on the front porch. He tugged on the brim of his hat. She waved.

CHAPTER THIRTEEN

I am weary with my groaning:
all the night make I my bed to swim;
I water my couch with my tears.
PSALM 6:6

"NOT BREATHING."

Charlotte held back her own tears as she watched Laina touch her baby's perfectly formed nose, then brush a fingertip across the closed eyelids. Only moments ago, as Charlotte cheered her on, Laina had made the final tremendous effort to birth her son. The two women's eyes had locked as they shared an instant of rejoicing. And then Charlotte's father frowned. Charlotte held Laina's hand while they waited for the cry that never came. She remained motionless when her father pronounced the two words that brought a weight of grief into every corner of the little room.

"Not breathing."

"I'm so sorry, my dear," Charlotte's father spoke again. "But there's still more work to do. Push now." Gently he directed Laina to the completion of the birth process.

While her father worked with Laina, Charlotte wrapped the baby boy in a blanket. Somehow, she found the strength not to collapse into sobs. How well she remembered this helpless, empty feeling. She had felt it three times, the third time no easier than the first.

Leaning back against her pillow, Laina closed her eyes. "Caleb," she said. "I want Caleb."

"I'll see to it," Charlotte said, handing the baby to the doctor and heading for the kitchen where she motioned for Nathan.

"Where's CJ?" she asked.

"Outside with Will."

Charlotte took in a deep breath. "The baby." She closed her eyes, unable to say the words.

"Oh, no," Nathan said. He shook his head.

"She's asking for Caleb."

"He'll be here in the morning," Nathan said, and left.

"What's wrong with my ma?" CJ came to the door.

"Your ma's fine," Charlotte said. Her voice wavered. "I'm afraid your baby brother . . ." She swallowed hard. "He's in heaven."

CJ grabbed Will's hand and held on. "Can I see him?"

Charlotte's father entered the kitchen. He shook his head. "I think your mama needs to be alone for a little while, CJ."

Charlotte's eyes filled with tears. Her presence seemed so accidental. Will and Lieutenant Boone had returned from the Four Pines Ranch at sundown, bedded their horses, and came back to Dr. Valentine's house to be treated to a piece of Garnet's fresh gooseberry pie. Charlotte marveled as Will recounted the details of his first western roundup, described his adventure with an enthusiasm Charlotte had never seen in him before. He was demonstrating branding, by standing over an imaginary calf, when CJ pounded on the back door in search of Dr. Valentine. Before anyone had time to think, they were all clustered in the kitchen at the trading post, trying to assuage CJ's fear and waiting half the night while Dr. Valentine came and went.

Not far into the night, Charlotte had been surprised

when her father came out to the kitchen and said Laina was asking for her. Laina was apologetic. Charlotte was touched. As the hours went by, she applied cool compresses to Laina's furrowed brow and stroked her arms. At one point, she even sang a hymn, joking about her wobbly voice until Laina actually smiled.

Now the birthing was over, Laina in mourning, and Will's best friend, CJ, was clutching his hand in fear while she tried to process what had happened.

Charlotte took charge. "You come on home with us, honey." She held out her hand to CJ. "You can come back after your ma has had time to rest."

Maude DuBois spoke up. Turning to Charlotte she said, "You're exhausted, too. You don't worry about a thing. I'll check in on Mrs. Jackson from time to time. That elixir your father gave her will keep her asleep, likely until mid-morning tomorrow."

CJ allowed Charlotte to lead her away to Dr. Valentine's house. As they walked along across the darkened fort grounds, Charlotte put her arm around the girl's shoulders. "It'll be all right, CJ," she whispered. "Don't worry."

Charlotte rose at dawn. She roused Garnet and asked her to delay CJ as long as possible, then headed to the trading post to be with Laina. She stroked the back of her friend's hand while they talked. "I've been through this three times, but I don't know of anything I can say that will help. I wish your Granny Max was here. Maybe she'd know what to say."

Without opening her eyes, Laina recited, " 'I don't understand it, honey-lamb. No, I don't. But I know God is still on His throne. We just got to trust Him.' " She looked at Charlotte. "That's what she'd say."

Charlotte nodded. "That sounds good." She patted

Laina's hand. "I can tell it's helping you."

Laina pulled her hand away. She shook her head. "I know God's ways are not our ways. I know He is the Potter and I'm the clay. But right now, those things just sound like empty words." Her eyes filled with tears.

"I don't understand why this has happened," Charlotte said. "If anyone deserves happiness, it's you. It seems to me you've been through enough."

Laina snorted. "Apparently not." She shook her head. "The only thing I've asked God for in quite a while is sons for Caleb. He wants sons so badly." She stared at the foot of the bed, talking to no one in particular. "What could possibly be wrong with that? Why on earth would God say *no*?" She reached over and touched the edge of the blanket that still held her baby. Tears rolled down her cheeks.

"I'm so sorry," Charlotte said. "Try to get some sleep. I asked Garnet to keep CJ occupied as long as possible so you would have some time to yourself. And Caleb should be here soon."

"I know Maude's worn out from keeping watch last night," Laina said. "Would you . . . could you . . . stay. . . ."

"Of course I'll stay," Charlotte said, stroking her arm. "Try to get some sleep. I'll be right here."

Once, Laina woke with a jolt. "The baby! Where's the baby?"

The panic in her voice brought tears to Charlotte's eyes. "Right here, Laina. Right here at your side."

"Why isn't Caleb here? What's taking so long?"

Charlotte looked out the window. "The sky is really overcast. Maybe he had to wait out a cloudburst."

Laina looked down at her baby. "Oh," she moaned softly, bringing her hand to her breasts as her body awakened the timeless response of a mother to its child.

"I'll be right back," Charlotte said. She slipped out and returned with a length of muslin from the trading post shelves and tore it into strips. "Let me help you bind yourself," Charlotte said. "It will help."

"How do you know about this?" Laina asked.

"I've been through it."

Laina closed her eyes. "I'm sorry. I forgot." Tears streamed down her cheeks. "It hurts."

"I know," Charlotte said.

⋄⋄⋄◆⋄⋄⋄

At last, Caleb arrived, his footsteps muffled by the rag rug on the floor. Laina stifled her sobs and opened her eyes just in time to see Charlotte pat Caleb's shoulder and slip out of the room. For all their married years, Caleb had always had a way of soothing her woes. His hands were large and rough, but when he stroked her forehead, following her hairline down one temple and to the tip of her chin, he was as gentle as Granny Max had ever been. She'd once told him that his touch was like being soothed by God. When he stroked her that way, he always hummed a raggedy melody. Off-key. Then he'd stretch open his fingers and massage her head, easing the tingling along the left side of her head where a bullet had once sliced her scalp, leaving a wide scar. Whatever old wounds or fears assaulted her, Caleb's presence had always stilled them all, bringing her back to the present and to a place where she was safe and loved and as secure as any woman could be.

It was only natural for Laina to expect that Caleb would reach out to her that way again, show his love without saying a word, stroke her forehead, maybe trace a line between her eyebrows to the tip of her nose. She closed her eyes. *It's all right, baby girl* he would say.

But instead of reaching out to her, Caleb touched the edge of the baby's blanket. "Let me hold him," he said.

She knew that voice. It was low and gravelly—the voice he used when he was having trouble controlling his own emotions. She heard it when a calf was found half eaten by wolves or a prized mare died or when he didn't know if they were going to be able to make the next payment on the ranch. She'd heard it at the worst times of their lives.

When she held the baby out to him, Caleb took the bundle and stood up and went to the window. He turned his back to her. She saw his shoulders shaking. He must be crying. But he didn't share his tears with her.

The quiet in the room nearly smothered her. The tension came back to her midsection and a weariness settled over her. Pulling the covers up to her chin, she closed her eyes.

"Not breathing."

The night before, Laina had thought hearing those words was the worst thing she would ever have to endure. As Caleb left with the baby without saying a word to her, she realized she was wrong. Dreaded words could rip a woman apart inside. Words could break a heart. But sometimes silence was worse.

◆

Caleb and Laina Jackson buried their infant son on a bleak May morning made even more dreary by a cold wind heavy with moisture. Laina stood beside her husband, thanks to an herbal tea supplied by Garnet Irvin and CJ's clinging to her hand. Taking Caleb's proffered arm brought her no comfort. Before his son died, Caleb always walked with his arm around her waist, not caring about the shocked looks such a public display of affection garnered them both. But that was then. And this was now. In the hours since his son's death, Caleb Jackson had undergone a transformation.

Dr. Valentine was reading the Shepherd's Psalm. But Laina could not listen. All she seemed to be able to hear were the words he had spoken a short while ago when, after a brief examination, he summoned Caleb to his wife's room.

"As I told you yesterday," the doctor had said, looking apologetically at Caleb, "I had some concerns after the delivery. There is good news. The bleeding has stopped. That's a good sign in regards to *your* health, my dear." He patted the back of Laina's hand. "I think it will be all right for you to ride in the carriage over to the cemetery for the service. However," he continued, "I am very sorry to have to say this, but future pregnancies are no longer possible."

"What?" Laina said. She looked at Caleb, who was staring out the window. She looked back at the doctor. "What do you mean? I'm fine. Of *course* there will be more babies. We're building a ranch to pass on to our children. Our *sons*. We expanded the house to make room. Maude knows a woman who didn't have a baby for years and years—but then she had five in the next five years. That's what we want, isn't it, Caleb? Tell him. Tell him we're going to have—"

Caleb turned around and faced her. He shook his head. "No," he said. "We're not." He stayed by the window, barely looking at her. "Tell her, Doc," Caleb said. "Tell her how you explained it to me."

At least he walked over and put his hand on her shoulder while Dr. Valentine explained things. Tissue had been expelled in the delivery, he said. And the loss of that *tissue* made it impossible for her to conceive again. "I recall, Mrs. Jackson, that when Clara Joy was born I told you she was something of a miracle. Having also attended this birth, I can tell you that with even more certainty. He turned to look up at Caleb. "And I can also say that you are blessed that your wife survived this birth."

They still call it birth. How odd, Laina thought.

"Will she be all right?" Caleb asked.

"She needs rest and time to heal. But she'll be fine," Dr. Valentine said. He issued a few more directives, encouraged

Laina to rest, to spend most of her time in bed for the next week, then to gradually take short walks until her energy returned. He complimented Charlotte's "binding," and offered to bring over one of his women's medical books if Laina thought it would help answer her questions. And then he left.

Caleb looked down at her. "You must be exhausted. I've got to check in with the commanding officer. He promised to put me to work right after roundup." He patted her head twice. Kissed her on the cheek. Left without another word.

"Will she be all right?" Caleb had asked. Dr. Valentine had said she would be, with time. Now, while the doctor's voice droned on through the reading of the Shepherd's Psalm at her baby's graveside, Laina thought how very wrong Dr. Valentine had been. She might heal physically, but something had happened to make Caleb pull away. And Laina was quite sure she would never be all right again.

···◆···

CJ Jackson told Will she had never experienced having her parents barely speaking to each other. Will had never experienced anything else. "Don't worry," he said. "My folks practically lived in different parts of the house sometimes. At least yours aren't fighting."

CJ frowned. "You don't understand, Will. It's not like that for Ma and Pa. I mean, they were *embarrassing* the way they always acted around each other, always kissing or hugging or just—you know, just *looking*. Like they had a secret or something." She was sitting on the side porch at the doctor's residence with Will. "It's been a week. Ma sleeps most of the time, and Pa . . . well, Pa is always working. He hasn't even had supper with us." CJ stifled a sob. "I'm scared."

It felt awkward, but Will made himself put his arm

around his friend. "Don't be afraid," he said. "Things will work out." He added, "You can eat with us tonight. Lieutenant Boone is coming to talk to Ma about Spirit."

⋯⋯

Dinner at the Valentines' residence was over, and it was nearly sunset when Nathan finally found Caleb, still at work installing windows in one of the new buildings on the West End. "I had dinner with Charlotte and Will and the doc tonight," Nathan said after a quick greeting. He cleared his throat. "CJ was there, too. She's worried about her family."

Caleb frowned. "According to the doc, there's not going to be much family." He went on to tell Nathan what Doctor Valentine had said.

"I'm the last person in the world to preach any sermons to you, and I know it," Nathan said brusquely. "But, Caleb—you do need to take a look around."

"At what?" Caleb said. "At the loft back at the ranch that's going to be empty? At the new brand I'll never need?"

Nathan scrubbed his jaw with a closed fist. "How about you take a look at the tombstones over in the cemetery. Start with the one that says Lily Bainbridge Boone. Realize everybody loses people they love. Everybody has dreams they didn't manage to live."

"And I suppose the fact that your wife died makes you an expert in this kind of thing," Caleb mumbled, taking one of the nails from between his lips and nailing a board in place.

"Hey," Nathan said. "You've already got a preacher in your life. You don't need another one, and I know that. But blast it, man—" Nathan looked away. "Laina *survived*. You've still got a beautiful wife *and* a terrific daughter. And they need you. Charlotte can't even get Laina to go for a carriage drive. CJ tells Will the two of you hardly talk. She says Laina spends most of the day in bed." He cleared his throat. "I know you don't want to hear this—neither did I when Lily died. But when it comes right down to it, your problems aren't all that special. God sends rain to fall on the just and the unjust."

Caleb placed another nail, speaking before he hammered it down. "I hear what you're saying. And I know I've got things to be thankful for. Dorsey rode in this morning, and once he quit grumbling about his bum knees, he said Jack has a good start on breaking three colts. Rachel's garden is coming along well. We're going to have a good crop of foals. And with me working here at the fort, we'll have money to expand the herd, maybe even bring Banner out, and put a down payment on the Dawsons' place if they decide to move into Crawford. Things are looking good for the building of a ranch." He hammered another nail, then another, before looking up at Nathan.

"But blast it, man, what's it all *for* if there's nobody to leave it to? We've done nothing these past ten years but dream about building something that's worth passing on." His voice was bitter. "And now this." He bent the nail he was trying to drive. Swearing under his breath, he pulled it out and held it down as he hammered it back into shape. When Nathan still didn't speak, he finally grumbled, "I know. I know. And you're right. I got to get my thinking straight." He shook his head. "I *really* got to get it straight when the man who doesn't talk to God is quoting Scripture at me."

"Scripture? What are you talking about?"

"'God sends rain to fall on the just and the unjust,'" Caleb replied.

"I was quoting Granny Max," Nathan said.

Both men chuckled. Caleb shrugged. "Well, you're right, anyway." He stood up straight and looked at Nathan. "I appreciate you caring enough to walk over here tonight. Really, I do. And I'll be all right. But I need some time."

"Then take time," Nathan said. "But don't let Laina *see* how you're struggling. She'll blame herself. It'll kill her."

Caleb shook his head. "That's where you're wrong. She's strong. And it's not like she doesn't know what's going on inside me. It wasn't just my dream. It was hers, too."

Tattoo sounded. "I've got to get going," Nathan said. "I'm sorry, Caleb. You two deserve better."

"I'm inclined to agree with you." Caleb nodded. "But we'll be all right. Laina's strong. She'll bounce back. We all will."

CHAPTER FOURTEEN

Trust in the Lord with all thine heart;
and lean not unto thine own understanding.
PROVERBS 3:5

IN SPITE OF WHAT HER HUSBAND SAID ABOUT HER, Laina Jackson showed no sign of being strong. And those who knew her best saw that she was far from being "all right."

Charlotte invited her on a walk every day. Laina was too tired.

Maude Dubois suggested Laina check over the new bolts of calico in the trading post and get started on a new dress for the Independence Day festivities. Laina declined, saying she doubted they would attend this year.

Caleb wanted her to go with him into Crawford. Laina didn't feel strong enough for such a long drive.

Charlotte suggested they attend a women's tea together. Laina had no energy for "small talk."

Garnet Irvin offered her special healing tea. Laina claimed she was healing just fine and left most of it in the cup.

CJ asked for her help with a school assignment. Laina told her to ask her pa.

Nathan Boone offered to have Private Blake drive Laina and CJ back to the ranch. Laina wasn't ready to go.

Caleb began to work longer days and took to sleeping in a tent on the East End instead of "coming in late and disturbing you, honey."

Everyone was concerned, but no one knew what to do.

Charlotte wondered why Laina's faith, which had seemed so real, did not help her more.

Nathan wondered why Caleb's faith, which had seemed so real, did not help him more.

* * *

"I'm really worried about her," Charlotte said to Nathan Boone one morning several weeks after the funeral. He and Will and CJ had arrived at the Valentines' back door without Laina, who had once again refused an invitation—this time a ride up into the hills for a picnic with the children.

Nathan had dismounted and come to the door to fetch Charlotte. "She won't come." With CJ and Will out of earshot, he lowered his voice and added, "She's never cared much for riding, but I really thought she'd come for CJ's sake."

"I thought part of the problem was her being homesick for the peace and quiet on the ranch," Charlotte said. "You'd think she'd welcome an afternoon away from all the construction noise."

Garnet spoke up. "No reason you two shouldn't let Will and CJ have their outing," she said.

"Bess isn't anything so fine as you're used to riding," Nathan said. "But she's gentle. And it *is* a beautiful day."

"Come on, Ma, *please,*" Will begged. He'd jumped down off Bones and come inside. He looked back over his shoulder. "CJ needs cheering up."

Looking past Will to where CJ waited aboard a rangy spotted mare, Charlotte nodded. "All right. Let's go."

They rode north and picked up a trail leading toward the high bluffs overshadowing Fort Robinson.

"Even old Bones can feel summer coming," Charlotte said to Nathan as Will kicked the horse into a canter and sped away. "I didn't think Bones could move that fast. Will has been complaining about the old boy's stubborn tendencies."

Nathan said, "Have you had time to think any more about Spirit?"

"The gray filly at the Four Pines?" Charlotte said. "Will can't go a day without mentioning her. She sounds pretty."

"She is," Nathan said. "Black legs, long black mane and tail. Interesting face." He drew an imaginary line diagonally across his own face. "Half white, half black."

"You said she's *feisty*—I think it was—at dinner the other night."

Nathan nodded. "But there was definitely a connection between her and Will." Nathan went on to describe the scene he'd witnessed the first night Will noticed the horse.

Charlotte nodded, murmuring, "I know what that's like."

"Isaac?" Nathan asked.

"Yes. Isaac." She looked into the distance. "I do hope Major Riley is treating him well."

She looked over at Nathan. "Will said he calls her Spirit because she looked like she was floating above the ground that night he first noticed her. I assume that means her movement is good."

"She has a beautiful, fluid gait. I definitely think you'd approve." Nathan nodded at the trail, which was narrowing to where they would begin to climb single file. "You sure this is all right?" He nodded at her still-bandaged wrist.

"Of course," Charlotte said, and nudged her mare forward. From above them, they could hear CJ and Will calling to one another, laughing and screeching as their horses climbed the steepest part of the trail.

"Get on, Bones, get on!" Will shouted.

Charlotte smiled at Nathan. "I'd say his confidence level is definitely improving."

For a few minutes they both gave their attention to the steep ascent. Finally, they emerged at the top to find that CJ had already spread a cloth on the ground and was opening her saddlebags to unpack the lunch Garnet had sent along.

Nathan reached up to help Charlotte down. She blushed as his hands encircled her waist. As soon as her feet touched the ground, she mumbled a thanks and walked toward the edge of the bluff. "I'd forgotten how breathtaking the view is from up here," she said. "When Emory used to tell his mother about Nebraska, he only mentioned the barren hills. It was as if he'd never seen this." She pointed to the valley below.

"The Colonel came out here?" Nathan asked.

Charlotte nodded. "Once. When Will was a toddler."

"You didn't come?"

Charlotte shook her head. "The Colonel didn't want the distraction."

"Lunch is ready!" CJ called.

After lunch CJ and Will headed off to explore.

"I'm thinking a horse to train might be just the thing to keep Will out of trouble," Nathan said. He leaned back on his elbow and stretched out his long legs. Turning his face up toward the sky, he closed his eyes.

"Heaven knows he's going to need something to keep his attention now that school is ending," Charlotte agreed. "And you're right—he has definitely outgrown Bones."

"I've put in for an extended leave," Nathan said. "Once the school session closes, if you approve, I thought maybe Will and I could head back up to the ranch for a few weeks. He could work to earn the horse. I'd have time to visit the Dawson place and talk to the old man about buying him out."

"I didn't know you were interested in ranching," Charlotte said.

Nathan shrugged. "I don't know that I am. Land is a good investment, whether I'm personally living on it or not. And I don't think it would be too hard to get someone to work the place."

Charlotte smiled. "You're talking about Rachel and Jack," she said. "Will told me about them. So do you think Rachel is closer to saying yes?"

Nathan hesitated. "I don't know if Jack has asked her recently."

Charlotte looked at him. "I wasn't talking about Jack." She smiled. "Will's young, Lieutenant. He isn't blind." When Nathan didn't respond, she apologized. "I'm sorry. It's really none of my business." She sighed. "And here I've been congratulating myself on how much I've changed from that little gossip Charlotte Valentine used to be. For whatever it's worth, Lieutenant, I haven't said anything to anyone, and I won't."

"Good," Nathan said. "Because there's nothing to say." He turned and looked at her. "Rachel Greyfoot is a good woman. I like her. The same could be said for any number of women I know. Including the one sitting next to me watching the clouds from this hill."

Embarrassed, Charlotte got up and went to look for Will and CJ.

* * *

The Reverend Erastus Barton III, who was simply known as Preacher Barton by his supporters and friends, had spent most of spring ministering to the outfits working roundup, among them the boys hired by Caleb Jackson for the Four Pines Ranch. He'd spent two weeks at the Four Pines, making no headway at winning Rachel, Jack, or Corporal Dorsey over to Christianity. He'd also failed to get a positive response from Lieutenant Nathan Boone during their late night discussions, and he'd left the area feeling defeated, except for having witnessed the blossoming friendship between Mrs. Jackson and the surgeon's daughter at Fort Robinson. Barton could sense that the Widow Bishop needed to hear about the Savior. *Trust that to Mrs. Jackson, old man. Her faith is sure.*

With roundup concluded, Barton had thought about heading for Fort Robinson again to check on the Widow Bishop and to follow up with Nathan Boone. He and the lieutenant had had some good talks around the campfire. Talks about eternal things. Thanks to his deceased wife and his association with a woman he called Granny Max, Boone seemed to have a lot of head knowledge about spiritual things, but he was holding a grudge against God. In the end, Barton had decided he didn't have the wisdom to argue the young lieutenant into the kingdom. He would instead pray that Boone would read the book of Job, as Barton had suggested, and perhaps think more on God's omniscience and less on his own human understanding.

So, in spite of the coming heat of summer, Barton decided to head up to the Black Hills. But then his faithful horse, Elvira, threw a shoe, and for some reason he could not quite discern, he felt he should visit Crawford before heading north. In all his years of wandering around the Sandhills, the Reverend Erastus Barton III felt he had accomplished very little for the kingdom of God. He was, he often thought with a sigh, long on perseverance and short on results.

In Crawford, Barton walked the streets for the better part of a morning, arguing with God about the wisdom of street-corner preaching in such a rough town. The fact was it scared him spitless. He wondered if the apostle Paul had been nervous on Mars Hill and chastised himself for the thought. Paul might have mentioned preaching with "fear and trembling," but Barton doubted he would have minded being laughed at by a few drunken cowboys, which was probably the worst thing that would happen in Crawford.

This morning, the boomtown buildings served to funnel a cool wind down the main street, penetrating his threadbare wool jacket and making him shiver. It took all his willpower to step up onto the crate he'd dragged out of a pile of rubbish and upended in the space between two unfinished buildings. Barton cleared his throat and began to recite words his aging eyes could not see in the small book in his trembling hands. Two or three men who had been on the opposite side of the street crossed over.

"Preach it, brother!" one of them yelled.

Barton blinked. *Did you hear that, Lord? Mocking. They don't want to hear from you.* The wind ruffled the pages of the book. The old man didn't hear a voice, but his heart recited familiar words. *"Blessed are ye when men shall revile you and persecute you."* He held the book closer, blinking, squinting, hoping the print would come clear. When it didn't, he held the little book farther away with the same unsatisfactory result.

Two men snickered.

Preacher Barton looked up. Both hecklers had better than a day's growth of stubble on their faces—although it was hard to tell where beard ended and dirt began.

More memorized words came to mind. *"Therefore thou shalt speak all these words unto them; but they will not hearken to thee: thou shalt also call unto them; but they will not answer thee."*

All right, Lord. All right.

The familiar words of Scripture, and an added fleeting prayer, helped steady the old man's hands and quiet his pounding heart. Odd, he thought, how, after all these years, he still got so nervous. He would have thought by now his skin would be thicker.

"Love your enemies, bless them that curse you, do good to them that hate you, and pray for them which despitefully use you, and persecute you."

The preacher recited another familiar passage of Scripture. He called upon the gathering of men to do something he called "consider Christ."

One drunk nudged the other and hollered "Amen!" The effort made him stagger sideways. Losing his balance, he fell to the ground. When his partner tried to help him get up, the drunken man waved him away. "I can hear jus' as well from down here. 'Sides . . . I'm closer to hell down here, which is where I b'long—ain't it, preacher?!" The man guffawed, slapping his leg.

The preacher hesitated. Was he just casting pearls before swine after all? More words came to mind. *"If ye love them which love you, what reward have ye? Do not even the publicans do the same?"* The wind blew the long white hair away from his face. He gave up trying to adjust the book so he could read the words. Instead, he recited yet another passage from memory.

"This morning I declare unto you the gospel . . . the good news . . . by which ye are saved. . . . How Jesus Christ died for our sins according to the scripture; and he was buried, and he rose again the third day. . . ." He looked at the drunken man sitting on the ground. "And that, my boy, is the best news you'll ever hear. And as to whether you are closer to hell or to heaven, I say that's up to you this very minute and how you answer this question: What will you do with Christ?"

The drunk was leaning against a barrel, his eyes closed. He drawled, "I'm not doin' anything with 'im, preacherman. I ain't seen Him all morning. Guess He heard about a change in the weather and had the good sense to stay home."

A few of the men laughed. One let out a loud belch and started to walk away.

Preacher Barton raised his voice, "That's where you're wrong, boy. Christ is here, even now. He was raised from the dead, and He is here, calling you to himself."

"He *is*?" One of the men held up his hand to his ear. "I

must be going deaf! I can't hear a thing! Heal me, preacher! Heal me!"

"Now settle down, boys," Barton said. "And listen. Someday we're all going to be called out of our graves, and there's only one thing that's going to matter"—he raised the little book up over his head—"and that will be what we did with Christ. It says right here, 'That if thou shalt confess with they mouth the Lord Jesus, and shalt believe in thine heart that God hath raised Him from the dead, you shall be saved.'"

The drunk hollered, "I don' need savin'. I'm jus' fine, thank you very much."

"You listen up, son," the old man said earnestly. "You won't be fine at all when Judgment Day comes. That's what I'm trying to tell you." He looked around him at the small group of men. "None of us will be all right on Judgment Day unless we have Christ."

"Yeah, yeah, yeah," one of the bystanders yelled. "I heard all that before. At my mama's knee."

Someone else made a vile joke about mothers. Before Barton knew what had happened, a brawl had started and was gaining momentum. Someone got knocked against the crate he was standing on, and he fell, tumbling to the ground, clutching his arthritic knee.

"You all right, Preacher?" Someone was reaching down to help him up. Someone with whiskey on his breath. Grabbing his small testament, Barton allowed himself to be hauled upright. He looked behind him, relieved to see the brawl was dying down fast.

"Come on. Let's find Elvira. Get you something to eat."

"Give me a minute, son," the preacher said. After leaning for a moment against the one finished wall of what a sign claimed would soon be Crawford's *Newest and Best General Merchandise Mercantile,* he bent over to catch his breath, straightened his rumpled collar, and tucked the testament in his breast pocket. Looking into his rescuer's face, he started to say *thank you,* but instead he blurted out the man's name. "Caleb? Caleb Jackson?"

Caleb looked away. "Not proud of it. But it's me."

Barton put his wrinkled hand on Caleb's forearm. "Elvira is at the livery just up the street, son. She threw a shoe, and I'm getting her a whole new set, thanks to your generous pay for the little work I did on roundup."

Caleb nodded. "Good."

"You come with me," Barton said. He took hold of Caleb's arm. "We'll both have breakfast. Strong coffee and something in your stomach will do you as much good as it will me."

By the third cup of coffee and his second plate of eggs, Caleb Jackson was feeling clearheaded enough to be ashamed of himself. "I don't know what got into me," he said. "I came into town yesterday for supplies for the foreman." He put his coffee mug down. "Too much time to think on the way in, I guess." He looked out the window. "They told me the order wasn't due until today, so I started back to the fort. Then I saw Mr. Dawson headed into the saloon. I've been wanting to talk to him about buying his place, so I followed him in. Didn't think there was anything wrong with having one drink."

"It's not one drink that got you into trouble, son," the preacher said.

"I know it. I never should have gone through those doors in the first place." Caleb shrugged. "I thought my drinking problems were enough years ago that I didn't have to worry. I should have known better. Especially now." He took his hat off and raked his hands through his raggedy beard.

"What do you mean . . . especially now?" the preacher asked.

Caleb's eyes filled with tears. "We lost our baby, Preacher. Our *son*."

The preacher leaned forward. "I'm so sorry. Is the missus all right?"

Caleb shook his head. He leaned forward and put his elbows on the table and his head in his hands. "No more children." His voice broke. "That's what the doc says, anyway."

"But Mrs. Jackson is all right?"

Caleb lifted his head. He nodded. "Physically."

The preacher stared at him. "Let's hear it, son. Let's hear it all."

"I know it rains on the just and the unjust. I know everyone has tough times. A man has to expect his share. But . . ." He took a deep breath. "Every time she looks at me I feel it. And I can't stand it."

"You feel what?"

"Like I've done something wrong. Something to hurt her. Like she's waiting for me to say something. Only I don't know what I'm supposed to say."

"Well, in my short-lived experience as a married man," Barton said, "I found that *I love you* goes quite a ways."

Caleb shook his head. "Laina knows I love her. It's not enough. I've tried to love her. She pulls away. That's how I ended up sleeping in the tent with the crew. It got to where I couldn't stand the way she was pressing against the wall on the opposite side of the bed. Like she couldn't stand to be near me."

The preacher took a sip of coffee, then spread butter on a biscuit. Presently he cleared his throat. "I am claiming no special expertise with the species of creature Adam named *woman,* young man. But I do have some knowledge of *love.* And I believe God defines it pretty well. My testament uses the word *charity.*" Barton recited, "'Charity suffereth long, and is kind. Charity doth not behave itself unseemly, seeketh not her own.' Do you understand what that means, young man?"

"I thought I did. But obviously I'm missing something."

"Well, I'd say that's fairly obvious even to the casual observer," Barton said. "Does it look like love for you to be sleeping on the opposite side of Fort Robinson from your grieving wife?"

"I'm grieving, too," Caleb said.

"Of course you are. Both of you are in a time of mourning. So is CJ, I'm sure. But that's not my point, son. My point is that 'charity seeketh not her own.' This may be a time when your faith is being tested to see if you can look past your own hurt. Don't wait for Mrs. Jackson to turn to you. If she's learned she can't give you sons, she's probably frightened to death."

"Frightened?" Caleb asked. "Why would she be frightened?"

"For the past few years, every time I've visited your ranch, you've talked about your plans for the future. You've literally raised the roof about it—getting that loft ready for more children—a passel of boys, I believe you said. Mrs. Jackson has been told she can't give you your dream. And you're sleeping in a tent clear across Fort Robinson. What's she supposed to think?"

Caleb scratched his beard, then ran his hand across his chin to smooth it down. "I haven't handled this well. I just don't understand what was so wrong with our dream that God had to rip it away."

"Wasn't necessarily anything wrong with it," Barton said. "Sometimes God takes away good things so He can replace them with something *better*."

"I don't see any way that having only CJ could be better than a loft full of boys," Caleb protested, but even as he said the words he heard how "only CJ" sounded and realized how his behavior must look to his daughter. He'd hurt her, too. God forgive him.

"Don't be so earthly minded, son," the preacher was saying. "Those of us who claim faith in God are supposed to look at life differently. Whether you have a passel of boys or not won't matter in twenty thousand years. What will matter is whether or not you trusted God. If you and your sweet wife can find it in yourselves to trust and obey now, you will be enjoying rewards for that trust long after the Four Pines Ranch is nothing more than a memory in some Dawes County history book." Barton smiled. "And I'd better be right, because the belief that the next life is more important than this one is the only motivation strong enough to make me climb up on a crate and preach Jesus to a bunch of drunken cowboys."

Caleb took a deep breath. He looked across the table at the white-haired preacher. "I want to trust and obey. But . . ." He swallowed hard. "He was such a beautiful boy, Preacher. You should have seen him." His voice wavered.

"Trust and obey doesn't mean you don't hurt, son."

"So, where do I start?"

Barton leaned forward and put his hand on Caleb's forearm. "Hold on to your wife and daughter. And don't let go."

Caleb nodded. "I'll try. The supplies should be arriving soon. I'll head back as soon as we get it loaded." He folded his napkin and put it on the table before standing up.

The preacher paid the bill and together they headed toward the door. Barton reached out and put his hand on Caleb's shoulder. "And be forewarned, young man. I can lasso *you* as easily as I can a steer, and if I get wind of you near a saloon again, I'll be obliged to prove it."

CHAPTER FIFTEEN

A good man sheweth favor, and lendeth.

PSALM 112:5

FOR A MAN WHO HAD SPENT MORE THAN A DECADE avoiding women, Lieutenant Nathan Boone had more than his share of female troubles.

Laina Jackson's situation was the most pressing. He was not going to stand by and do nothing while her life fell apart. If her husband and God weren't going to do something for her, then he was.

Because of Laina Jackson's problems, Nathan also had concerns for Clara Joy. The usually feisty young girl had become unusually subdued in recent days. Her heart was breaking over the difficulties between her parents. And because CJ's heart was breaking, Will Bishop was a simmering pot of trouble just waiting to happen. Whether Laina would go or not, Nathan decided he had to find a reason to get CJ and Will away from Fort Robinson and back to the ranch.

Then there was Charlotte Bishop. He had originally called on her out of respect for Dr. Valentine. Circumstances had continued to throw them together. He'd done his duty and been a gentleman. That was all. It was Rachel Greyfoot who was stirring up feelings he thought had died with Lily. But then roundup was over and he came back to the fort. He and Charlotte took CJ and Will on a picnic, and a simple thing like putting his hands on Charlotte's waist to help her down from a horse changed everything. Charlotte said she was happy for him and Rachel. And he didn't know why, but he didn't really want Charlotte to be so approving of the idea of Nathan Boone and Rachel Greyfoot being together. He began to catch himself thinking about Charlotte with a kind of gentle sadness. He noticed the way she smiled. And that it happened all too infrequently. He realized that a light shone in her eyes when Will hugged her that made her almost beautiful. He decided he had misread Rachel's response to him. She was grateful to him for the past. That was all. He decided he was grateful for the attention, though. Rachel's smiles had awakened a part of him that had been sleeping for a long, long time.

Ever present in all of Nathan's musings about the women causing him to lose sleep was the memory of Granny Max and the knowledge that somehow he was failing her because he had yet to make his peace with God. He felt differently about all of that these days. Like maybe it could happen. In all the years he'd been away from Fort Robinson, he had remained closed to the idea of God. But the words of Granny Max kept coming to mind. He'd even quoted her to Caleb Jackson and been surprised when Caleb said it wasn't just a *Granny-Maxism,* but something out of the Bible. Believers kept coming into his path—people like Private Blake and Preacher Barton. The preacher had told him to read the book of Job. Nathan was doing it.

Barton was like no other preacher Nathan had ever met. During the roundup he worked as hard as any of the wranglers and was a passably good cowboy in spite of his advanced age. In the evenings around the campfires he laughed and joked. He never acted sanctimonious or self-righteous, even when some of the men slipped up and swore in his presence.

Between Carter Blake, Erastus Barton, and Job, Nathan had been getting very close to reevaluating his opinion of God. And then the Jackson's baby died, Laina fell apart, Caleb fell apart, and Nathan began to wonder. The seemingly unanswerable questions loomed again. Where was God at times like this? If He could control everything, why didn't He protect his children from pain?

Job had asked the same questions. As far as Nathan could tell, the only answer he got was "Where wast thou when I laid the foundations of the earth?" Which, Nathan decided, was God putting Job in his place. Once put there, it seemed like Job stayed humbled. "I will lay mine hand upon my mouth," he said. No more questioning God. "I repent in dust and ashes," Job said. As nearly as Nathan could tell, the answer to *why* was pretty much, *because I'm God and you're not, you speck of dirt.* He wasn't sure he was ready to be a speck of dirt. But he was beginning to realize that the people who lived by faith—who accepted things they didn't understand and still trusted in a loving God—were, for the most part, happier than he. They weren't perfect. They had their moments. Like Caleb and Laina. But, Nathan reasoned, he'd been bitter and miserable for more than enough years. He was getting a little tired of demanding answers to questions God had decided not to answer.

In the midst of all his wonderings, Boone decided to follow through with plans to help Caleb expand his ranching operation, and he rode into Crawford intent on a meeting with a local banker. At the first livery stable on the edge of Crawford, both front and back sliding doors were open, giving a clear view of the blacksmith's yard out back. Nathan peered through the open doors and caught sight of a white horse chowing down on a pile of oats while the blacksmith filed her rear hoof. *Elvira.*

The sight of the preacher's horse and the idea that he had

"just happened" to ride into Crawford and see her in the livery stable gave Nathan an odd feeling. In one of their campfire talks on the roundup, the preacher had made it clear he didn't believe in coincidences. In his reading of Job, Nathan had been challenged to think about the idea of what the preacher called God's sovereignty. He remembered something Charlotte had said just the day before.

"I wish we had a regular chaplain at Fort Robinson. The Jacksons might benefit from a visit. That night Preacher Barton showed up at Fort Robinson to see how I was doing, he said the Lord just impressed on his mind that he should come and check on me. That was strange. But it really was the beginning of my friendship with Laina. If he's still in tune with whatever powers that be, maybe he'll be impressed to head back this way before too long. The Jacksons surely could use a visit from him right about now."

Of course, Nathan thought, as he headed up the main street of Crawford in search of a white-haired preacher, it was only a fortunate coincidence that he had seen Elvira. The old horse had thrown a shoe. Surely not something God would use to plant the preacher in his path. *Or was it?* He knew Granny Max would have told him not to be so sure.

He must be crazy. Completely. That was the only explanation for Nathan's interrupting his search for Preacher Barton to step inside a general store and look at things like hair ribbons and lace.

"May I help you?" The shopkeeper approached from the opposite end of the store. Nathan pulled his hand back like he'd been burned. He could feel a blush crawling up the back of his neck.

"Shopping for the missus?"

Nathan frowned. He shook his head. "A girl." He stretched out his arm and indicated CJ's height. "This tall."

The shopkeeper looked confused.

"The daughter of a friend."

"Ah," the shopkeeper nodded. "How old is the young lady?"

"Ten, I think."

"Well, this," the shopkeeper said, indicating a wide lavender velvet ribbon, "should make her eyes light up with pleasure."

Picturing CJ Jackson with lavender velvet hair ribbons almost made Nathan laugh. He looked around the shop. "Just some candy," he said, crossing the store to where a row of glass jars displayed sweets of various shapes and colors. "Those," Nathan said.

He was about to leave with the sack of candy when a small figurine in a glass display case caught his eye.

"Those just arrived. Fine craftsmanship. Hand-carved ivory."

Nathan bent over to inspect the small, intricately carved figure of a white horse.

"That," he said. He'd give it to Will. The minute he thought of it, he had another idea. Exiting the general store, he headed for the telegraph office.

After sending the telegram, Nathan combed the east side of the town of Crawford looking for Preacher Barton. He was crossing back to the west side when he caught a glimpse of shoulder-length white hair just as the man beneath it ducked out of sight between two buildings. Hurrying up the street, Nathan slipped between the same two buildings and yelled, "Preacher! Preacher Barton!"

The preacher emerged from the rear of the building, holding his hand up, palm out, as he tried to block the sun and focus on Nathan's face.

"It's Lieutenant Boone, Preacher Barton."

"Well, my boy, if this isn't the day for meeting up with old friends." The preacher pumped Nathan's hand.

"Am I ever glad to see you," Nathan said.

"Why? What's happened, son?" the preacher asked. He

frowned. "It's not Mrs. Bishop, I hope? She was doing so well—"

"No, not her," Nathan said. "Laina Jackson. Both of the Jacksons, actually. The baby died. And they aren't doing well. Caleb's sleeping in a tent on one side of the fort, and Laina's barely left their room at the trading post for weeks. Charlotte and I have tried everything we know to—"

"Calm down, son," the preacher said. "I just came from having breakfast with Caleb."

"Caleb is here? In Crawford?"

The preacher nodded. "We had a fine talk over breakfast." The preacher patted his stomach and belched. "Too much of a fine breakfast for me." He grimaced. "Anyway, Caleb is heading back to Fort Robinson to see Mrs. Jackson. And I believe things are going to be all right."

"Laina just hasn't been herself," Nathan said.

The preacher nodded. "I promised Caleb I'd head their way as soon as Elvira gets shod." He smiled. "The Lord works in mysterious ways, doesn't He? Elvira threw a shoe. I took a detour from my planned route to visit the blacksmith. Decided the Lord might have me say a word on His behalf while I was here. Caleb scooped me up out of the middle of a brawl—"

"What?"

"My sermon wasn't too well received," the preacher said. "But Caleb came to the rescue. Seems he'd come into Crawford for supplies and then had a meeting about adding on to his ranch. At any rate, he spent the night in town and was there to rescue me. We had breakfast over at the hotel, and I sent him packing. He was going to talk to the bank about expanding his operation and then head back to the fort. What brings you to Crawford, Lieutenant?"

"I thought I could maybe help the Jacksons if I talked to the bank. Thought I might ride out to the Dawson place and talk to them about the sale." Nathan noticed the preacher looking at the package tucked under his arm. "Trying to cheer CJ up," he said, "and something for Will."

"Well, Lieutenant Boone," the thick-waisted banker reached across his desk and pumped Nathan's hand. "Glad to meet you in person. What brings you to us this morning?"

"I want to ask you to think about something," Nathan said. "Something involving the Four Pines Ranch."

"Strange how things happen," the banker said. "I haven't heard from the Jacksons in weeks, and now everyone I see is talking about the Four Pines."

"Really?" Nathan said.

The banker nodded. "Yep." He chewed on the stub of the cigar jutting from the corner of this mouth. "Too bad."

"Too bad?"

"Hate to hear those things about a good man."

"Excuse me?"

The banker looked around as if checking for eavesdroppers. "See here, Lieutenant, I know you're a friend of the Jacksons. Maybe you can do something. I had a meeting first thing this morning with Elmer Dawson." He motioned for Nathan to sit down, then followed suit, extinguishing his cigar stub in a shallow ash-littered tin bowl on the corner of his oversized oak desk. Leaning forward, he motioned to Nathan to do likewise before he said, "I've always liked Caleb Jackson. He's always been good to do business with. You know anything about his recent problems? I like to give a man the benefit of the doubt."

"You mind telling me what it is you're talking about?"

"Like I said, Elmer Dawson was in here this morning. It seems your friend followed him into the saloon last night. And had more than one too many."

"Caleb and Mrs. Jackson have had a tough couple of weeks," Nathan said. "They've had a personal setback. But things are looking up for them both. And if Mr. Dawson wants to sell then we want to buy."

The banker switched back into business mode. "What terms were you thinking of?"

Nathan smiled. "Cash." He pulled out his copy of his telegram. "And I have another matter I'd like you to handle."

CHAPTER SIXTEEN

The Lord is nigh unto them that are of a broken heart;
and saveth such as be of a contrite spirit.

PSALM 34:18

"LAINA? ARE YOU AWAKE?"

Laina turned away from the door. She had taken to putting Caleb's pillow lengthwise against her side, so that during the night his absence was not quite so evident. Now she wrapped her arms around it and pretended she was still asleep. But Charlotte did not take the hint. Instead of giving up and going away, she came into the room and put her hand on Laina's shoulder.

"Laina." She shook her gently. "You need to wake up. There's something you need to attend to."

"Get Caleb," Laina mumbled. "He's working just across the—"

"Caleb went into Crawford yesterday to get supplies. His foreman said he isn't back yet," Charlotte said. "There must have been some kind of delay."

"Can't it wait until he gets back?"

"No. It can't."

Sighing, Laina turned over and opened her eyes halfway. Charlotte had retreated to the doorway and was standing behind CJ, her hands on the young girl's shoulders. CJ was a rumpled mess. Laina lifted her head and blinked. The drapes were drawn across the window, but it was daylight and enough light filtered through the thin fabric to illuminate CJ's dress . . . with tattered hem . . . her rumpled hair . . . and . . . Laina sat up.

"What happened? You look like you've been in a fight!"

CJ pressed her lips together and stared at her mother, defiance in every muscle of her dirty face. "So what?" she blurted out.

Laina sat the rest of the way up. "You're going to have a black eye."

"So?" CJ said. One eyebrow arched just slightly. The girl's expression caught Laina's attention. This was more than defiance. It almost appeared to be . . . dislike.

"Speak up," Laina snapped. "What have you done now?" She pressed two fingers against her forehead, wishing the headache would go away.

"What do you care?" CJ spat out.

"Don't use that tone with me," Laina said again. "Or you'll find yourself waiting on the stool in Mrs. Dubois's kitchen until your father comes home."

"Hmpf," CJ said. "I won't hold my breath." She looked at the floor.

Laina looked past CJ to Charlotte. Charlotte shook her head slightly from side to side and cast a warning glance in Laina's direction.

Laina took a deep breath. "Please tell me this didn't happen at school."

"This didn't happen at school," CJ recited in exact replication of Laina's weary tone.

"School's been out for several days now, Laina," Charlotte said gently.

"Where, then?"

"Behind Troop F's stable," Charlotte replied.

"All right, young lady," Laina said. "You go on out to

the kitchen. I want to talk to Mrs. Bishop. I'll be out directly." She pushed the quilts aside and slid to the edge of the bed, calling after CJ, "And you'd better have a very good explanation for such outlandish behavior."

Laina heard a chair scrape the kitchen floor as CJ pulled it out and sat down. Standing up, she asked Charlotte, "Do you know anything about this?" Laina wobbled to the dresser across the room and looked in the mirror, then moved closer. She hardly recognized the creature who stared back at her. Matted hair framed a pale face marred by great, dark circles beneath her eyes. *You look almost as bad as that creature Granny Max brought back to sanity.*

Charlotte leaned against the doorframe. "Private Blake broke up the fight. He wasn't too clear on the particulars. Said it was something said about Caleb. I don't know exactly what. Private Blake wouldn't tell me."

Laina leaned closer to the mirror, looking at Charlotte's reflection. Taking a deep breath, she reached up and shoved a matted piece of hair out of her face. She looked around at the room. Her gray shawl and yellow sunbonnet were still hanging on a hook by the door. Wrapping herself in the shawl, she headed up the hallway toward the kitchen, where CJ was sitting at the table, head bowed, her right leg crooked up off the floor, her right ankle positioned on her knee, her foot jiggling constantly.

Charlotte passed through the kitchen ahead of Laina, closing the curtain that separated the kitchen from the trading post.

Laina slid into a chair opposite CJ. She was trembling just from the effort it had taken to get out of bed. When had she gotten so weak? It hadn't even been a month since the baby—*I've been in bed for nearly a month?* It didn't seem possible. The past weeks were a blur. She forced herself to focus on CJ. "Well," she said, "I'm waiting."

CJ raised her chin and stared back. "For what?"

"I am waiting for you to tell me what happened."

CJ shrugged. She tilted her head to display her puffy left eye. "Pretty obvious, isn't it?"

"Don't be impertinent," Laina said. "Or do you prefer to wait on that chair and talk to your father instead of to me?"

Silence.

"Well?"

Silence.

Laina took in a deep breath. Coffee. She needed some coffee. Standing up, she went to the stove and poured some. She took a sip. Sat back down. "I need to hear your voice," Laina said. "Am I going to be getting a visit from the other girl's mother?"

CJ curled her lip. "I wouldn't fight with any *girl,*" she sneered.

Pondering the information, Laina took another deep breath. She forced herself to sound calm. "All right, then. Am I going to be getting a visit from some young man's mother?"

"Or his ma *and* his pa," CJ said abruptly. Her hands curled up into fists. She made a little boxing motion with each hand. "Because he's gonna have *two* black eyes."

Maude came to the doorway that led to the trading post. "Excuse me, Laina, but Private Blake is here to talk with you."

Blake's hulking frame loomed behind Maude, who let him pass before she retreated into the trading post. Laina motioned him into the kitchen. "Please," she said, indicating a chair. "Sit down. Can I pour you a cup of coffee?"

"No thank you, ma'am," Blake said. "I was just checking on the little one here. Wanted to see if she's all right."

"She'll be fine. Until her father gets hold of her," Laina said. She looked at CJ. "What's it going to be, young lady? Are you going to tell me what happened, or am I going to have to rely on Private Blake to fill in the blanks?"

CJ shrugged. "I told Farley to shut up. He wouldn't. So I shut him up. That's all."

"Farley?"

"Farley Hopkins," CJ said.

"And who, pray tell, is Farley Hopkins?"

CJ rolled her eyes. "I *told* you this before."

"Well, I don't remember."

CJ shook her head. " 'Course not. You never listen."

"That will do, young lady," Laina said and popped the back of CJ's hand.

CJ snatched her hands off the table and put them in her lap.

"Now tell me about Farley Hopkins."

"He hates me. Almost as much as he hates Will."

"You can't get in a fight with people just because they don't like you. You know that."

"I didn't," CJ said.

"You didn't . . . what?" Laina set her coffee mug firmly on the kitchen table, hoping CJ would read the signal that she was nearly out of patience.

"I didn't get in a fight with Farley Hopkins because he doesn't like me. I got in a fight because of what he said about—" CJ stopped abruptly, pressed her lips together. She looked up at Carter Blake with wide eyes that suddenly filled with tears. Taking in a deep, ragged breath, she paused again.

"Honey-lamb," Laina said as she moved to the chair beside CJ and put a hand on her shoulder. "Tell me. Please."

The minute Laina's hand touched CJ's shoulder, it was as if a floodgate opened. "He said his father was in Crawford and he saw Papa go into the saloon. He said . . . things. About Pa."

Laina looked across the table at Private Blake, who nodded agreement with CJ's version of the fight. "Well," Laina said. "I'm sorry. But that doesn't mean you had to get into a fight."

"Well, he wouldn't stop saying them, and he started calling Pa names, and so I told him I'd stop him, and he said I couldn't, and I said I could and to meet me behind the

Troop F stable. And he did." A shudder coursed through CJ's body. "And I stopped him."

"Where was Will when all this was going on?" Laina asked.

"He went riding." CJ cast Laina an accusing look. "With his *mother.*"

"Laina," Maude's voice sounded at the door again. "Mr. and Mrs. Hopkins are out here, and they want—"

Laina sighed. She looked at Private Blake. "You don't suppose you could try to find Mr. Jackson, could you? And ask him to hurry over here?"

"I would, ma'am. Gladly. I tried to find him earlier. Miss Irvin knew you'd want him to handle this." Blake shrugged. "But he's not back from town yet."

So it was true. Caleb had gone into Crawford. And he had stayed overnight. A sense of dread washed over her. What else was true? Had Caleb really gone into the saloon? She closed her eyes. *Lord, have mercy.*

"You come with me, CJ," Laina said, and stood up. Relieved when she didn't feel quite so wobbly, she managed to smile at Carter Blake. "Thank you for coming to check on CJ. And thank you for rescuing her."

"Wasn't any rescuing necessary," Blake said matter-of-factly. "Unless it would be the Hopkins boy. Little missy here had him down on the ground when I came around the corner."

"Well, then," Laina said, "thank you for rescuing her from herself." *Please, Lord. For CJ's sake. Help me. Rescue me. From myself.*

Blake put on his hat and turned to leave.

"Private Blake, would you please ask Mr. and Mrs. Hopkins to give me a few minutes?" Laina said. She took CJ's hand. "We need to clean up a bit."

Back in the bedroom, Laina had CJ sit on the edge of the bed while she poured clean water into the washstand bowl.

Laina wiped her own face, then handed the towel to CJ

while she reached up and began to remove her hairpins. "Remember when you used to comb my hair for me when you were little?" Her hair fell down her back in a tangled mass of auburn waves. On impulse, she took the used towel from CJ's outstretched hand and replaced it with her hair comb. She sat down on the edge of the bed. "When you were little, you used to like to comb my hair for me. That always felt so nice." Closing her eyes, she waited, giving an inward sigh of relief when CJ crawled up behind her. She tilted her head to one side and then the other while CJ worked out knots and tangles.

"That's all I can get out," CJ said, and handed her mother the comb before scooting against the headboard of the bed and clutching a pillow to her midsection.

Laina stood up. She could almost hear Granny Max's voice offering advice. *Just do the next thing, honey-lamb. Just do the next thing.* She got dressed and braided her hair, then wrapped the braid around her head. She perched back on the edge of the bed. Without looking at CJ, she said quietly, "Will you take a walk with me when I get back?"

"To where?"

"Oh, anywhere. Just a walk. I need the fresh air." She inhaled and made a face. "It stinks in this room. Stale air." She went to the window, threw back the drapes, and raised the window. "So . . . what do you say?"

"Sure," CJ said. "We can take a walk." Her tone was resignation, laced with a measure of doubt. And who, Laina thought, could blame her.

"You get changed while I talk to Mr. and Mrs. Hopkins. Leave your dress out so I can mend it," Laina said. She paused at the door. "I'm weak as a kitten. It's past time I started building up my strength. Don't you think?"

CJ only nodded.

Laina did what she could to calm Farley Hopkin's parents. She apologized for CJ. She promised it wouldn't happen again. When she went back to her room, CJ lay asleep on the bed. Her face was scrubbed clean, and she had pulled her hair into two separate bunches, one tied over each shoulder with a length of red string, much like the way Rachel Greyfoot wore her hair. Her torn dress lay at the foot of the bed. She had pulled a clean smock over her petticoat before falling asleep.

Laina leaned over the bed. At her touch, CJ roused. "Shhh, shhh, honey-lamb," Laina whispered. "You take a little nap. We'll talk later." Pulling up the bottom of the quilt so it covered CJ and formed a kind of bedroll around her, Laina leaned down and kissed her daughter's cheek before taking the yellow sunbonnet down from its hook and heading outside.

I did the next thing, Lord. Now what?

She made her way down the trail toward the river, past the log hospital, past Soapsuds Row. She walked along the riverbank, disappointed when an old familiar picnic spot proved to be overgrown. Out of breath, she settled on the grass and leaned against a red granite boulder jutting out of the earth beside a bend in the river. Lifting her face to the spring sunshine, she closed her eyes, thinking back over the recent weeks. *I've been like Jacob. Running away. Wrestling with God. Only there's been no ladder sent down from heaven. No answer.*

The mental image of Granny Max's Bible sitting on the dresser in her room at the trading post flashed in her mind. It had been weeks since she'd opened it. She remembered the saying Granny had written on the cover page. *I want to master this book so the Master of this book can master me.*

It had been weeks since she'd prayed anything more than *help me, help me, help me*. In recent days, she'd stopped saying even that.

How did it come to this, Lord? Where did it all go? The strength to manage life. I lost it. And now . . . look what's happened. That dirty face . . . the torn dress . . . the swollen eye . . .

the defiance. The mental image of CJ curled up asleep on her bed brought tears.

Laina wrapped her arms around her legs and rested her chin on her knees. *Caleb.* How she longed for Caleb's arms around her. *Do the next thing, honey-lamb. Do what you can. Give God the rest. Give Caleb to God. Give your love for him to God. Trust and obey, honey-lamb. Trust and obey.* She was back to the same place she'd been all those years ago when Nathan Boone first brought her to Granny Max. Maybe not half crazy . . . but certainly at the end of herself.

"Ma!" CJ's voice called out.

Laina sat up and looked around.

"Ma!"

She scrambled to her feet, calling and waving, "I'm over here!"

CJ came running. In the space between the trail and Laina's arms, she started to cry. In the time it took for her to sob out all her fears, Laina started to cry, too. "I'm so sorry, honey-lamb," she finally whispered. "I won't go away again. As long as God gives me breath, I promise you, I won't go away from you again."

The sigh of relief that coursed through her daughter's wiry young body pierced Laina's heart. *Do the next thing. Just do the next thing.* For the first time in a long time, Laina knew what the next thing was.

"So tell me, CJ, how a girl your size manages to get a hulk like that Hopkins boy on his back in the dirt?" Laina asked. They were walking along, hand in hand, making their way around the parade ground and toward the doctor's residence.

"I watched Jack," CJ said.

"Jack Greyfoot taught you to fight?"

"Of course not," CJ said quickly. "Jack wouldn't do that. But he likes to wrestle with the other Cheyenne who come on roundup. Sometimes they have wrestling matches."

"And the men on roundup let you watch these things?"

"No. They make me go to the chuck wagon. They told me it isn't fitting for a lady to see such things," CJ said glumly. "But I climbed up on top of the wagon and watched anyway."

"I see," Laina said. "Well, there will be no more fights with the Hopkins boy. Or anyone else, for that matter."

"I won't let him talk about my pa that way." Stubbornness sounded in the girl's voice.

"We're going home," Laina said.

"What?"

"I said," Laina repeated, "we're going home."

"When?"

"Now." She motioned toward the doctor's residence. "And we're going to see if Mrs. Bishop and Will want to come with us."

"Did Pa say we could?"

"I haven't talked to your pa," Laina said. "But I'm sure he won't mind. We'll leave him a note. And when he's finished with his work here at Fort Robinson, he'll come home." *Or not. What if he doesn't come home?* The inner doubt clutched at her midsection. Laina took a deep breath and forced a smile.

CJ bounded ahead of her, around the doctor's residence and up to the back porch. She was already knocking on the door when Laina caught up.

* * *

"Is Will here?" Lieutenant Boone stood at the front door holding a small package wrapped in brown paper.

Charlotte looked at the package. "You've been to town," she said. "Did you find Caleb?"

Nathan shook his head. "Just missed him. But I saw the preacher. He'd had breakfast with Caleb. He thinks things are going to be all right."

"Lieutenant!" Will called a hello from the hallway. He looked at Charlotte. "Did you tell him, Ma?" Without waiting for her to answer he blurted out, "We're going to the ranch!"

Nathan looked at Charlotte, who nodded. "Laina invited us."

"When are you going?"

"Later today," Charlotte said.

Will broke in. "Ma's going to see Spirit. And maybe we'll buy her. And I'm going to learn how to lasso. Spirit will be my cow horse! What's that?" Will pointed to the package in Boone's hand.

Nathan held it out. "For you," he said to Will. "But I want you to take it back to the kitchen while I ask your mother something. And don't come back in here for a minute."

"Secrets?" Will asked.

Boone nodded. "For now."

The boy pounced on the package and exited the room.

"What happened in Crawford? Is something wrong?"

From the kitchen came a whoop of pleasure. Will called out. "I'm gonna go show CJ!" The back door slammed.

"So tell me, what went wrong in Crawford?" Charlotte repeated.

Nathan smiled. "Actually, things went great. I didn't find Caleb, but I did run into Preacher Barton." He told Charlotte what Barton had said about Caleb. "Both of them should be back here before you all leave for the ranch." He smiled. "I think things are going to be fine."

"Laina needs to hear that."

"I agree . . . but not from me. I've put my nose as far into that business as I think I should." He paused. "For all I know, Caleb's at the trading post right now."

Charlotte shook her head. "It's amazing. The timing of it all is just amazing." Quickly, she told Nathan about CJ's fight and the effect it had had on Laina. "It seems to have jolted her back to life."

Nathan nodded. "That plays into what I wanted to ask you. I've mentioned it before, but I'd like to know what you've decided about Will maybe staying at the ranch this summer and working toward owning Spirit. To tell you the truth, I was just going to buy the horse and surprise him, but—"

"I couldn't allow that," Charlotte said quickly.

"Yeah," Nathan said. "I realized that. So . . . will you think about this other idea? I'll ride out to Four Pines in a couple of days. By then you will have seen Spirit. If you're agreeable, then I'll talk to Laina and Caleb about Will spending the summer on the ranch."

"I don't know what to say."

"*Thank you* would work." Nathan smiled down at her.

Charlotte looked away. She stepped back and put her hands behind her and nodded. "I'll think about it." She turned back to him and smiled. "And thank you."

CHAPTER SEVENTEEN

Now faith is the substance of things hoped for,
the evidence of things not seen.
HEBREWS 11:1

"HE HASN'T COME," LAINA SAID. SHE WAS STANDING outside Charlotte's back door clutching her shawl around her. A gust of wind caught Laina's hair and blew it around her face. She brushed it back with a trembling hand.

Charlotte opened the back door and pulled Laina inside. "With that storm brewing," she said, "he probably decided not to drive the team back. You know how it is, Laina. There's a shortage of good teams, and some of them are barely harness broke. He probably didn't want to head into the face of a storm. And I imagine Preacher Barton thought the same thing. Especially with that old mare he rides. I remember you said he treats her almost like his child. He probably would save her from a storm if he could." She pulled out the kitchen chair and motioned for Laina to sit down.

Laina shook her head. "No, no . . . that's all right. I just wanted you to know."

"I understand. Will and I can visit the ranch another time. It'll give us both something to look forward to."

Laina smoothed her hair back. She looked out the kitchen window. "I didn't walk over here to tell you we aren't going," she said. "I haven't changed those plans. Nathan stopped by a while ago. When he didn't find Caleb he headed back into town. Said the men are going on maneuvers tomorrow." Laina paused. "That means if we don't go today, we might not have anyone available to drive us. Now, I'm a determined woman, but even I'm not fool enough to head out across the prairie alone. Unless"—she forced a smile—"you have experience with a rifle I'm not aware of."

Charlotte smiled back. "As a matter of fact," she teased, "in another life I was a sharpshooter in a Wild West show. However," she said, holding up her bandaged wrist, "I'm a bit off my game at the moment. So a soldier with a rifle is probably a good idea."

"We might be in for a real drenching. On the other hand, if we can scoot up the trail, the worst of it might just blow over. It's hard to say."

"Father has an old oilskin. We can hunker down under that," Charlotte said. "If you're really going, I'd still like to come along now. Will would never forgive me for keeping him away from Spirit. And I don't want to have to be left here worrying about what mischief he might think up without CJ around."

"I never thought of CJ as a mature voice of reason," Laina said.

"Compared to Will, she's twenty-five. She's undoubtedly kept him out of more trouble than I care to know about."

"Maude thinks I should wait for Nathan to round up Caleb," Laina said abruptly.

"You have to do what you think is best. And I'll support you no matter what you decide." Charlotte patted her friend's hand. "I'm the last one on the earth qualified to give marital advice. It only took me about six months of being

Mrs. Colonel Bishop to realize I had no idea what I was doing."

Thunder rumbled. Laina headed for the door. "I want to go home. I've prayed on it and asked God, and I still want to go home." She inhaled sharply. "And when Caleb is ready . . . he'll know where to find me."

"Then let's get going," Charlotte said. "Maybe the rain will wait. Or blow over. If it doesn't, we won't melt."

• • • ◆ • • •

Caleb Jackson went to the hotel room window and moved the lace curtain aside so he could see up the main street. Clouds on the horizon promised a good drenching was on its way. Someone knocked on the door.

"What in blazes do you think you're doing?!" Nathan Boone sounded off as he shoved past Caleb into the hotel room. He was brought up short by the sight of Preacher Barton lying in bed, his white hair spread out on the pillow, his chest rising and falling in rapid, shallow breaths.

"How'd you know I was here?" Caleb said.

"Saw the preacher. Saw the banker. Thought you were on your way to your wife, so I headed home. Then you didn't show up. Laina didn't know what to think, so I told her I'd come back into town and check on you. No sign of you or the preacher. The guy down at the livery suggested I check hotel registries. What's going on?"

Caleb motioned to where the preacher lay. "I was on my way back to the fort when I found him doubled over in Elvira's stall."

"What's wrong with him?"

"Bad meat. That's what the doctor here in town thinks, anyway."

"Just be glad you didn't order the steak for breakfast," the preacher spoke up, his voice barely a whisper. "I'm sorry . . . son, but I need—"

Caleb swooped across the room, grabbed the chamber pot, and assisted the preacher, wiping the old man's mouth and offering him a drink of water before he said to Nathan, "I couldn't exactly leave him alone. The doc's so busy with calls he couldn't stay." Caleb shook his head. "I sure am glad this hotel isn't serving Four Pines beef. Half the town is sick according to the doc." He walked back to the window and nodded toward the west. "Looks like we're in for it." He shook his head. "I don't like the idea of Laina sitting at the fort worrying."

Nathan recounted Laina's plans to go to the Four Pines. "Blake's driving them. They'll be all right," he said, then smiled and winked. "And you can enjoy a reunion at home."

Caleb smiled back, nodded, then cleared his throat and changed the subject. "You said you talked to the bank? Was it Wade Simpson?" When Nathan nodded, Caleb took in a deep breath. "Oh, brother. What did he have to say?"

"He said you're a good man and he hopes things are all right."

Caleb let the surprise he felt sound in his voice. "Really?"

"Really."

"Well, that's a relief."

"I imagine the fact that I said we can pay cash for Dawson's place helped his attitude a little."

"We?"

"Sure," Nathan said. "If you still want me for a partner."

Thunder crashed and the skies opened. The preacher moaned.

◆

It was near sunset when the Jacksons' farm wagon finally topped the last rise and headed down the gentle incline toward the Four Pines Ranch.

"That's the farmhouse," Will said, and proceeded to give

Charlotte a verbal tour of the ranch, from barn to bunkhouse to corrals to hen house. "Lieutenant Boone and I stayed there in the bunkhouse with Dorsey and Jack." He prattled on about Dorsey and Jack Greyfoot, and then, as the wagon drew closer, he began to talk about Spirit. "Jack said he'd keep her in the barn and gentle her some."

The minute the wagon pulled up to the ranch house, Will started to jump down, then hesitated and looked doubtfully at Charlotte.

"Go on," she said. "I can wait a few minutes to use your muscles. But don't be gone long." Will and CJ shot down the trail toward the barn without a glance behind them.

Private Blake helped Charlotte and Laina down from the wagon. He nodded at Rachel when introduced, but didn't waste any time moving the women's two trunks to the edge of the wagon in preparation for unloading. In less than an hour, Rachel and Jack had moved CJ's things into the loft and Charlotte's trunk into CJ's room. Jack took Will's small trunk down to the bunkhouse and returned for the team.

"If you don't mind, ladies," Private Blake said, untying his horse from the back of the wagon. "I'll be going now."

"But don't you want some supper?" Laina said. "You've never eaten stew until you've tasted Rachel's."

"I believe you, ma'am," Blake said, smiling. "But as you know, you've never eaten pie until you've tasted Miss Irvin's. And she promised me a piece if I get back before taps."

◆

"You were right," Charlotte said the next evening. "The silence out here is wonderful. If you could can it and sell it, everyone in Detroit would likely want some."

"I thought you might find it . . . boring. You aren't used to this kind of life." Laina settled on the rocking chair next to Charlotte's. "And shelling peas all day isn't exactly mentally challenging."

"That's what I liked about it," Charlotte said. She flexed the fingers of her left hand. "There's something comforting about the simplicity of it. And I really do think my fingers benefited. They ache—but it's a good ache, if that makes any sense." She leaned her head back against the rocker and closed her eyes. "And we certainly do have something to show for the day's work. Something much more useful than two yards of lace for a tablecloth no one needs." She opened her eyes and looked at Laina as she explained, "Mother Bishop worshiped at the altar of the cult of domesticity."

"What?"

She laughed under her breath, "That just means that while the servants did the real work, Mother and I sat by the fire and did fancywork."

"I didn't think you liked to sew."

Charlotte murmured, "What I liked or didn't like was never much of a concern to the Bishops."

"You really were miserable, weren't you?"

"I was," Charlotte said. She held up her right hand and swept it toward the horizon. "But I'm not now. This is . . . astounding. I can see why you love it."

•••◆•••

"What are you doing out here in the middle of the night?" Charlotte said. "I heard the front door open." She walked to where Laina was standing beside Spirit's stall and touched her friend's shoulder. When Laina glanced at her, Charlotte could see the tears.

She took a deep breath. "I said all the right things. I believe them. I have to raise CJ and do what's right . . . regardless of Caleb's choices." Her voice wavered and she swiped at another tear. "But now I'm home . . . and the bed is empty . . . and I didn't really think I'd have to *do* it . . . without him."

Charlotte put her arms around her friend.

"I'm sorry," Laina apologized.

"For what?"

"I'm not being a very good . . . example."

"I don't know what you're talking about," Charlotte said.

Laina sniffed and wiped her nose. She turned around to the stall and scooped up a hand of grain. Spirit's black ears went forward. "Here, girl," Laina said, and held her hand out. Spirit stepped forward and accepted Laina's offering, then stood quietly while Laina rubbed the filly's ears and stroked her soft muzzle. "I'm not a very good example of faith. I mean, if I really believe that God is in control of my life, I shouldn't be such a mess."

"Don't be so hard on yourself," Charlotte said. She thought for a few minutes before speaking again. "That first night you visited me in the hospital, do you remember how I reacted?"

Laina shrugged. "You were hurting."

"I was just on the edge of rude to you," Charlotte corrected her. "Because I thought you were just doing your Christian duty by visiting me. I never expected you to call on me again, and the last thing I wanted was another hypocrite checking me off her list of things to do like I was a chore."

"Ouch," Laina said. "It sounds like you have experience with that."

"The Bishops were very involved church members," Charlotte said. "But their religion never really had much to do with what went on inside the four walls of that house. With one exception. The Colonel was fond of quoting the proverbs about meting out corporal punishment just before he disciplined Will." She swept her hand across her forehead. "But you, Laina . . . you aren't self-righteous. Your faith is real. Even in your worst moments, you cling to it."

"Like a cat clinging to a tree limb—just barely hanging on," Laina said, mocking herself.

"Did you really expect God to spare you the pain of the

loss when your baby died? I always thought people were religious so they could hang on to God while they were going through bad times. Not so He would make them not feel the pain. He didn't even do that for His own son—at least not according to the Sunday school lessons I remember."

Laina's eyes widened. "I haven't thought about it that way. Ever. I didn't think I would hurt as much when hard things happened. Because I believe." She paused, speaking slowly. "You're right, Charlotte. I had things all wrong. It hurts just as much. The difference is, God provides the strength instead of my having to go through it on my own." She sighed. "Except I didn't really tap into His strength."

"How would you have done that?" Charlotte wanted to know.

"Praying. Talking to Him. Reading the Bible Granny Max left behind. You wouldn't believe how marked up that book is. I remember Preacher Barton saying you could tell a lot about people by looking at their Bible. He said sometimes a Bible will almost fall open to a person's favorite passage. Granny's Bible doesn't fall *open*. It's falling *apart*. She has things underlined, and even some notes written in the margins. Dates, too. I always wished I knew what those dates meant." Laina shook her head. "Anyway, I suspect that if I'd been reading those words like I should have, I wouldn't have been quite so helpless. But I was so angry, I stopped. We both did, Caleb and me. And then we stepped away from each other and stopped talking." She sniffed again. "And now he's . . . gone." Her voice broke on the last word.

"Don't give up," Charlotte said. "I can't imagine God has it in mind to break your heart again." Charlotte put her hand on her friend's shoulder.

"I hope you're right."

* * * * * * *

Caleb—CJ and I are going home. Please forgive me for failing you. It breaks my heart to think that I can't fulfill your dreams. I will do my best to understand whatever decision you make about the future.

Charlotte Bishop and Will have gone with us. Will is so sure he wants Spirit, and Charlotte needs to see her. I hope you won't mind. CJ was very excited about it, and it was good to see her smiling again. It's been a while since any of us have smiled, hasn't it? You may have wondered, but I have never stopped loving you.

Your L

As he stood at the trading post reading his wife's note, Caleb frowned. He looked up at Maude. "I sent a note with Nathan Boone for Laina. Did she get it?"

Maude shook her head. "I don't know anything about a note. Lieutenant Boone left on maneuvers. He and Private Blake and all of Company B headed out to Chadron for the readiness drill two days ago."

"But I sent word," Caleb repeated. "Nathan would have seen to it that someone else got the message to her, even if he couldn't do it himself."

"Maybe you'd better take it in person next time," Maude said. "And not make her wonder."

Caleb nodded. "You're right."

"You bet your britches I am," Maude said. "Now get going!"

Caleb swung back into the saddle. He rode to the hospital and was pleased when the preacher stepped out and swung onto Elvira at his approach. "Doc says I'm fit as a fiddle," the old man said. "Let's get you home."

Charlotte grabbed the saddle horn with her right hand and hauled herself astride a rangy dun mare Jack Greyfoot had assured her was the perfect horse for her. She looked down at Laina, grinning. "Mother Bishop would be appalled."

"No doubt," Laina agreed. "But we don't own a side-saddle, so this is the only way."

Charlotte rubbed her palm against her denim pants. She hugged the horse with her knees and flexed her feet in the too-large boots Emmet Dorsey had loaned her. "Slow down, CJ," she called to the girl who was mounted and waiting outside the corral. "Give me a chance to get the feel of things here in the corral before we head out, okay?"

Charlotte nudged her horse into a trot. In a few minutes, she was moving with the animal, sensing its rhythm—and feeling in control.

"That's it, Ma," Will encouraged. He was riding an ancient buckskin gelding—after a protracted discussion with Jack, who would not agree that Spirit was ready for trail riding.

"Are we having company?" CJ asked, and motioned toward the top of the rise in the direction of Fort Robinson.

Laina turned to look into the distance.

"Hey . . . it's the preacher!" CJ called out. "I can see his white hair . . . and . . . Pa!" CJ squealed. "It's Pa!" She whirled her horse around and set off.

Charlotte walked her mount to the side of the corral where a pale-faced Laina waited with her hand at her throat. Charlotte found herself casting a *Help her, Lord,* toward heaven, even as she watched CJ ride up next to her father and lean over and hug him without ever leaving the saddle. "That girl's a good rider," she said.

Laina nodded. "I told you she'd rather be in the saddle . . . helping her Pa . . . than in the house with me any day of the week." She reached up to touch the left side of her hair.

"You look fine," Charlotte said, waiting alongside her friend, her own heart beating rapidly as she hoped for the best and feared lest it not happen.

Caleb and Preacher Barton headed for the house, but then Caleb saw the women out at the corral and detoured.

He rode up to Laina, swung down off his horse and swept her into his arms.

Charlotte heard very little of what Caleb Jackson said to his wife as he buried his face against her neck, but she knew they were both crying, and she knew it was good. A pang of emotion shot through her as she rode out of the corral and to where Will and CJ were waiting. She frowned at the next thought, which was the image of Lieutenant Boone in his dress uniform. *Even if it were possible, which it is not, the last thing on earth you would want is another soldier. The very last thing.*

"Let's go," she called to CJ and Will, and led the way.

CHAPTER EIGHTEEN

He that trusteth in his own heart is a fool.

PROVERBS 28:26

CJ WOKE WITH A START.

It was time.

She couldn't believe she had let Will talk her into such a crazy plan.

For over a week now, things at home had been wonderful. She didn't understand all the details, but she'd overhead snippets of a talk between the grown-ups that hinted at a lost letter from Pa. A letter that would have made Ma feel better those couple of days after they got home and before Pa and the preacher arrived. Apparently something had happened to the paper as it passed from Pa to Lieutenant Boone to another soldier who was supposed to deliver it to the ranch. There had been orders to go on maneuvers and the letter was lost. But it didn't matter now because Pa was back home and Ma was smiling again.

Even Mrs. Bishop, usually quiet and subdued, had laughed aloud at dinner last night. Lieutenant Boone had gotten his leave and was staying at the ranch for a while, and he and Pa spent hours together, talking about horses and land. Even Will seemed happier these days. When Pa complimented Will on being such a good worker, CJ could see how pleased Will was. Jack Greyfoot claimed that Will's hard work in keeping the barn clean freed him up to spend more time breaking and training Rebel and Spirit. CJ figured Jack's extra time with the horses must be the reason why he never ate meals with them at the house anymore. CJ was proud of Will, although the closest she got to telling him that was when she said his riding was "not too bad, for a city boy."

It was in the midst of this same week that CJ and Will had started planning an adventure based on something Will had seen on their ride with his mother the day Pa came home. When CJ told him it was too dangerous, it seemed to make Will all the more determined. "Ma's birthday is coming up. She's never even seen an eagle egg." Will went on to describe the glass dome at their home back in Michigan that had once protected a beautiful, decorated ostrich egg from dust and fingerprints. "It was a present," Will said.

"Well, it might be all right if we can get someone to help us," CJ finally said. "And maybe we could go into town and get some pretty buttons and beads and things. We could decorate it for her."

Will nodded. "That's a great idea. I bet Lieutenant Boone would help us."

"I bet he would," CJ said, grinning. "He likes your ma."

Will frowned. "Sure he does."

"No, I mean he really *likes* her. How would you feel about getting a new pa, anyway?"

Will looked at CJ like he thought she was crazy. "I don't know what you're talking about."

"Well," CJ explained, "My ma was telling Pa just last night how she's been praying for them both, and she thinks it would be just fine if God would 'open their eyes and make them realize what's really going on.'" CJ took a breath, "and what she *means* is they like each other. Only they don't seem to know it yet."

Will shook his head. "That's crazy. Lieutenant Boone is being nice, that's all. He was making eyes at Rachel all during roundup. She came out and watched him bulldog the cattle. And they took a walk together. In the dark. Your pa even teased the lieutenant about it."

"Grown-ups!" CJ said. "My folks talk about how God is in control all the time. But they sure spend a lot of time making sure God is doing things right."

Will returned to the subject of the eagle egg. "My father broke the ostrich egg Ma liked so much."

"Why?" CJ said.

Will shrugged. "I dunno. Captain Danley gave it to her. He liked to dance with her. She told Pa it didn't mean anything. But Pa got mad and broke the egg the captain sent her."

"Your pa was jealous," CJ said matter-of-factly.

"I guess he was," Will said. "But I don't know why. He never let Ma go anywhere without him."

CJ shook her head. "I'll never understand grown-ups. Ma and Pa think your ma should marry Lieutenant Boone, and you think Lieutenant Boone likes Rachel. And Jack likes Rachel, and—"

"He does?" Will said.

"Of course," CJ said in a tone of an adult explaining something to a child. "Why do you think Jack quit eating with us?"

"So he could spend more time with Rebel and Spirit," Will said.

CJ shook her head. "Naw. That's not it. That's just an excuse."

"How do you know all this?" Will asked. "I haven't seen anything different."

"Well, tonight at dinner you watch. Rachel makes sure Lieutenant Boone's cup is always full of coffee. And she sneaks him extra biscuits. And pie. She makes sure he gets two pieces."

"My ma doesn't do any of that stuff when Lieutenant Boone eats with us," Will said.

"Maybe not," CJ said. "But Ma says your ma smiles more when he's around. And she's happier."

Will thought for a moment. "She does like to go riding with him," he said. "But she always liked to ride."

"I thought you said she hated riding with that Major Riley."

"That was different."

"Of course it was," CJ said, rolling her eyes. "Because she didn't like Major Riley. Honestly Will, for a smart boy you can be really, really dense sometimes."

"I don't care about all that stuff," he said.

"Maybe you should," CJ said. "You just might be getting a new pa. So, I'm asking you again, what do you think about that?"

"Ma wouldn't do that."

"She might. With somebody nice like the Lieutenant."

Will was quiet for a minute. He looked at CJ. "Ma's been sad for a long, long time. Lieutenant Boone makes her smile. He even made her laugh the other night. If he can make Ma laugh, then I'll be glad to call him Pa. But I still want to give her that egg. And I don't want any grown-up help, either. Lieutenant Boone isn't the only one who likes to see her smile."

Will had insisted and planned and schemed until CJ was ashamed of her fear and overcame her reluctance.

Even so, this entire night had been one of waking, looking for daylight, trying to fall back to sleep, and then tumbling into a dream from which she woke again. Lying in the dark, CJ listened, half fearing she would hear Rachel or her father moving around in the kitchen, half hoping she would get caught. But it was so early even they weren't stirring yet. CJ sat up in bed. Bending over, she felt beneath her bed for the gunnysack Will had given her the night before.

"You'll need pants and a shirt," he'd said as they went through his trunk in the bunkhouse. "And my extra boots. And some socks. How you going to sneak them into your room?"

CJ had assured him it wouldn't be hard, and indeed it wasn't. For the first time in her life she saw some practical use for skirts and petticoats as she had tucked the bag out of sight up under her petticoat and headed for the house. Once inside, she made some excuse about needing something from her room and walked past Laina and Rachel and Will's mother, all three hard at work in the kitchen canning green beans. She quickly tucked the gunnysack beneath her bed and then went back to the kitchen to offer help with the harvest. As far as she could tell, no one suspected a thing.

And now the time had finally come. Dawn was breaking, and she needed to hurry and find a way to sneak out. She put on socks and pants while still beneath the covers, then sat up, pulling her nightgown off and Will's flannel shirt on. Arranging her pillows to look as much like a sleeping girl as possible, she pulled the covers back up and, with Will's extra boots in hand, crept to the door, looking each way to make certain no one was stirring.

Just as she stepped out into the hall, she heard the front door creak open. *Blast.* Rachel must have already gone down to the barn to get fresh milk. CJ ducked back in her room. Hoping no one heard the scraping of wood against wood, she raised the one small window she had closed when the night breeze proved too cold, slithered through the opening, and dropped to the ground. Slipping around the corner of the house, she made a dash for the chicken coop. Her heart pounding, she made another dash for the thickest stand of cedars behind the coop, scrambled across the steep incline behind the trees, and ducked into the canyon where Will waited astride . . . *Spirit.*

"This is a bad idea," CJ said immediately.

"It's an easy ride," Will retorted. "You said so yourself."

"I don't mean going after the eggs," CJ said. "I mean you and Spirit. She's not ready." As if agreeing, the little mare tossed her head and sidestepped.

Will reached down and patted her neck. "She's fine," he said. "She's just excited to finally get outside the corral."

"My pa or Lieutenant Boone or Jack would've already had you going for short rides up into the hills if they thought Spirit was ready," CJ said. "You should trust them. Pa says a rider and a horse have to be a good team. You and Spirit aren't a team yet. She knows more than you."

"I'm riding Spirit," Will said. "Now are you coming or not?"

CJ stared up at her friend. His jaw was set, and even in the dim light she could see the familiar glint in his eye that meant he was set on something and it was futile to contradict him.

"What if I go wake up Jack or the lieutenant?" CJ threatened. "They'll stop you."

"Go ahead," Will said. "Just don't ever expect me to talk to you again."

CJ hesitated. If she went along, she could at least make sure nothing bad happened. "Oh, all right," CJ said, and took the reins of her horse, Pappy, as Will held them out. Together they headed west. Morning light had just begun to gild the tips of the bluffs looming above them when CJ noticed a gathering of dark clouds on the distant horizon.

"Hey," she called to Will's back.

Will pulled on Spirit's reins and waited for CJ to come alongside.

She pointed at the dark clouds.

Will shrugged. "Probably nothing."

"That's rain. Or hail," CJ said. "You haven't been out here long enough to know, but I sure do. Weather moves in fast. And if it comes this way—"

"If it comes this way, we'll hightail it back to the ranch,"

Will said. "We can probably outrun it. And if we don't, we'll get wet. You afraid to get your new duds wet?"

CJ looked down at Will's flannel shirt. "Of course not," she said. "But you haven't sat out a hailstorm. Believe me, we don't want to get caught. Out here you can't always outrun a storm."

"Maybe Pappy can't," Will said. "But Spirit can."

"There's prairie-dog holes and all kinds of things. You—"

"Stop lecturing me," Will said abruptly. He was frowning. "I'm not afraid of a little rain or hail."

"I'm not talking about you, silly," CJ said. "I'm talking about Spirit. Pappy's an old army horse. The soldiers fire blanks over their heads to get them used to gunfire. Pappy's not going to be scared of a little thunder. But Spirit—"

"I should have known not to ask a *girl* to come with me," Will said. "I should have known you'd chicken out. You just don't want to climb up to that cliff."

The gauntlet had been thrown down, and CJ picked it up. Kicking Pappy's sides she said loudly, "Don't you worry about me, Will Bishop." She called over her shoulder, "You just worry about keeping up!" She urged Pappy into a run and tore away.

Spirit leaped after Pappy the second Will touched her flanks. Dodging this way and that, the surefooted pony quickly caught up with and passed Pappy. It was all Will could do to cling to the little horse's back. Suddenly CJ was yelling from behind him. Grabbing Spirit's reins, Will finally managed to pull the horse up, albeit with much prancing and foaming at the mouth and a couple of stubborn little bucks that nearly unseated him. CJ was waiting far behind him, gesturing and pointing up above her.

"Gosh you're fast," Will said to Spirit, patting her sweaty withers even as he tried to make his own voice sound calm. "Just settle down now," he said, relieved when the horse's black-tipped ears twisted toward his voice. Spirit shook her head and arched her neck, dancing sideways. "Whoa there, now. We're done running. CJ's found the nest. Let's go back and check it out." He barely touched Spirit's sides, and the horse leaped ahead, trying to run again. With great difficulty Will managed to keep her in check, almost getting thrown off again when Spirit gave an enthusiastic hop with her hindquarters that put daylight between Will's backside and the saddle.

"Whew," Will said when he was finally alongside CJ. "She likes morning runs!"

"I warned you." CJ nodded toward the west again, where a mountain of dark clouds was piling up, obscuring the familiar buttes in the distance. "And I'm telling you, if that turns into a bad storm that comes this way, Spirit is going to—"

"If you'd stop yapping and start climbing we'd have the egg and be home before anybody even knows we're gone," Will snapped.

CJ jumped to the ground. Letting Pappy's reins drop, she headed up the incline that lead into a cleft in the bluff and a narrow rocky trail.

"Hey," Will called, "aren't you going to tie Pappy?"

"He *is* tied as far as he's concerned," CJ called back. "It's called *ground* tying. Jack taught her. As far as Pappy knows, when his reins are down like that he's tied to a post. He's not going anywhere." She paused and put her hands on her waist. "But since you couldn't wait until Jack worked with Spirit more, you'll have to figure something out for her if you expect her to be within a mile of here when we're done." She turned back around and began to scale the rocky trail.

Will looped Spirit's reins over a low-growing bush three times and scrambled to catch up to CJ, oblivious to Spirit's nervous snorting.

CJ and Will climbed together, finally reaching the first ledge. Above them, sticking out from the bluff, was a narrower ledge barely visible beneath the impressive pile of sticks and brush gathered by two eagles over years of nest building.

"There," Will said, pointing upward. "There it is."

"I'm not blind," CJ snapped. Her next step on the trail sent her sliding backward. Rocks tumbled down, bouncing off the sides of the bluff. Below them, they could hear Spirit snort.

"It's okay, girl," Will called down. "Just a bunch of rocks. Nothing that will hurt you." He held his hand out to CJ. "Come on. I'll help you up."

CJ brushed her open palm against her jeans. Inspecting it, she spit on the skinned place and wiped the blood off on the backside of her borrowed jeans. She pretended not to hear Will and, ignoring his proffered hand, scrambled back up and past him.

Thunder sounded in the distance. "That's not good," CJ said.

Will looked toward the oncoming storm. "Maybe it'll blow by."

"I don't think so," CJ said.

"Well, maybe it'll go south of us," Will said. "Lots of storms do."

CJ shrugged. "If it doesn't, we're in for a drenching."

"I don't care," Will said.

CJ looked at him soberly. She looked down the trail and then back at the clouds. "All right," she said. "Let's go." She turned around and began to scale the rocky trail again.

Will protested. "Wait for me," he said. "This was my idea. I should get to go first."

"Fine," CJ said, and hunkered over to the side of the trail, clinging to a seedling tree while Will scrambled past. There was barely room for him to pass between her and the vertical wall of the bluff.

"That's rain," CJ called after Will. She reached up and felt the crown of her head. As she did so, another drop of rain landed on the back of her hand. She turned around. "Oh brother," she exclaimed. "Here it comes."

"Well, hurry on up," Will said, climbing harder. "We can sit out the storm on the ledge."

CJ hurried, pulling herself onto the ledge just as the storm broke.

"Is it always like this?" Will shouted above the roar of the storm. They were hunkered together against the looming wall of the bluff in a sliver of space left open in the amassing of the great nest before them.

"It's been abandoned," CJ shouted after an especially loud peal of thunder.

"How do you know that?" Will shouted back.

"See those two broken eggs?" CJ said. "Something got at them. And that one"—she pointed to the lone remaining egg—"must be infertile."

"What?" Will asked.

"City boy!" CJ shouted. "It won't hatch. So they left it."

"Why didn't it get broken, too?" Will said, as he picked up the egg to examine it.

CJ shrugged. "So some fool boy could come steal it, I guess." She wrinkled her nose. "You aren't going to like the way that smells when you try to empty it out for decorating."

The storm grew even more intense. Water came down in sheets. They could no longer see beyond the edge of the ledge.

Will shivered. "How long do these storms usually last?"

"Don't be afraid," CJ said. "I've seen worse."

"I'm not afraid!" Will said. "I just wanted to know!"

At that moment a flash of lightening revealed the valley floor below.

"The horses," CJ said.

"What about the horses?"

"They're gone. Even Pappy."

Will shrugged. "They'll run home."

"Of course they will," CJ said. "But then everyone is going to worry about us, and we're going to be in trouble."

"Not if we hurry back right now," Will said.

"We can't," CJ said. "I don't even know how we're going to get back down the trail after this rain. Look at it!" She pointed to the narrow trail, now a mud slide running with water.

"Just sit on your backside and slide!" Will said. With the next flash of lightening, he stood up and, stepping forward, clutched the egg. Just at that moment a roaring wave of water spilled from above them. One second CJ could see Will clinging to the nest, the egg cradled in his hands, the next he was gone. She screamed his name and leaned forward. A second wave of water took her over the edge, too. The last thing she remembered was the sensation of something cold slashing at her as she rolled over and over and over—down, down, down.

* * *

Jack Greyfoot landed inside the ranch kitchen door to report missing horses at the same time Rachel came rushing out of CJ's room after discovering the pillows positioned to look like a sleeping child.

"Will," they both said at the same time, and hurried out of the house, down the trail to the bunkhouse.

Just as they neared the door, Nathan Boone emerged. "Will's—"

"—gone." Rachel finished his sentence for him. "CJ too."

"On Pappy," Jack chimed in. "And Spirit."

"Spirit?" Nathan frowned. "I told that boy Spirit isn't ready for trail riding."

Jack nodded. "We all did." He looked toward the west. "And if they get caught in that . . ."

"Spirit will throw a fit, dump Will, and hightail it home." Nathan dragged his fingers through his beard, then scratched his head in frustration. "That boy," was all he could say, even as he headed for the barn.

Jack followed him.

Rachel turned to go back to the house, calling out, "I'll tell everyone else and get some warm blankets ready. They'll be drenched," she said.

Within minutes, Caleb joined Nathan and Jack. The three men had no sooner set out when the rain hit them like a wall, coming down in such thick sheets they were momentarily blinded. Pulling their hats down over their eyes, they gave their horses their leads and were soon standing sidled up to a clump of cedar trees.

Just as quickly as it came, the storm was gone, leaving in its wake broken branches and rivulets of water gushing down every crevice in the bluffs. The meandering creek that wound its way through the Four Pines had become a rushing torrent of water. About the time the men managed to force their mounts through the raging water, Spirit and Pappy came charging toward them, heads high, tails flying in the wind. Spirit leaped over the raging creek with one easy bound. Pappy screeched to a halt and eyed the water suspiciously. Deciding not to cross, he dropped his head and began to graze.

"Well, wherever they are," Caleb said, "those two are going to get a talking to."

Nathan shook his head from side to side, muttering, "What were they thinking?"

"They weren't thinking," Jack said.

"You have any idea what kind of plan they'd hatched up?" Caleb asked.

Jack shook his head. "We all told Will that Spirit wasn't ready for trail riding. We didn't have to tell CJ. She knew that. The only thing I can figure is CJ went along because she couldn't stop Will."

The longer the men rode, the more quiet they became. Nathan swore at the rain. "Washed out any hope of tracking them," he muttered. He pulled up, took his hat off his head and flailed it against his thigh, then rolled up the brim, pressing the excess water out. "Ruined my new hat." He swore again.

"CJ! CJ Jackson!" Caleb called.

"Will Bishop!"

Their voices bounced back at them off the bluffs. Unanswered.

With the departure of the fast-moving storm, the prairie glistened in the morning sun. Droplets of moisture dripped from every pine needle and every leaf. The heads of blooming flowers bowed down with the weight of water, painting the prairie floor with a mass of subdued color. As they rode, the sun came out and began to dry off the rain, the flower heads lifted toward the light. Still, there was no answer to the men's repeated shouts for CJ and Will.

CJ rolled over onto her right side and looked around. The sun was shining brightly, making the droplets of water on the pine boughs looming above her sparkle like jewels. It made her head hurt. Squeezing her eyes shut, CJ grunted and raised her hand to her forehead. "Will?" With her eyes closed, she tried to listen, hoping to hear the sound of a horse grazing nearby. "Pappy?" *You dumbbell. He's back home by now.* The idea sent a chill through her. She was going to be in so much trouble.

She managed to pull herself to a sitting position, grunting again with the pounding of her head. Slowly, she turned and looked up the bluff, shivering a little when she realized just how far she'd fallen. She looked at the trees around her.

If she'd hit one of those . . . Carefully, she checked her wrists, shrugged her shoulders, turned from side to side, lifted first one leg, then the other. Every muscle screamed, just like the time she kept getting thrown by a rambunctious pony. She'd climbed back on, over and over and over again, until the meanspirited varmint gave in and let her stay on its back. Once she'd conquered the beast, she decided she didn't want to ride it anyway and had hobbled home. The next morning she'd felt a lot like she felt right now, which was sore but not permanently hurt. There was a difference though. After conquering the pony she'd felt proud. Right now she felt ashamed. And a little frightened.

"Will. . . ? Will Bishop? Can you hear me?"

An eagle screamed and CJ looked up. She caught a glimpse of the great bird soaring high above and, for a moment, felt a pang of regret on behalf of the bird. Maybe that was the one whose nest got washed away. She imagined how it would feel to have the ranch house swept away in a flood. Looking up at the bird, she murmured, "Sorry."

Will. She had to find Will. He'd gone over the ledge before her, which meant he might be farther down the hill. Or did it? Calling out his name, CJ bent over and pushed herself to a standing position, surprised at how dizzy she was. She blinked and brushed the back of her hand across her forehead. Finally, she leaned against a tree. Which way was home? She didn't even know that . . . and she *never* got lost. That fall must have addled her brain. It sure hurt enough for something to have shaken loose.

Breathing in deeply, CJ looked around her. The horses were gone, that was certain. If she stayed put, someone would eventually come looking for them. But what about Will. What if he was hurt? What if—

Stumbling a little, CJ stepped away from the tree and reached for the next. She made her way down the incline groping her way from tree to tree. When she'd gone what seemed an impossible distance, she slid to the ground to rest.

She just couldn't seem to clear her head. No matter how much she blinked, everything seemed fuzzy.

"Will? Can you hear me, Will? It's CJ."

Deciding to lay down for a minute, she leaned over. That was when she caught a glimpse of red sticking out from beneath the low-hanging branches of a cedar tree. Rubbing her eyes, CJ tried to focus. There was a *hand*!

"Will!" CJ shouted. "Will!" She rose and scrabbled across the few feet between the pine trees, across a small clearing to where the boy—yes, it was Will's hand—had come to the end of a long tumble down the mountainside.

CJ called his name again and again, but Will didn't answer. Afraid to pull on his arm in case it was broken, CJ lay close and ran her hand underneath the branches, along his sleeve, up his back. She could barely touch his neck, but the feel of something warm and sticky made her shudder. Blood.

"Will," she shouted. "Will, can you hear me? Please answer me!" She began to cry. She shook his shoulder. He moaned. "That's good, Will. You just keep breathing. You hear me, Will Bishop? You keep breathing! I'm bringing help and . . . and . . . and you've got to help us break Spirit. You hear me? You keep breathing, Will Bishop!"

Stumbling and crying, CJ made her way down the incline into a clearing. Her head was pounding and she still couldn't focus. Which way? Which way was home? She looked skyward. Nothing looked familiar. Nothing looked—

Wait. Calm down. Look around you. Isn't that what Jack Greyfoot had taught her when she begged him to show her how to track animals? "I can't see anything," she had whined. Jack had told her to wait. To calm down. To look. Inhaling deeply, CJ closed her eyes. She listened. She waited. She calmed down. When she opened her eyes again, she looked around. For a few moments nothing made any sense. *Find the sun, stupid. You headed west. Home is east. Where's the sun?* Looking east, CJ saw the sign she was looking for. The thinnest plume of white streaked the sky in the distance. Someone might have mistaken it for a cloud, but CJ knew it wasn't. That was Rachel's cooking fire. That was *home*.

She wanted to run. But she couldn't. Every muscle in her body screamed every time she moved. She did her best, though.

"You listen to me, Will Bishop," she called back up the hill. "I'm running home and I'm bringing help and you'd better be ready to get moving because I'm not growing up without you. You hear me? I'm not!"

CJ headed east, tears streaming down her dirty cheeks.

CHAPTER NINETEEN

He hath shewed thee, O man, what is good;
and what doth the Lord require of thee,
but to do justly, and to love mercy,
and to walk humbly with thy God?

MICAH 6:8

KEEP WALKING. KEEP GOING. DON'T STOP.

CJ stumbled along, wiping tears, rubbing her aching head, talking to herself. Her entire body ached. She'd taken off her coat and tied it to Pappy's saddle before the climb, and now the damp morning air made her shiver.

Keep walking. Keep going. Don't stop.

The mental image of Will lying unconscious beside a cedar tree kept her moving in spite of the urge to stop and rest. Finally, the wind carried a voice. Voices. Calling out. Calling . . . her name. Will's. CJ paused, squinting into the distance. Movement. Three dots on the horizon. Strength came from deep inside, and she began to run. She forgot her aching head, her sore muscles. She kept running, pumping her arms, sobbing, crying out loudly, "Here! I'm here!"

Pa and Lieutenant Boone and Jack flung themselves down off their horses all at once and ran to her, encircling her in their arms.

"Are you all right?" Pa asked. He put his hand to her skinned forehead.

CJ nodded. "My . . . my head hurts. But . . . Will." She began to sob. "Will's hurt."

"Where?" the men said in unison.

"Back there. By the . . . the split tree. Under a . . . cedar."

"Catch your breath, CJ," Pa ordered. "Calm down a bit."

CJ inhaled deeply. Her heart slowed enough for her to talk. She looked from Jack to her father. "You know the big tree. The one split by lightning last year. And the ledge. The eagle's nest?"

They nodded.

"We climbed up . . . the storm. There was a big *whoosh*. It washed us down." She gulped. "He isn't moving. I couldn't get him to . . . answer . . . me." She began to sob again.

The men mounted their horses. Pa leaned down, his arm extended. CJ wrapped her arms around his and hung on while he hoisted her up. "Hang on," he said. "Tight."

CJ clasped her hands around her father's waist.

"You ready?"

"Ready," CJ said.

The horses leaped forward. Together, they charged across the wet earth. CJ squeezed her eyes shut and pressed herself against her father's back, grasping the horse with her legs. *Just hold on. Just hold on. Don't let go. Don't let go, Will. Don't let go.*

It seemed to take forever to get to the split tree, but when they finally did, Jack leaped off his pony first, calling Will's name.

"Show us," Pa said, helping CJ down while he searched the area with his eyes.

"There," CJ said, running toward the cedar tree.

Will lay curled up like a baby, his hands pulled in toward his body, his eyes shut.

Lieutenant Boone ducked beneath the cedar's low-hanging branches and hunkered over him. He leaned down and listened. "He's breathing," he said.

"Will," he said loudly. "Will Bishop. Wake up, son. It's Lieutenant Boone. Will? You hear me?"

Will didn't move.

Gently, he checked the boy's arms and legs. "I don't think anything's broken," he said.

Will moaned softly.

"I'm gonna pick you up, son. We're going for help. You hear? You just stay with us, son. You're going to be all right."

CJ stood back while Jack and Pa used their bodies to press some of the cedar branches out of the way. Lieutenant Boone scooped Will up into his arms. Halfway to his horse he asked Jack to check the side of Will's head that lolled against his shoulder.

When Jack lifted Will's head he grimaced. "He's bleeding. Not bad, but it's swollen up. Looks awful."

"Is he gonna be all right?" CJ asked.

"I don't know," the lieutenant said. He looked at Jack. "He needs a doctor. The question is, do we wait the half day it will take for one of us to ride and fetch him on horseback, or do we take Will to the fort."

"Just get to the house," Pa said, and once more climbed into the saddle and reached down for CJ. "Maybe we'll know more when we can take a closer look."

The minutes it took to get to the house seemed like hours. Nathan held Will close and wondered again how such things could be allowed to happen. First Laina and Caleb, and now Will and Charlotte. Sometimes it just seemed to him that the worst things kept happening over and over again to the nicest people. How, Nathan wondered, was Charlotte Bishop going to get through this. Just when it was beginning to seem like things were going to be all right.

Charlotte took one look at her unconscious son and said, "We're going to the fort."

"Do you think we should put him through that?" Nathan said. "It's a rough ride."

"I'm not sitting here for half a day waiting for someone else to rescue my son," Charlotte said.

"Are you sure?"

"I'm not sure of anything," Charlotte's voice wavered. She closed her eyes and inhaled deeply. "But I remember my father talking about things like bleeding on the brain. I don't know if that's what's causing the swelling, but if it is . . . then time means a lot."

Laina was already moving around the house gathering blankets and quilts. "We'll cushion it as much as possible," she said. Rachel joined her, emerging from her own room with two blankets and her pillows. CJ ran for her room and followed suit. Jack and Nathan headed to the barn, hitched the wagon, and rumbled up to the door. The women climbed into the back, spreading first their pillows, then all the blankets on the wagon bed. Nathan lay Will atop the mound of feathers and blankets. Charlotte climbed in and perched herself at the head of the makeshift bed, elevating Will's head gently, pulling a pillow into her lap, then positioning herself so she could stroke her son's forehead.

Rachel handed Laina a bucket of water and a cloth.

When CJ put her foot on the wagon wheel to climb aboard, Laina held up her hand. "Honey, you should st—"

"I'm going," CJ said. "I can help." She plopped down beside Will.

With a glance at Caleb, Laina nodded. "All right."

"I'll catch up," Caleb said, and headed for the barn to saddle his horse.

Nathan gathered the reins and lashed at the team. The wagon lurched ahead, sloshing water out of the bucket onto CJ's dress. She dipped the cloth her mother had handed her into the water, wrung it out, and passed it to Charlotte, who did her best to wash Will's face clean.

"It doesn't look bad," Charlotte said. "Not that deep. May not even need stitches."

"So why doesn't he wake up?" CJ asked.

Charlotte closed her eyes and bent down to briefly press her lips to Will's forehead. "I don't know, CJ. I don't know."

They reached the fort in record time.

It felt like it had taken a lifetime. Nathan wanted to lash the horses and make them run full out, but he forced himself instead to watch the trail and try to keep the ride as smooth as possible while pushing the team at a steady lope.

As promised, Caleb had caught up with them, shouted he would alert the doctor, and raced ahead to the fort. Orderlies were waiting with a litter when the wagon pulled up to the hospital. They moved Will inside, the doctors examined him. Dr. Valentine came out into the hallway and explained the situation. He used words like *hematoma* and *trepanning*. Nathan had once seen a surgeon open a box containing the tools for that procedure. He'd winced at the sight of the drill and the saw. And now it was Will's skull they were drilling. Nathan's stomach reacted to the idea. He almost reached for Charlotte. Instead, he put his hand on his hip and shook his head. Apparently she knew the details, too, because when the doc said "trephine," she went pale and sat down on the bench in the hallway. She looked up at Nathan, then reached for Laina's hand, leaned her back against the wall, and closed her eyes.

"C-could we pray for him?" CJ asked, her voice distorted by fear and barely controlled sobs.

Without opening her eyes, Charlotte said, "Please."

"Help us," Caleb prayed. "God, help us. We're afraid. Doc said there's blood pressing on Will's brain. That sounds bad to us, but you are the Lord, and we are asking for a miracle. Guide Doc's hands to the right spot to drill. Let it be all right."

"Please," Charlotte said aloud. "Lord God, help my boy." She swallowed hard before adding, "I haven't asked you for anything in a long time, Lord. But Will's just getting started. Please, Lord. For my boy's sake. Please."

Even Dr. Valentine prayed. "It's my grandson, Lord. And I love every mischievous bone in his body. Please take my hands and help me help Will. Bring him back to us."

Charlotte took in a deep, ragged breath. Laina took her hand and whispered a prayer. The words were simple, but so natural, so heartfelt.

When even CJ talked to God, Nathan found himself wishing he knew more about praying for other people. Given a moment longer, he thought he might have tried it.

But then Dr. Valentine put his open hand on the top of his daughter's head and spoke aloud. "You keep praying, daughter." He looked at Laina. "Thank you for being here." With a pat on CJ's shoulder and a nod to Nathan and Caleb, he hurried off down the hall.

"Would you mind, terribly . . ." Charlotte opened her eyes and looked at Nathan.

"Anything," he said. "Just say it."

"Garnet."

Nathan hurried outside.

"Oh, my Lord." Garnet Irvin raised her hands to her face, one palm against each cheek. She stood just inside Dr. Valentine's back door, staring at Nathan. "Will he be all right?"

"God knows," Boone said.

Garnet reached for the shawl hanging beside the back door. As she stepped out on the back porch, she asked Nathan to find Carter Blake. "He'll want to know."

Grateful to have something more to do besides sit and wait, Nathan went to find Private Blake.

Nathan found Carter Blake and sent him to the hospital. He drove to the trading post and told Maude Dubois about the accident. Then he unhitched the team, took them into the stable and rubbed them down. All the while his mind raced, second-guessing the decision to move Will, thinking of ways they could have made the trip easier on the boy, wishing he would have heard CJ and Will ride away early that morning, wondering if somehow he'd neglected to fully warn Will about taking Spirit out on the trail, thinking back over the last week, asking himself if he'd missed some hint at what Will and CJ were planning.

When he ran out of things to do, Nathan stepped outside the stable and looked up at the sky and said aloud, "If anything happens to that boy . . ." He scolded himself. *That's good, Lieutenant. Threaten God. That's worked so well in the past. Surely God trembles when Nathan Boone talks.* He took his hat off and raked his hands through his hair. *He probably doesn't even listen. And why should He? By now He's probably tired of hearing you blame Him for everything that's wrong in the universe.*

Thinking back to the scene at the hospital made Nathan reluctant to return. It had been strange standing in that circle of people, listening to everyone else but him say a prayer for Will. He'd always felt uncomfortable around that kind of thing, but this time, something was different. His discomfort wasn't because he thought they were wasting their time. Today he was uncomfortable because he was the only one who didn't pray. It bothered him not to be able to offer Charlotte the same kind of comfort the others had. He'd seen the change that came over her while they prayed. She visibly relaxed. The concern didn't disappear from her lovely face, but the deep lines of agonizing fear seemed to recede. Nathan wished he could have been part of that. Part of helping Charlotte.

Something else niggled at him. He realized that of all the people around Charlotte Bishop, he was the only one who had reacted with anger toward God. Everyone else had seemed to just naturally turn to Him for help. Will's situation had him—just a friend of the family—pacing back and forth in a stable while Will's own mother sat quietly on a bench over at the hospital, no less concerned . . . but much more in control.

"All right then," Nathan said aloud. "If it makes any difference to you, I'm asking. I don't expect you to listen. But just in case you are, I'll ask. Is that what you want me to do? Ask you?" He looked into the distance. The morning storm was moving east. Bright blue sky was beginning to appear between thick clouds on the horizon toward the west, and the tip of Turtle Butte was bathed in sun while off to the east, low-hanging storm clouds still obscured the tip of Crow Butte. Nathan looked toward the ribbon of blue in the west.

"I'm not asking for me. It's for them. For Charlotte and Will. Please let Will live." Nathan pulled his hat back on, started to go to the hospital, then stopped again and looked up. "And if there's anything I can do—" His voice broke. "I really like that kid, God." Sniffing, Boone looked around him to make sure no one had heard or seen the embarrassing display of emotion. He pulled his hat back on. He didn't know what else he could do. But one thing he did know. He couldn't stay away from the hospital any longer.

By the time Nathan Boone got to the hospital, Will had been brought out of surgery and moved into a small back room at the far end of the ward. Dr. Valentine was leaning over him listening to his chest with a stethoscope. When Nathan looked in, the doctor glanced up and shook his head in reply to Nathan's questioning look, then his eyes directed Nathan's attention to where Charlotte sat, her head bowed, her eyes closed, her hands clutching a black book.

Nathan didn't recognize Granny Max's Bible until he sat down next to Charlotte and she held it out. "Laina said she grabbed it at the ranch as we were leaving. She said it might bring me some comfort."

"You know where to read for that sort of thing?" Nathan asked.

Charlotte pointed at the Bible. It lay open, and many passages on the two pages Nathan could see were heavily underlined. It looked, he realized, a lot like Lily's Bible.

Charlotte read aloud, "'God is our refuge and strength, a very present help in trouble. Therefore will not we fear, though the earth be removed, and though the mountains be carried into the midst of the sea; though the waters thereof roar and be troubled, though the mountains shake with the swelling thereof.'" She paused, put her finger on the text, and repeated the words, "'God is our refuge and strength. . . . Therefore will not we fear.'"

"Does that bring you some comfort?" Nathan asked.

Charlotte's eyes filled with tears. She nodded. "Yes," she croaked. "It does."

"Then keep reading," Nathan said.

Moistening her lips, Charlotte looked back down. "'The Lord of hosts is with us; the God of Jacob is our refuge. . . . Be still, and know that I am God. . . . The Lord of hosts is with us; the God of Jacob is our refuge.'"

Charlotte looked up at Nathan. "I haven't tried making God my refuge in a long, long time." She smiled through her tears. "I had sort of decided the people were right who say God started it all and then just sat back to watch. I used to picture Him sitting up on a hill somewhere just watching." She shook her head. "I don't want to believe it's that way anymore. I want to think He was in the operating room guiding my father's hands. And that He's in this room right now."

Nathan only nodded.

Doctor Valentine finished his examination and pulled a white sheet up to his grandson's chin before turning toward them. "Caleb and Laina went over to the trading post to get

CJ cleaned up and so they could all get some supper," he said. "I'm glad you came back, Lieutenant. I need to check on another patient, but I didn't want Charlotte left alone."

"What about you?" Nathan said to Charlotte. "You need to eat, too."

"Garnet's bringing me something," Charlotte said.

"Garnet's a good woman," Nathan said. "A good friend."

"Yes," Charlotte agreed. "She is." She took in a deep breath. "You know, she didn't have to move all the way out here with me. I sure am glad she did." She paused, then said quietly, "She prayed for Will. You should have heard her." She swiped at a tear.

Doctor Valentine put his open palm on Will's bandaged head. "He did well through the surgery, sweetheart," he said. "Now, we wait." He stepped across the room to kiss Charlotte on the cheek. "I'll be back directly." He headed for the hospital ward.

"Is there anything else I can do?" Nathan asked, and started to stand up.

"Wait," Charlotte said. "We have to wait."

Nathan sat back down.

"I didn't mean *you* have to stay," Charlotte said. "I just meant that's all that's left to be done." She ran her thumb over the printed page of Granny Max's open Bible.

"You must be exhausted," Nathan said.

"I'll be all right." Charlotte lifted her chin and straightened her shoulders. She tilted her head from side to side and arched her back. Finally, she laid the Bible on the bench, stood up, and went to the tiny window that looked north toward the trading post and the distant bluffs. "We told Will not to ride Spirit outside the corral yet," she said. "We told him it was too dangerous." She rubbed her hand across her forehead. "I didn't think to add that he shouldn't be climbing rocky ledges in the rain." She closed her eyes. Her shoulders slumped. She began to cry.

Nathan got up and went to her side. Feeling awkward

about it, he put his hand on her shoulder, half expecting her to flinch and pull away. When she didn't, he stepped closer. "I haven't prayed in a lot of years, Charlotte. But I prayed for Will. And you."

"Thank you," Charlotte said. She closed her eyes. "I appreciate that. I'm grateful for all you've done for Will. He loves you, you know."

"I'm flattered," Nathan said.

"Don't be flattered," Charlotte said. She looked up at him, her eyes shining with tears. "Just don't give up on him." She looked over to the bed where Will lay motionless.

"I won't," Nathan said. He lifted her chin and looked down at her. "On either of you."

Offering Charlotte a shoulder to cry on was the manly thing to do. Offering her his strength and his friendship made sense. What didn't make sense, Nathan thought as he wrapped his arms around Charlotte, was the way his heart thumped when she lay her head on his chest and gave in to her tears.

"Don't let go," Charlotte said, closing her eyes as she leaned against him.

"I won't," Nathan whispered.

◆

"I don't know."

"Time. He needs time."

"We released the pressure. But we can't know yet."

"It all depends."

"All we can do is pray."

"I've seen remarkable recoveries."

"Give it time."

"We don't know."

"There's no way to know."

"Only God knows."

A week after her son's accident, Charlotte was no closer

to knowing his fate than she was two minutes after his surgery. Laina and Caleb and CJ had reluctantly gone home, with a promise to return as often as possible to visit.

From her place at her son's bedside, Charlotte had heard snatches of the Independence Day festivities at the fort. Through the open window of Will's hospital ward, she'd caught glimpses of the dozens of Sioux in full regalia who had ridden down from the reservation for the celebration.

Nathan took up his soldiering responsibilities again. "Will and I can go back to the ranch together when he's better," he promised.

Charlotte's father said that every day was a step in the right direction. To Charlotte, it looked like every day was a step into nothingness. And yet, in the moment of her life that she should feel most desperate, there was a voice of reason. Somewhere deep inside her, hope flickered and would not be extinguished. The knowledge that half a dozen strong believers were praying for Will brought comfort. Charlotte read the forty-sixth psalm so many times she could recite it from memory. She went on to read other psalms, and began to cling to the God revealed in them.

One morning while she was sitting beside Will's bed, Charlotte fumbled through the unfamiliar pages of Granny's Bible trying to find a string of verses Granny had written on the inside cover of the old book. They talked about God being holy and just. They mentioned sin and the sacrifice Jesus made because of it. Charlotte read phrases like "whosoever will may come." She puzzled on the verses and asked Garnet about them. Garnet said they had talked about such things before.

"I know," Charlotte said. "But this time your answers make sense." Charlotte decided to step forward with what she thought of as a trembling kind of faith—cloaked in things she didn't understand but would trust to God. As a result, God was no longer a remote spirit watching from a distance to her. He became a "refuge" and her "present help in trouble." She was still terrified about Will. But in the midst of the fear was a sense that she was no longer alone.

The days took on a routine. They moved Will home. Garnet stayed in his room at night. Every morning Private Blake, who was officially a striker for Dr. Valentine now, carried Will into the kitchen, where a makeshift cot had been set up near the window.

"I just want him to hear our voices and be part of the family," Charlotte said. "I can't explain it, but I think it has to be good for Will to hear us talking."

Garnet, who had long since stopped reading aloud to soothe Charlotte's mind, took up the habit again, reading every afternoon from books Lieutenant Boone brought from the post library. And she sang. She filled the kitchen with music, sometimes accompanied by Carter Blake on a mouth harp.

Will did not open his eyes, but he could swallow, and between Charlotte, Garnet, Carter, and Nathan, his young body took in a steady stream of gruel and fresh milk. One day nearly two weeks after Will's surgery, Charlotte was feeding Will fresh applesauce.

"Mmm."

Charlotte's eyes widened. "You like that, honey? That's an apple. I put cinnamon and sugar on it."

"Mmmm. Mmmmhmmm."

"If you can hear me, Will . . . if you know what Mama's saying, could you show me? Do you think you could open your eyes, sweetheart?"

And there they were. The most beautiful gray eyes in the universe.

Chapter Twenty

A friend loveth at all times, and a brother is born for adversity.

Proverbs 17:17

For all his experience with chairs, Will Bishop had always thought of the mahogany chair in Grandmother's entryway back in Michigan as the worst. That was the chair where he waited for his father to come home on days when he had been particularly naughty. He thought he'd never hate any chair as much as that one. He was wrong. As the weeks went by after his accident, and he was able to sit up and be more aware of his surroundings, Will grew to despise the rocking chair on his grandfather's porch more than any chair he'd ever inhabited. He couldn't get out of it on his own because it wobbled. And he couldn't rock in time to anything, so the creaking sound it made was irregular—just like his body and brain since the accident. He hated being trapped in the chair, and he hated the way it talked to him, reminding him how different things were.

Even if he did walk oddly now, Will couldn't see the reason why he had to just sit on the porch or hobble around the house. Loot Boone had said as much one night when they thought Will was asleep. He'd almost argued with Ma, asking her how Will was going to learn to walk any better if he was never allowed to exercise, Loot Boone had said Will ought to be walking around the parade ground every day, even if it took all morning. He argued that the walk would be good for him and maybe he'd get better. Will thought that made sense. But he couldn't quite figure how to get down the three stairs between him and the ground. And then how to get back up to standing so he could take a step. That was a puzzle he hadn't solved. He had to be able to do it fast, too, before Ma found out, or she'd throw a fit. But he was determined to do it or die trying, because if he had to spend many more days in that rocking chair on Grandfather's porch, he was going to lose what was left of his mind.

Everyone treated him differently now. Even Ma. Although she still stroked his head and said she loved him, she was different. Always hovering, as if there was some unseen evil just waiting to hurt her baby. Will tried to show her he was still Will inside, but every time he tried to talk, she interrupted him. "It's all right, honey," she'd say. "Don't upset yourself." And she'd pat his hand and give him something to eat. He was beginning to hate cookies.

When he tried to take a walk, Ma called him back and said he had to wait until she could go with him. And when she called his name, her voice was laced with fear. If he could form the words, he could tell her it was all right. That he knew he couldn't do the same things as before. That his mind still worked pretty well, except that he couldn't find words any more. At least not the kind he could say. His tongue just wouldn't do it. And for some reason when he tried to write the words down, his fingers wouldn't act right either. But the words were still in his head. He remembered the way to the Four Pines Ranch, even though he hadn't been there in a long time. He remembered all the faces from before and the names that went with them, although sometimes he suspected a little part of the names might be scrambled. *Loot Boone* didn't seem quite right, but that was the best he could do. He wondered if he were allowed to walk around the parade ground like Loot Boone had suggested, if that would make his brain work better so the names would come back just right.

If he had the names, Will thought, maybe people would stop treating him like he wasn't there. Sometimes when people came to the house and saw that he was sitting on the porch, they walked right past him. Like he was invisible. Even if he looked right at them, they didn't even nod. He could have been a giant doll for all the attention they gave him. Didn't they see his eyes? Couldn't they tell he was smiling? Didn't they hear his voice? Even if it was only a grunt, surely they realized he was grunting at them. They should talk back. But they didn't. Most of them glanced at him, averted their eyes, and knocked hastily on the door, looking around nervously while they waited for Garnet.

There were exceptions. Loot Boone always slapped him on the shoulder and said hello. So did Private Blake. Will understood everything they said. He wished he could talk back. But he could only lift one corner of his mouth and try to smile—and he always slobbered when he did it. It was embarrassing. Especially when he was so awkward with his hand and couldn't always manage to wipe his own mouth. He looked away when that happened. Sometimes people sighed with the sound that said they pitied him. That made him mad.

It was the *pity* that finally got to Will. He couldn't stand all those sappy women walking by him to knock on his mother's door. News of his accident had spread fast, and the women at Fort Robinson had turned out in droves to comfort his ma. From the things they said, you would have thought Will couldn't understand a word. Surely, he thought, if they knew he understood them, they wouldn't have said the things they did. Sometimes they lowered their voices so he couldn't hear the words, but he remembered that tone. It was the same tone women had used in their murmurings when Father's body was laid out in the dining room at Grandmother's back in Michigan. Such voices had made his mother cry back then, and they made her cry again now. Will was sure of it, although Mother never let him see the tears. But he saw her red eyes often enough. She talked about God helping them and she prayed now before they had a meal. But she still cried. A lot. It made him want to scream. Except he couldn't. It made him want to run away. Except he couldn't do that either.

One July morning Will finally got them to listen without his having to talk. Ma had decided to have a quilting, which was a first, since Ma hated to sew. Will suspected it was another way for her to provide entertainment for him. She seemed to think that hearing other people talk would somehow help him get his own words back. She and Garnet scurried around all morning, moving the parlor furniture back from the middle of the room and setting up the quilting frame so they would be ready when Mrs. Barstow from up on Officer's Row arrived. Mrs. Barstow was the one bringing the quilt top. It would be put on the frame along with some filler and back fabric, and the women were going to "tie" it, Ma had explained. That meant they would be there all day, putting needles with yarn on them through the fabric layers and tying a million knots before it was finished. It also probably meant Will would be ignored all day. He could hear the scraping of chairs on the floor inside and the excitement in Ma's voice as she and Garnet got ready. They had taken Will out onto the porch to "enjoy the sunshine."

Just about the time the aroma of fresh coffee wafted through the windows, making his mouth water so that a bit of saliva ran out the corner of his drooping lip and made a dark spot on his blue shirt, the women started to come. Mrs. Barstow was the first, followed by five more. And not one of them said a word to Will as they paraded past him. Mrs. Barstow hugged her quilt top to her body and frowned as she walked by. Another glanced at him and then looked away, shaking her head. Another one made that clicking sound against the roof of her mouth he hated so much. The last two were quiet, but when they got onto the porch they sort of drew their skirts aside. As if Will might have lice or something. Those skirts were the last straw.

Sitting in the rocker, Will realized that if he waited for his mother to understand or for anyone else to listen, he was going to be sitting in this rocker on Grandfather's porch for the rest of his life. He was going to see those looks and endure those sounds of pity unless he put a stop to it, and he *was* going to stop it. He would show them. Ma would stay occupied with her guests, and Garnet would be busy in the kitchen, and that would give him time.

The first problem was getting himself out of the rocking chair. He inched his bottom to the edge of the seat and looked down at the porch, thinking he might as well be peering over the edge of a cliff. He was going to fall, no doubt about it. But if he could break the fall so he didn't land with too big a thud, then he would be able to roll to the edge of the porch and tackle the next big hurdle, which was the steps. Leaning over as far as he could, he felt the blood rush to his head. With a grunt, he pitched forward so that the top of his head was the first thing to land on the porch. Quickly, he rolled his head to one side, feeling the pull of the muscles as first his shoulder, then his entire right side landed on the porch. He lay quietly for a minute, breathing hard, waiting for Ma's screech. But the only thing he heard was laughter from the women inside.

Rolling toward the steps took another few minutes. But he made it, and even managed to sit up after a few tries. That was when he realized something wonderful. His legs were long enough to stretch across the top of all three stairs. His feet almost touched the ground. Bracing himself with his hands, he pushed himself forward until his bottom slid onto the top step and his feet were resting on the earth. If it weren't for the stair rail, he could have swung his feet to the side of the stairs and pushed off and been standing up. But the stair rail was a problem. Unless . . . Reaching up, Will lobbed his hands across the top of the rail, dismayed when his bad left hand was too weak to grip firmly enough for him to pull himself up.

How long it took, Will didn't know, but Ma caught him just as he had managed to get himself to the bottom step, wrap his forearms around the stair railing, and inch his torso along the rail until he was positioned at a crazy angle—half sitting, half standing—and completely worn out.

"Will Bishop!" she called out from the doorway. "What do you think you are doing?"

Will couldn't get his head turned around to see her, but he didn't have to look to imagine every woman at the quilting standing behind her, looking at Widow Bishop's idiot son. Closing his eyes, he could hear their sympathy. It made him mad. So mad that when his mother's hand touched his shoulder he tried to shrug her off. He shook his head angrily, becoming even madder because of his inability to speak. *No no no no no.* Why couldn't his mouth even say *that*. Angry tears sprang from his eyes.

"What is it, baby," Ma was saying, "what hurts? Did you twist your ankle? Does your back hurt? Show Mama, darling." And without even waiting to see his answer in his face, she was calling for Garnet.

Garnet came, her face a mask of kindness, a hint of apology in her eyes as she helped Will stand upright. "Put your hands on my shoulders, baby," she said. "Then you can lower yourself back onto the stairs while I get Carter to help us."

No no no no. Will struggled, lost his balance, fell back, crashing onto the edge of a stair. Pain shot up his back, making him even angrier. The tears flowed. The women came out onto the porch. With monumental effort, Will pushed himself to sit up, raised his fists to the side of his head and sat, his eyes scrunched shut, the tears flowing.

"Run get help, Garnet," Ma was saying. She sounded out of breath.

Will leaned against the railing, his hands clamped over his ears, trying to shut out the clucking and murmuring of the women behind him. It seemed like it took ten years for the murmurings to stop. Even after Ma suggested the ladies go back inside and quilt, and even after they did, he could hear their voices through the window, imagine the things they were saying, and picture their pitying looks—like hens clucking over a wounded chick.

Ma was leaning over, looking up at him, rubbing his back, trying to calm him down when Loot Boone's voice sounded. "Is everything all right?"

Ma's answer made Will mad. "Of course not," she almost snapped. "Will's fallen. He must have been trying to walk again. Alone. Garnet's gone for Father."

"Doesn't look to me like you need a doctor," Loot Boone said.

"Help me get him back up to the porch, will you?" Ma asked as she stood up.

When she reached for his arm, Will pushed her away, shaking his head. He looked at Loot Boone, and then at the parade ground and back again.

"Why don't you let me take him for a walk?" Boone said. "I've got nothing pressing this afternoon. You can go back to your quilting, and Will and I will just take a stroll." Loot Boone looked at Will. "That all right with you, son?"

Taking a deep breath, Will did his best to smile. He knew it came out as more of a grimace, but Loot Boone must have seen the intent rather than the result, because he said, "See, Charlotte? I've got it right. A walk is what the boy wants." He glanced past Will toward the parlor window. "And it's no wonder, with him having to listen to a gaggle of women all morning long. That would wear any boy out."

Ma opened her mouth to protest, but Loot Boone interrupted her. "You can trust me, Charlotte. I won't let anything happen. But you can't expect the boy to spend the rest of his life in a rocking chair on his grandfather's porch." He went on without giving Ma a chance to speak. "Now go on back inside with your women friends and enjoy the afternoon." In one easy movement he hauled Will to his feet. "Will and I will be just fine. I'll bring him back to you for dinner, and I predict he'll be hungry as a mountain lion."

Ma closed her mouth. Will saw the doubt in her eyes. She looked back up toward the parlor and back at Loot Boone.

"Trust me, Charlotte," Boone repeated, his eyes never leaving Ma's.

Ma looked up into Loot Boone's eyes, and Will could see that something inside her let go. The effect was not unlike what Will had sensed happening when Father left on an expedition. The minute he was gone, Will stopped tiptoeing around the house and Mother smiled more. Just like she was smiling now as she said, "All right, Nathan. If you're sure."

"I'm sure," Boone said.

Ma nodded, smoothed her apron, and turned to go. But not before she pulled a kerchief from her apron pocket and swiped the place at the corner of Will's mouth where the spit sometimes rolled out.

"All right, young man," Loot Boone said, the minute Ma was out of sight. "Think you can make it all the way around the parade ground?"

Will nodded eagerly, and took a step, grunting with dismay when his right foot refused to step and he nearly toppled to the ground.

Boone was quick to catch him. "Whoa, there," he said. "What if you just slide that bum foot along without trying to pick it up. Can you do that?"

Sweat broke out on his forehead with the effort, but inch by inch, Will managed to slide his bad foot forward, throw his weight on it, and bring his good foot alongside.

"Outstanding," Loot Boone said, clapping him on the shoulder. "That will work for now. Let's go." Cupping his left hand under Will's right elbow, Boone stepped forward, bracing himself and holding tight while Will struggled to take another step.

Will sighed with dismay and looked up at Boone, who grinned back. "Want to give up?"

Will frowned and shook his head.

"Didn't think so," Boone said. "Not much fun sitting in a rocking chair, is it?"

Will shook his head again.

"Well then," Boone said, tugging on Will's sleeve. "Let's keep moving."

◆

It took the better part of the afternoon for Will to walk the perimeter of the parade ground. Halfway around, Loot Boone made Will sit down on the front stoop of one of the new barracks. "Wait here," he said. "Catch your breath. I need to run over to the trading post for a minute. I won't be long."

While Boone was gone, Will watched Company G of the Ninth run through their drills on the parade ground. He frowned suddenly, wondering what had happened to Carter Blake's bay gelding named Dutch now that Carter was Dr. Valentine's striker. The fact that he even had the thought thrilled him. He'd forgotten a lot and he knew it. Garnet had taught him how to button his shirt, but try as he might, he could not figure out how to tie his own shoes. Still, with all the things he'd forgotten, he remembered Carter Blake and Dutch. Looking across the parade ground toward the stables in the distance, Will promised himself that the minute he was able to walk that far, he'd visit Dutch. Maybe he'd even hide a lump of sugar in his pocket. No, that wouldn't work. His hands didn't operate nearly well enough for him to dig a lump of sugar out of his shirt pocket. He'd have to ponder that. Maybe he could invent a way.

"Here you go," Loot Boone was saying, as he held out a brass-handled cane. "Frenchy has a half dozen canes behind the counter at his store. He was happy to loan us one. Now here's how he said it works," Boone said, and demonstrated how Will should step forward with the cane and his good foot, then drag the lazy foot up alongside. When Boone did it, it didn't seem hard, but when Will tried, it took all his concentration to move even half a foot. Looking ahead of him to the long walkway that ran in front of the row of barracks, Will hesitated.

"Too far?" Boone asked.

Will pondered. Taking a deep breath, he grasped the cane with his good hand and shuffled forward, carrying himself away from the barracks, away from his mother's quilting party and—thank you, God—away from that blasted rocking chair.

CHAPTER TWENTY-ONE

There is a friend that sticketh closer than a brother.
PROVERBS 18:24

HE NEVER WOULD HAVE THOUGHT IT POSSIBLE, BUT one day in late summer Lieutenant Nathan Boone realized that he was actually beginning to see the United States Army as an intrusion in the life he wanted to live. Or *lives* as the case seemed to be. He was getting increasingly confused about what the future might hold. Back in June he'd been at the Four Pines when Troop F was sent to Beaver Valley east of Chadron to check into rumors of "Indian depredations." Nathan was glad he hadn't had to be part of the "expedition" that spent several days finding nothing. Spending time as a cowboy had been great. And getting to know Rachel Greyfoot had been nice, too.

In July, when Troop I had been sent north to intercept Chief Red Cloud and some followers who had left the Pine Ridge reservation up in South Dakota, Nathan hadn't had to go with them either. As it turned out, the Sioux returned to the reservation long before they reached Soldier Creek—where the troops were headed. When the men rode back into the fort, grumbling about the wasted time, Nathan realized he felt his work with Will Bishop was more important than charging up to Hat Creek to do nothing. Dining with Will and his mother was becoming increasingly comfortable, too.

A new spiritual movement among the western tribes was ratcheting up the tension in the West. Periodically, all the men from Fort Robinson were ordered to "fall out" and camp just outside the post "to test their readiness for field service." Nathan had no choice but to participate, but every time he was gone from the fort he caught himself wondering how Will and Charlotte were doing in his absence. Every time he returned, he looked forward to seeing Will's lopsided grin and Charlotte's welcoming smile.

In spite of visits from nervous citizens who were certain the Ghost Dance religion spreading through the western tribes was going to result in a renewed Indian war, life at Fort Robinson continued to be ruled by 5:30 A.M. reveille and a routine number of bugle calls throughout each day until taps sounded at 9:15 every evening. Nathan began to resent the rigidity of military life. He got in the habit of checking in on Will every night after taps. Sometimes they played chess, with Nathan encouraging Will to use his "bad hand" to move the pieces, and sometimes they took a walk. Boone grew to look forward to the sounding of taps and the lamplight in the window at the surgeon's residence that meant they were expecting him.

Nathan's negative feelings about the direction his own life was headed reached a new high early in August when an expedition from Princeton University in the East arrived at the fort. The leader of the expedition, a Professor Scott, stayed as the houseguest of Commander Tilford, and the rest of the expedition members were treated almost like visiting royalty. Nathan didn't see why Dr. Valentine had to invite some of them to dinner every blasted night. Especially the one named Gabriel Moser.

Moser had an opinion on everything from what he called

"the Indian problem" to the origins of man to the future of Nebraska in the national economy to the impossibility of earning anything approaching a respectable living in ranching. In spite of Nathan's personal resentment of the man's high opinion of himself, he was glad about one thing. Moser knew a specialist back east who might be able to help Will. But even that caused Nathan's hackles to rise, just because of the way Moser put it. "If anyone knows how to return the boy to normal, it would be Doctor Faucett."

"I don't think anyone who knows Will thinks of him as not being normal," Nathan said, staring across the table at Moser, who was seated next to Charlotte. Nathan got up and excused himself before Moser could respond. He went outside to join Will, who had long since excused himself from the table and headed outside.

When a few minutes passed and the sound of Charlotte's laughter lilted through the parlor window to where Nathan and Will sat talking, Boone stood up. "It's all right if you'd rather stay here with your company than come with me," he said to Will. "We can always ride tomorrow."

In response, Will pushed himself upright and grabbed his cane.

Boone nodded. "All right, then. I'll just tell your mother, and—"

The door opened and Charlotte came out, followed by the fresh-faced man Nathan and Will didn't like. She turned to shake his hand. "Thank you again, Mr. Moser. I'll write Doctor Faucett tomorrow."

"Be sure to mention my name," Moser said. "He and my father studied together."

"Not following in the old man's footsteps?" Nathan asked abruptly.

Moser shook his head. "No. I always had my heart set on Princeton, where my grandfather studied." He motioned to the new buildings of the West End. "Professor Scott is very impressed with the improvements made here since his first visit." Moser looked around. "He said it was quite primitive back then."

"Well," Boone said, unable to stop the sarcasm in his voice, "we had to cope with the buffalo and the Cheyenne and the Sioux, you know. There wasn't a lot of time to hang wallpaper."

Will nudged Nathan's arm and smiled up at him. He nodded toward the stables.

"We'd better get going," Nathan said. "Will wants to climb aboard old Bones before it gets too dark."

"Are you sure this is going to be all right?" Charlotte asked.

"Why don't you come and see for yourself?" Nathan said.

Charlotte hesitated.

Moser spoke up. "Why don't we all go."

Will frowned. Nathan sighed.

"That's a wonderful idea," Charlotte said. "I'll get my bonnet and my shawl and be right out."

* * *

"You're . . . what?" Nathan didn't think Charlotte Bishop could surprise him.

"We're going with the Princeton expedition. Father is to be their surgeon. You should see him. It's given him a new lease on life to be part of the project."

"Do you think Will is ready for something like that?" Nathan asked. "And do you have any idea how miserable it is up in that country in *August*?"

"I don't mean we're going fossil hunting," Charlotte said. "We'll only go as far as Four Pines and stay there while Father is gone."

"But *I* was going to take Will to the ranch as soon as I get back from my trip east."

"Well, now you won't have to. It's all arranged." She

looked up at him. "I'd think you'd be happy Mr. Moser came up with the idea. Now you won't have to hurry back just because of us."

Nathan chewed his lower lip while he formulated a reply. The fact was, he didn't understand what it was about Charlotte and Will's going to the ranch without him that should make him so upset. *She'll be right where you want her when you get back. It's perfect.* And it would have been perfect. If only Gabriel Moser wasn't in the picture.

•••◆•••

"Please, Laina," Charlotte said. "Give it a rest." The women were sitting on the front porch at the ranch. "You were mistaken about Lieutenant Boone and me, pure and simple. He's written to Will twice since he's been gone, and I'm grateful for that. The fact that he *didn't* write to me is evidence enough."

"You're wrong," Laina insisted. "Nathan's just . . . slow about letting his feelings show."

Charlotte closed her eyes. "This is embarrassing," she said. "I wish you would just drop it. He's a good friend, and I'll always appreciate that. But that's where it ends."

"You can't tell me you don't feel . . . something." Laina objected.

Charlotte flexed the fingers of her left hand and went back to snapping the green beans in the bowl in her lap. She and Will had been at the Four Pines for two weeks now. The summer garden was bearing vast quantities of food, and the women worked hours every day preserving the bounty. "All right. If it makes you feel better, yes, I feel something," Charlotte said. "And I'm grateful God woke up that part of me. I really thought the Colonel had probably destroyed every last trace of that kind of thing for me. It's nice to know he didn't. That's probably what God intended when He brought Lieutenant Boone back into my life. I'll admit that lately I've been hoping it might be more. But I'm determined to be content with whatever happens." She smiled at Laina. "And I believe a certain Mrs. Jackson is the one who first said that kind of thing to me about being content with whatever God provides."

"I did no such thing," Laina snorted. "I never wanted you to give up on Nathan."

"That's not what I meant," Charlotte said. "I mean the idea of contentment and letting God be in charge."

"Oh . . . that," Laina said. She looked at Charlotte. They both burst out laughing. "You mean that little item of eternal importance. Trusting and obeying God."

Charlotte nodded. "Uh-huh."

Laina sighed. "All right. I repent. But I still have to say one more thing about all of this. And that is . . . you cannot possibly tell me you are truly interested in Gabriel Moser."

"Why not?" Charlotte asked. "Because he's a few years younger than me?"

"Charlotte," Laina said. "He's a *century* younger than you when it comes to life experience."

"And I find that refreshing," Charlotte said. "But lest you worry, I'm not interested in him the way you think." She lowered her voice. "But, Laina, for the first time in a long time, someone sees me for myself. To Mr. Moser, I'm Charlotte Bishop. I'm not 'Will's mother.' That's nice. And now," she said with a flourish, "could we please talk about something *besides* my nonexistent love life?"

Laina laughed. "All right. Jack put a saddle on Spirit weeks ago. She's going to be a wonderful little ride."

Charlotte sighed and shook her head. "I don't know if Will will ever be ready for Spirit. I was amazed when Nathan got him up on Bones a few weeks ago."

"Don't give up on that," Laina said. "Being around Spirit just might spark some part of Will's willpower you haven't tapped into yet."

"Or it could discourage him to the point he'll give up,"

Charlotte said. She sighed. "I don't know what to do. It's taking so *long*."

"What does that doctor out east say?"

Charlotte shook her head. "I haven't heard from him. But there was an article in one of my father's medical papers not long ago. The latest research, supposedly. And it reiterated exactly what my father has been telling me. Every case is different. They see miracles every day. Don't give up hope. Keep him working at everything. Fine-motor skills come back last. He could eventually be completely normal . . . or he might never talk again. There's no way to know what was destroyed permanently or how much he might be able to relearn." She blinked back unexpected tears.

"You," Laina said, "are a wonder of patience and love, Charlotte Bishop."

"I," Charlotte said, "am tired." She sighed and closed her eyes.

"Which is why," Laina said, "you belong here. New scenery. Rachel and Jack and old Dorsey to help. Who knows, we might just witness that miracle your father prayed for that first night before surgery."

"I don't think I'm standing in the right line for miracles," Charlotte said.

"What do you mean?"

"I mean, that some people get miracles . . . and other people get the patience to handle things without the miracles. I'd like a miracle, don't get me wrong. But if God isn't going to do the miracle, he'd better pass out some patience and perseverance."

Laina nodded. "He does."

"I know," Charlotte said. "He has. 'It is of the Lord's mercies that we are not consumed, because his compassions fail not. They are new every morning: great is thy faithfulness.'" Charlotte smiled. "See? I took your advice. I'm reading the Bible."

"Has it helped?"

"Oh my goodness *yes,*" Charlotte said. "Just when I fall on my face and tell God I can't, He picks me up. And I can. Most of the time. Although," she said, with a grin, "I did almost lose my head and run off into the badlands in search of fossils with my young lover."

"Charlotte Bishop!" Laina looked appropriately shocked. She brought her hand to her chest in mock horror. And they giggled like schoolgirls.

• • • ◆ • • •

The hardest thing, CJ thought, was that Will couldn't talk to her any more. That was the thing she missed most. She didn't mind so much that he walked with a jerk or that he drooled a little. And his crooked smile was almost cute. Anyone who knew Will at all could see he was still *in* there, behind those gray eyes. But he didn't talk. And she couldn't get him to try.

"Please, Will," she'd say. "Just try. I don't care if you can't say it good. But it's like walking. You had to have a cane when Lieutenant Boone first took you around the parade ground. And now you barely need it. I bet you won't even have a limp by Christmas. I bet it would be the same way with talking. If only you would try."

Will would listen, press his lips together, and shake his head. He was staying in the bunkhouse with Jack and Dorsey, just like always. But as far as CJ could tell, he didn't try to talk to them, either. It drove her crazy.

• • • ◆ • • •

Late in August, the expedition from Princeton was back at the ranch before heading for Fort Robinson and the railroad and the long ride back east. The Jacksons hauled their bathtub out to a place behind the barn and, one by one, the members of the expedition washed the grit and grime of weeks in the badlands from their sunburned skin. Will sat on the front porch of the ranch house grinning as he listened to the whoops and hollers as the men doused one another with ice-cold well water. The fossil hunting had been a success, and the students and Professor Scott were in high spirits.

Behind him in the ranch house, Mrs. Jackson and Will's mother and Rachel were preparing food and bringing it out to the table they had set up on the porch. Toward evening, one of the more energetic students hauled out a violin and began to play. Before long, someone suggested a dance. Even CJ was invited to join in, which she did, much to Will's amazement. He had almost forgotten that CJ was a girl. Seeing her dancing reminded him. Made him wish he could dance, too. From where he sat on the porch watching, Will tapped his foot to the music. He nearly laughed aloud when the old soldier Emmet Dorsey did an arthritic version of a jig that had everyone rolling with laughter—including Dorsey.

He was having a wonderful time until he caught a glimpse of his mother. Dancing. With that Gabriel Moser. He did not like the way his mother looked up at that man. *"You might get a new pa,"* CJ had told him. He'd said that was all right with him. And it was. As long as it was someone like Lieutenant Boone. *Lieutenant. See? He knew the right name now. It wasn't "Loot Boone" anymore. He was normal. Boone knew it. Why didn't this Moser guy?*

The music ended. Moser held on to Ma, and she didn't seem to mind. Will got up and shuffled toward the barn. He leaned his cane against the door and continued inside, making his way to the last stall on the right where a gray filly stepped forward and thrust her head over the top board. She watched him approach with her wide dark eyes, her ears both brought forward to take in every sound. As Will came up alongside her, Spirit put her head down. She kept it lowered while Will buried his face in her mane and reached around her neck. Spirit didn't move. She didn't bob her head up and down, as was her manner. She stayed very still, except for a gentle whicker that vibrated her black muzzle.

Will slid his hand down her face and to the muzzle. Spirit opened her lips and nibbled. Will laughed.

"S-s-s . . . pir-r-r-r . . . it-t-t," Will whispered. "Hey, gir-rl-l-l-l."

Spirit whickered again and nudged Will gently. She took in a deep breath and sighed.

CHAPTER TWENTY-TWO

The Lord is good unto them that wait for him, to the soul that seeketh him. It is good that a man should both hope and quietly wait for the salvation of the Lord. It is good for a man that he bear the yoke in his youth. . . . For the Lord will not cast off for ever: but though he cause grief, yet will he have compassion according to the multitude of his mercies.

LAMENTATIONS 3:25–27, 31–32

EARLY IN SEPTEMBER, CHARLOTTE AND WILL RETURNED to Fort Robinson. Charlotte's energy and attention were given to the planning and execution of a wedding between Garnet and Private Blake. Dr. Valentine solved the quandary over the availability of living quarters.

"Why, you'll live at my house, of course," he said.

Blake, who had lost sleep over the idea of moving his bride from the relative luxury of the room behind the surgeon's kitchen into a shack down by the White River, offered his sincere thanks, to which the doctor replied, "Don't thank me, Private. I don't want to lose my cook and my striker."

Caleb Jackson rode into Fort Robinson and made sure Charlotte knew they expected both her and Will for a long visit soon. "Jack has Spirit trotting around the corral. She's just waiting for Will." He also told them that Nathan Boone was having great success out east, rounding up a good string of mares for the ranch, and that after protracted negotiations it looked like the stallion named Banner might be headed west to stand at the Four Pines, after all.

Charlotte answered Gabriel Moser's latest letter and enclosed Dr. Valentine's notes on Will's accident and surgery for Dr. Faucett's review.

Early autumn colors began to dot the bluffs in the distance, and the flat land around the fort turned golden as the grasses dried out and went dormant. The cavalry and infantry companies at the post made a long march and fought practice battles along the Niobrara River.

Charlotte did not hear from Nathan.

Dr. Faucett wrote that he had reviewed Will's case and could offer little more information than what Charlotte already knew about Will's prognosis. *I would, of course, be happy to evaluate your son here in my clinic.* Charlotte wavered between wanting to pack up and leave immediately and her desire to be at the fort when Nathan Boone returned.

But before Charlotte could decide what to do, the fervent prayers of many were answered. Will began to speak with words again. It came about when Garnet handed him a book one day, saying, "I've got work to do, young man. Suppose *you* do the reading from now on." As a result, Will's once impossibly garbled speech improved to the point where anyone could understand him. He continued to choose his audiences carefully, though, once he realized that strangers often assumed him to be mentally slow.

Lieutenant Boone wrote to Will. He was funny and took time to share anecdotes of the "city folk" he encountered who didn't know a "cattle prod from a rifle." Will laughed uproariously when he read the letter, telling his mother it was a "private joke." Charlotte scolded herself for being jealous of the two of them having private jokes. She admitted to wishing Nathan would add a note for her at the bottom of Will's letters.

But Charlotte didn't hear from Nathan.

• • • ◆ • • •

On a crisp September day, when frost dotted the landscape, Private Blake started the first fire of the season in the parlor fireplace. Charlotte was in the kitchen, helping Garnet load a basket with pies and cakes for a masquerade ball being planned for the officers' families, when footsteps sounded on the back porch. Charlotte felt the blood rush to her cheeks as she anticipated seeing Nathan Boone.

"Hello, Mrs. Bishop," Preacher Barton said, removing his hat and waiting to be invited in. "I'm on my way to the Four Pines and just wanted to check in on that boy of yours. Is he at home?"

Charlotte hid her disappointment and invited the preacher in. She made him coffee and coaxed him into letting her cut into one of the pies. She told him all about Will's recovery, ending with, "but you'll be able to judge for yourself. He's just over at the stables with Private Blake for a little ride. They should be back before long. Will wants to keep his riding skills sharp. We've been waiting for Lieutenant Boone to get back with a new string of horses for the ranch before we head that way. The lieutenant has written Will, and said he can help him deliver the new horses." She paused and poured herself a cup of coffee. "You'll have to be sure and ask Will about Spirit. He's really excited to see what Jack Greyfoot has been able to do with her."

The preacher stood up. "Well, if you'll excuse me, I think I'll just hurry on over to the stables and check in with your boy right now."

"I'll come with you," Charlotte said.

The preacher held out his hand. "There's no need. No need for that at all." And he hurried off, so abruptly that Charlotte was a little hurt by the obvious. The preacher did not want her along. She wondered why.

* * * ◆ * * *

"Tell me the truth, Emory William Bishop," Charlotte said firmly.

Will looked down at the piece of apple pie on his plate. He sighed. He picked at the roll of crust at the edge of the pie and pursed his lips. Finally, he said, "Yes, I s-s-saw him-m-m."

Charlotte looked away. "I don't understand what all this secrecy is about. Have I done something to offend Lieutenant Boone that he didn't even stop to say hello before he took the new horses to the ranch?" She paused. "I thought you were supposed to help him with that." She sighed. "I'm not angry with you, Will. You didn't do anything wrong. The same goes for Lieutenant Boone. I just don't understand his behavior." When Will looked at her, Charlotte said, "You're hiding something behind those beautiful gray eyes, William Bishop. I don't like it when you keep secrets from me."

Will picked up the piece of pie crust and put it in his mouth. He chewed so slowly Charlotte wanted to scream. "He tol' me not to tell. It's a s-secret."

"People who love each other don't keep secrets that hurt others," Charlotte snapped.

The corners of Will's mouth went down. His gray eyes grew wide and sad. "I sorry Ma. He coming back. S-soon."

Will looked ready to cry. But it was obvious to Charlotte that he wasn't going to betray Lieutenant Boone's confidence. Jealousy over Nathan entrusting Will with something fairly important gave way to irritation with him for burdening Will with something that erected a wall between Will and his own mother. She would speak to Nathan about that.

"All right, Will," Charlotte said, and reached across the table to pat the back of his hand. "Don't worry yourself about it. I'll just have to wait until the lieutenant decides to come back."

She changed the subject abruptly and asked Will about the day's ride up the bluff. "I'm so proud of you," Charlotte said, "how you just climbed back aboard Bones and learned everything again." She hesitated, then decided to tell him.

"The lieutenant's not the only one who has a secret, you know." She winked at Will. "I plan to make certain Mr. Jackson understands that we intend to buy Spirit."

Will's eyes grew wide. They filled with happy tears. He laughed. *Laughed*. It was a jerky, sort of sobbing noise, but to Charlotte it was a lovely sound. She sent a prayer of thanksgiving to heaven. Whatever Lieutenant Nathan Boone was up to, whatever disappointment was on the horizon for her personally, her boy was getting better, and that, Charlotte decided, was quite enough happiness for one woman.

◆

It came clear to her later that night. She was glad it had come to her while the world was quiet and she was alone. It gave her time to absorb the truth and rid herself of her own petty and unfounded emotions. She should have realized the truth when Nathan took care *not* to address her in any of his communications with Will while he was back east. It was so obvious, Charlotte scolded herself for being so dense. Hadn't Will even said that the lieutenant and Rachel spent time together during roundup? Hadn't everyone mentioned that Jack wanted to marry Rachel, but she repeatedly refused his attentions? That was it. Nathan wasn't hurrying to the ranch with the horses as much as he was hurrying to Rachel Greyfoot. That had to be it. His absence must have made him realize his true feelings for Rachel.

He hadn't written to her because he knew she had misinterpreted his actions during Will's injury and recovery. Knowing Charlotte cared for him, he didn't want to hurt her. So he didn't write. And he also didn't come to see her as soon as he got back. He was sending her a message. He cared for Will. He had seen Will. And he would see her . . . but in a more casual way. It took Charlotte the better part of the night to talk herself past the hurt and into a state of semiacceptance.

Dear God, she prayed, *I've let my mind fly to ridiculous places since Nathan has been gone. I was so sure you sent Mr. Moser to awaken the possibilities to me so that when Nathan—* She caught her breath. *Thank you for Nathan's love for Will. Help me not to do anything stupid that might come in the way of their friendship, which I know is a blessing straight from your hand.*

***

"R-r-riding," Will said at breakfast. "I wanna go riding."

It was as if he had read her mind. Or her mood. Charlotte wondered if the boy could sense her inner turmoil. She had prayed a long time last night. She had come to a place of peace. And then, with the rising of the sun, the questions and inner turmoil had come back. *You do not love Nathan Boone,* she had told herself while she brushed her blond hair and assessed herself in the mirror. Ten years ago she had had a twenty-two-inch waist. Ten years ago there hadn't been a single fine wrinkle around those big gray eyes. Sighing, Charlotte turned away from what she saw. *No wonder he wants Rachel Greyfoot. She's been through hard times, too, but she has that long river of dark hair. And that cinnamon skin.* Charlotte sighed. Fair skin certainly didn't weather the west very well. She looked down at the backs of her hands and shook her head, then made fists and closed her eyes. *Get hold of yourself. You have a son to raise.* She had looked outside at the blue sky and decided, if ever there was a morning for becoming a "watcher on the hill," this was it.

And so, after breakfast, with Will over at the stables with Private Blake, Charlotte went to the barn out back, saddled one of her father's horses, and headed away from the fort. She'd realized weeks ago that things took on a proper perspective when she rode to the top of a bluff. This morning was no different. Looking at the vast expanse of the scenery before her, Charlotte preached to herself. *Creation does not revolve around Charlotte Bishop.* She looked down at the fort, expanded to almost twice the size it had been only a few years ago. *It doesn't even revolve around that busy fort.* She gazed at the massive granite boulders jutting up from the earth, the white rock exposed on the sides of the buttes. *These rocks have looked down on that valley for centuries, and when Fort Robinson is little more than a pile of rubble on the valley floor, they'll still be here. The sun will still rise and make Crow Butte glow red in the morning, and the face of these cliffs will still glow golden on clear summer evenings.*

Charlotte smiled, remembering when riding up here and looking out on the scene had made her feel small and unimportant and alone. She looked up at the blue sky. *And now I come up here to be reminded that you, Father, who made all of this, are mindful of Charlotte Bishop and her future, and of Will and his physical challenges. You own the cattle on a thousand hills. You know when the mountain goat gives birth, and . . .* She smiled to herself. *You know whether or not Charlotte Bishop needs a husband, and if she does, you have one in mind. And, Lord, I don't want a man in my life who doesn't belong to you. So that means . . . I shouldn't want Nathan Boone. Fine as he is.*

Charlotte envisioned Boone's square shoulders, his thick dark hair. A handsome man by anyone's standards. A good man, full of caring and gentleness. *Good as far as his own humanity can take it.* But that wasn't enough. Not now. She wanted what Caleb and Laina had. The kind of love that sprang from a source beyond humanity. The kind that weathered storms. It didn't matter that Laina and Caleb had struggled so with their baby boy's death. In fact, Charlotte realized, it was almost comforting. They weren't perfect. Having real faith didn't mean people became perfect. Charlotte liked that. You could be a true believer and fail, and God didn't let go.

Don't let go. She had said those words in Nathan's arms while Will was in surgery.

Her eyes filled with tears. Caleb Jackson had let go. For a while. She supposed life could throw things at men that would make even the strongest of them tempted to let go. But in that entire awful time in the Jacksons' lives, when it looked like they might let go of each other, God had not let go of them. *That* must be what that Bible verse about the "everlasting arms" means. People let go. God never does.

•••◆•••

She was trusting God in a new way, but that didn't mean Charlotte's heart didn't thump a little harder the day Nathan Boone finally appeared on her doorstep. There he stood, his hat in his hand, his dark hair rumpled, his beautiful mouth smiling. He'd shaved his beard. She didn't remember that cleft in his chin. He was even better looking than she remembered. *Don't let go, Father. Don't let go.*

"Come in, Lieutenant," Charlotte said, hoping her smile looked natural. "I'll call Will in from the barn. He's brought Bones over from the stables for the day." She hesitated. "Or would you rather just walk on around to where he is?" She put her hands behind her back and looked away. *This is harder than I thought it would be.*

"Actually," the Lieutenant said, "I'm kind of glad Will isn't here. I needed to talk to you first."

Charlotte took a step back. "Should I make coffee? Garnet and Carter have gone over to the Bee Hive to visit some friends, but I can surely—"

"No," Nathan interrupted her. "That's all right. I don't want coffee. I'm wondering if you and Will can get ready fast enough for us all to head to the ranch."

"What? When?"

"Now. Today." He cleared his throat. "As soon as possible. I mean, Laina said you were planning a visit. I was hoping you might be packed. I brought the wagon. For your trunk. Will's things. We can take Bones, too, if you want. He's mostly retired from the army. I'm certain nobody will mind."

Charlotte had never seen the lieutenant so nervous. He was half apologetic. This would not do. She cleared her throat. "Nathan. Please. Calm down. I've been looking forward to a visit to the ranch. And I'm very happy for you and Rachel. So please. Relax. You don't owe me—"

"Lieutenant Boone!" The back door slammed in concert with Will's exclamation.

"Hello there, pard'ner," Boone said. He grinned at Will and winked.

"Ready to go," Will said. He looked at Charlotte. "Right, Ma?"

"Not completely," Charlotte said. Will made a face. She smiled. "But I can *be* ready to go. In an hour?" She looked up at Nathan. He nodded. "How about you two go on over to the Bee Hive. Find Carter and Garnet and let them know. Then go to the hospital to find your grandfather." Will nodded eagerly. "And I promise to be finished packing by the time you get back."

Charlotte felt like the drive to Four Pines Ranch from Fort Robinson took about three years out of her. She asked about the trip east. Nathan had little to say, other than that the string of horses he'd brought back was fine and, yes, Banner was a magnificent animal, and he hoped the price they had paid wasn't the downfall of their relationship with the banker Wade Simpson. "I've saved up," Nathan said, "but I didn't have the money for that kind of horse, that's for sure. And Caleb used all his savings for the rest of the horses. But Wade said 'all right' to fronting us enough to get Banner. He'll take his interest in breeding some of his mares soon."

"You took out a *loan* to buy a horse?" Charlotte said.

"I know what you're thinking. I hate debt, too. And initially I didn't expect to need it. But things just didn't go according to plan."

"Forgive me, Lieutenant," Charlotte said. "It's really none of my business. And I'm certain you were prudent in whatever risk you were taking."

"Please. Call me Nathan," he said. "We're friends, remember?"

"Here they *come*!" CJ could be heard shrieking with joy from the minute they got within earshot of the house.

"Well, she certainly had faith in our willingness to come at a moment's notice," Charlotte laughed as the wagon rumbled along.

Nathan only nodded. He had become increasingly silent the closer they got to the ranch. Now, as she looked down at his hands, Charlotte realized he was gripping the reins so hard his knuckles were white. She was going to have to pull him aside as soon as possible and wish him and Rachel happiness. And she was going, by God's grace, to do it with a sincere smile and not a tinge of regret in her voice. She hoped they wouldn't have to endure an awkward meal before she could clear the air.

Laina came at once, hugging her, laughing, a strange tone in her voice that made Charlotte think even Laina was nervous about the announcement that would be made about Rachel and Nathan.

"Where's Rachel?" Charlotte asked. *Might as well get it over with.*

"Rachel? Oh, she and Jack are over at the Dawson place," Laina said. "They'll be back later."

Nathan's plans were really moving forward. He'd already bought the neighboring ranch. Rachel was probably settling in. Poor Jack. It would be hard for him, too.

Nathan hauled Charlotte's trunk in and set it in the room Charlotte knew had originally been intended for the new baby. They all went back out to the front porch as Nathan and Will departed for the bunkhouse. As they walked down the trail, Charlotte watched as Nathan put his arm on Will's shoulder. They must have been sharing a joke because Will looked up at Nathan and nodded and smiled.

Thank you, Father. That's such a beautiful thing to see.

"That's a wonderful sight to behold," Laina said aloud, echoing Charlotte's thoughts.

Charlotte nodded. "Praise God, from whom all blessings flow." She turned toward the house. "Put me to work. What can I do?"

"You," Laina said, smiling, "can sit right there in that rocking chair and enjoy the view until the men come back from the bunkhouse. And then . . . we'll see." She grinned. "I'll be back in minute."

Charlotte could hear Laina inside, working in the kitchen. Once she went to the door, but Laina would not hear of her helping at all. "Just go sit down, Charlotte. Really. I want to do this on my own. I'm preparing a celebration. And I have a surprise or two."

"You didn't have to do that," Charlotte said.

"Yes," Laina said. "I did. Now behave yourself and do as you're told."

Charlotte turned around to see Nathan coming up the trail. Alone. He was walking with such purpose, Charlotte realized. *We're going to have THE TALK.* She took a deep breath and whispered a prayer.

"Can we . . . talk?" Nathan said.

"Relax, Lieutenant . . . Nathan," Charlotte said, hoping her smile was reassuring. "It doesn't have to be as serious as all this. I'm happy for you. Honestly, I am. Whatever you thought—"

"Down there," Nathan said, nodding toward the barn.

"What?"

"Thought you'd want to see the new horses. Thought you'd want to get a look at Banner for yourself," Nathan said.

She didn't want to go. Didn't want to walk alongside Nathan Boone and be tempted to imagine the impossible. Didn't want to be trapped in the barn and have to retreat to the house if her emotions didn't follow her intellect. She really *was* content in the role God had assigned her. Life was full. She really was going to be all right. But being alone with Nathan Boone didn't seem like a good idea. Not right now.

"Please, Charlotte," Nathan said, "just . . . just come and see."

She gave in. *Lord guard my heart. This is just looking at a few horses. Then make him leave me alone. Send him over to his own ranch. To Rachel. Please.*

"All right." She nodded toward the door. "Laina insists that she won't let me help anyway." She stepped off the porch, uncomfortably aware of the way he towered over her, remembering that night at the hospital when he had held her. How safe she had felt. "So," she said as they walked toward the barn, "tell me about these amazing horses that required a special trip east."

"Well," Nathan said, "actually, there's only one who's all that special. He's in that stall down there next to Spirit. Thought the two of them should learn to get along." He gave a low whistle. There was an answering whicker, low and . . . familiar.

Impossible, Charlotte thought, even as the occupant of the stall put his great, gray head over the stall door and looked their way.

Charlotte grabbed Nathan's forearm to keep her wobbly knees from collapsing. "Oh, my . . ."

"Major Riley took some convincing to let him go. He's a fine animal, but there seemed to be more to it than his just hanging on to a good horse."

"Isaac? You . . . found . . . Isaac?" She tried to keep herself from running to the stall. She wanted to maintain her dignity. But it was *Isaac.* He was bobbing his head, and when she spoke his name, he lifted his upper lip the way he always did and greeted her with his signature snort. When she came within reach, he pressed against the stall and thrust his head at her. He leaned down, and when Charlotte scratched just behind his jaw, he gave such a huge sigh, tears came to her eyes. She bowed her head and rested her chin against the place between the horse's ears. Tears rolled down her cheeks. Without looking at Nathan, she said, "I can't imagine how you managed to convince Major Riley to let Isaac come back to me—"

"Oh, I didn't let on that I knew anything about the horse or its previous owner," Nathan said. "I asked around at Fort Wayne a bit before making contact with the illustrious Major Riley, and I knew better than to mention your name."

"He's bitter then," Charlotte said.

"Only about losing the Bishop money," Nathan said, then immediately apologized. "I'm sorry, that sounded—"

"—truthful," Charlotte said. "You aren't telling me anything I didn't already know." She swallowed hard, rubbed her tears away with the back of one hand, and finally looked up at him. "However long it takes me," Charlotte said, "I will pay you back for this." She looked up at Isaac. "Thank-you just isn't enough. Words just don't begin to express—" She took in a deep breath.

Nathan cleared his throat. "He was expensive," he said. "I mean, *really* expensive."

"I can imagine," Charlotte said. "And he's a gelding. So he really is just a pricey toy."

"No," Nathan said. He took a deep breath. "Actually, he's a present. Sort of a . . . uh . . ."

"Good-bye." Charlotte interrupted him. "I know. It's all right, Nathan. Goodness, you didn't have to go to so much trouble or expense. You don't owe me such extravagance. If I gave you the impression I was . . . assuming . . ." She felt her cheeks color. "I'm sorry. I'm happy for you and Rachel, Nathan. Really, I am."

"If you'd be quiet for just a minute," Nathan said, "I'd like to finish what I was saying."

Charlotte stepped away from him. This was going to be harder than she thought. He had to make a *speech* about it all. *Help, Lord. Help me allow him to do whatever it is he has to do to feel better about all this.*

"First of all, I want you to know. I love Will."

"I know you do, Nathan. You don't have to tell me that."

"Well, the thing is . . ." He cleared his throat. "There was a time when I thought I should propose to you. For Will." When Charlotte said nothing, he sighed. "I'm not very good at this."

"You're doing fine, Lieutenant," Charlotte said without looking up at him. "You love Will. Like the son you never had." She drew herself up, put her hands behind her back. "And I am very grateful for that. I see it as a gift straight from the hand of a loving God. And I guess I understand how your convoluted brain could have convinced you that you should marry the mother . . . as a necessary accessory to your ongoing relationship with a boy you care about. But really, Nathan, I hope you know I'm not so shallow as to allow that."

"I don't—"

"Because," Charlotte took a deep breath, "I have been there and done that and I'm not ever making that mistake again."

"You've done . . . what?"

"Been a convenient accessory to a man's life."

"But it's more than that," Nathan said. "I *liked* you. I admired you. You're strong. You've got more guts than some of the men I've commanded."

Desperate to lighten the serious weight of regret pressing down on her, Charlotte saluted. "Thank you, Lieutenant, sir. I'll take that as a compliment, sir."

Nathan put his hands on his hips. He grunted. "I'm making a mess of this. Could we . . . could we sit down?" He waved toward the end of the row at a pile of hay bales.

"Really, Lieutenant, you are making such a mountain out of a very small hill. This is not necessary."

"I'd appreciate it if you'd let me . . . just . . . talk." He sounded almost annoyed.

Charlotte closed her eyes. *Help, Lord. Help.* Later she would mull over the never-ending speechmaking and try to make some sense of it. God certainly chose odd times to teach a woman patience.

Nathan didn't sit, he stood, pacing back and forth as he talked. "I've been attracted to you for a long time. First, it was just . . . admiration. For the way you've handled Will's accident, for the way you've handled everything that's come your way. When Lily died, I got bitter. When bad things happened to you, you got stronger." Seeming to anticipate her protest, he held up his hand. "I know, I know. It took a little while. But you did grow stronger. And then I loved Will. And so I hatched this plan to go east and get Isaac and make you love me. And marry me." He stopped and looked down at her. "For all the wrong reasons."

Charlotte nodded. Good. He realized it. Why he had to beat her over the head with it, she didn't quite understand. But at least he realized it. Maybe he had to say it so he'd be comfortable continuing his friendship with Will. Maybe he needed to clear the air.

"All these years I've been bitter and angry at God," he said. "But God didn't give up on me. He kept putting true believers in the ranks below me. Men like Carter Blake. He kept bringing Preacher Barton around at the most amazing times." He paused. "This last time . . . well, I realize there aren't that many choices when a man wants to return to Fort Robinson, so it isn't all that much of a coincidence, and yet . . ." He paused. "The preacher and I shared the train ride back here from St. Louis," Nathan said. "He was returning from the annual meeting of his missions board." He shook his head. "And you know the preacher. He's never been one to miss an opportunity to talk about God. Except this time, all those people I've been meeting over the years and all the little pieces of truth I've been hearing . . . Well, all my excuses just disintegrated." He swallowed. "I . . . uh . . . I decided to try it."

"Try. . . ?"

"Getting over myself and giving things up to God. And seeing what He could do about it."

"Do about what, Nathan?"

He swallowed. His dark eyes filled with tears. "This great big lump of . . . garbage." He made a fist and hit his midsection. "This gut full of—" He took a deep breath, a heart-wrenching sob. He looked at Charlotte and smiled through his tears and shrugged. "He did it. He took it. I'm . . . uh . . . well, I'm changed. Inside."

"Oh, Nathan," Charlotte whispered. "I'm so *glad*."

"I don't even know what happened," Nathan said. "It's like a lamp just . . ."

"Went on?"

He nodded. "Yeah. I realized my plans were all wrong. Marrying you for Will was just . . . wrong."

"Yes," Charlotte said. "Completely wrong." She started to get up.

"But . . . marrying you . . . for *me*," Nathan said. "That"—his voice lowered—"would be completely, absolutely, totally, *right*."

Charlotte sat back down. She frowned. "What?" She looked up at him. *Don't do this. Don't—do this. You are too beautiful and too near, and I am not strong enough to—*

"The truth is, Charlotte, I finally got things figured out. I don't love you because you're Will's mother. I love you because . . . you're . . . you."

"Stop it," Charlotte said. She raised her hand to her hair. "You're being kind and I appreciate it, but you aren't looking. You aren't seeing."

"I'm looking," Nathan said. He crouched down before her and touched the hair at her temple. "And I'm seeing."

"What?" She laughed bitterly and looked away. "A

widow who's aged before her time? A woman with lines and freckles."

"Stop it," Nathan said. He ran his finger along her jaw, touched the corners of each eye. "Every one of those things is a medal, Charlotte. A badge of honor. Proof of victory in battles waged in the most difficult place possible." He pointed to her heart. "Right there. And you fought them alone. And you won them."

She shook her head. "I didn't," she said, almost whispering. "*He* won them. God. Not me."

Nathan lifted her chin. He looked into her eyes. "I haven't been able to sleep, or eat—with thinking about how to say all these things to you. Knowing you wouldn't want to believe it. Fearing I've waited too long." He smiled at her. "The thing is, Charlotte, the horse is a gift. With a catch."

"A catch?"

His smile grew. "You have to take a retired cavalry officer along with him."

"Retired?"

He nodded. "I . . . uh . . . bought the Dawson place. For us. What do you think?"

Charlotte inhaled. "I think," she said, "that this is overwhelming. You've never shown . . . even tried to kiss—"

"I made up my mind, Charlotte, that the day I kissed you it had to be with a clear conscience. I had to come out here first. To talk to Rachel."

"Then I was right about her," she said.

Nathan shook his head. "We talked. And walked. And had some nice evenings together during roundup. Maybe we even flirted a little." He shrugged. "But the fact is she's happy for us. Even a little relieved, I think. She doesn't have a heart for anyone but Grey Foot." He reached over and covered her hands, which were clenched in her lap, with his own.

Avoiding his eyes, Charlotte murmured, "I've spent most of the past few weeks trying to convince myself that I have a very good life without you, Nathan Boone."

"You do have a good life," he said. "I just want to make it better."

"Well," Charlotte said, nodding towards Isaac. "You're off to a very good start."

Nathan leaned over to kiss her.

She didn't lean away.

Perhaps, after all, romance did not come into one's life with pomp and blare, like a gay knight riding down; perhaps it crept to one's side like an old friend through quiet ways; perhaps it revealed itself in seeming prose, until some sudden shaft of illumination flung athwart its pages betrayed the rhythm and the music; perhaps . . . perhaps . . . love unfolded naturally out of a beautiful friendship, as a golden-hearted rose slipping from its green sheath.

L.M. MONTGOMERY